Heartfelt Hope

LAINEY LAWRENCE

ISBN: 9798362119430

For Mum

xXx

1

Hope peered into the rear-view mirror, inspecting her makeup and wishing she could be beautiful just for today. Well, no, if wishes were to be granted, then she would wish it for the whole weekend. It would do her no good to look stunning today and then have to face Ben again tomorrow, only to have the magic wear off. *Benjamin Knight.* She sighed. Even the sound of his name gave her goose bumps.

Hope's friends had been very vocal about their opinions of the elusive Ben. Tomasz had told her she was no doubt being catfished. Her neighbour said Ben was probably married and had managed to 'get rid of the wife' for the weekend. Even Jess had said there was no way a total stranger could live up to Hope's fantasies, and she was setting herself up for a big disappointment. But Hope didn't listen. She would just have to find out for herself. And now that the day of their first date had dawned, she would.

Concealing her trepidation, Hope smiled sweetly at the elderly gentleman in the attendant's hut. He raised the barrier and waved her through. The wide-open space was functional yet surprisingly beautiful, with an array of blossoming shrubs and trees that evoked memories of camping holidays she'd enjoyed as a child. Several parked cars, abandoned temporarily by their undeniably rich owners, were barely noticeable through the greenery.

Hope chose a space next to an elegant Porsche and swung her not-so-elegant run-around neatly into it. The designer of this apartment complex had evidently showcased the serenity of the nearby waterfront. The development looked as if it were a part of nature, grown from roots deep beneath the ground. Hope breathed in the warm, fresh air. Everything was so peaceful, tranquil, and perfect here. So, why couldn't she shake the unpleasant sensation travelling from deep down in the pit of her stomach up to her throat?

Hope had first met Ben over a year and a half ago. Well, *met* wasn't quite the right word. He had stumbled into her life—or, at least, into her inbox—by mistake one day. Had this really been another one of life's little accidents, though, or was it in fact a well-engineered plan, painstakingly executed by some mightier force? She certainly liked to believe it was the latter.

One winter's evening, after she'd spent hours trying to remember how to sync her iPhone to her computer, her mood had turned as miserable as the weather. After admitting defeat and cursing technology, she'd spotted a random email from someone she was fairly confident she didn't know. The fact that he'd simply signed off with his first name, coupled with an e-mail address that didn't give away his surname, meant that she had to read the message a few times for a hint of who the sender might be. After a few minutes of scratching her head, she finally decided it must have been sent to her in error.

She composed a witty but polite reply, suggesting that she would love to take him up on his offer of dinner, but he should be warned that she might not be who he expected. Visions of *You've Got Mail* ran through her mind as she pictured the scene: her as Meg Ryan; him, Tom Hanks. Could this be the start of something special? She signed off and pressed send, realising that her romantic fantasies were no doubt futile. She would never hear from this stranger again once he realised his mistake. If she did get a reply, then he was probably a weirdo.

However, Ben's light-hearted response the next morning had prompted her to once again think of him as the Romeo to her Juliet. It was more fun that way because she could allow herself to revel in her daydreams. As further e-mails, then WhatsApp messages, had been exchanged over the following weeks and months, their two-dimensional friendship had evolved.

Since her first emails with Ben, Hope had been out on quite a few dates with other men, but none of them had led to a relationship. Always quick to make up her mind about a potential partner, she usually decided early on that something was wrong with the suitor and then let him down gently. Hope had been on so many dates with men who weren't interesting or tall or ambitious enough. Enough was enough! Or, in her case, it wasn't.

She conveyed her frustrations to Ben, who was

always happy to exchange messages, often whilst working late into the evenings. Hope had spent many an hour regaling him with her latest dating disasters, and he sent virtual hugs, winks, and raised eyebrows at appropriate times. Ben had enjoyed the anecdote about Pretentious Paul, who had wittered on and on about how great he was, blissfully unaware that he'd arrived on the date with a huge gravy splodge on his chin.

'Obviously not so great with a flannel and a bar of soap!' Hope had typed, followed up with a laughing emoji.

Ben acted as her agony uncle, always reassuring her that there were plenty more fish in the sea. *Perhaps it's time for me to stop casting my net and leave the sorry state of male marine life for all the other female anglers*, Hope had thought while flicking through a few more photos of potential partners on her dating app.

At that point, the only photo she had ever seen of Ben was his WhatsApp profile picture. The image was of poor quality, with the subject too close to the camera and his head therefore distorted into a peculiar shape. But assuming he wasn't the son of the Elephant Man and that only the camera angle made him look that way, she could at least make out a beautiful smile—if she scrunched up her eyes and peered through her eyelashes.

At thirty-two years old, Benjamin Knight was very eligible with a highly successful business under his belt. He had a fantastic personality to boot and an abundance of all the characteristics Hope wanted in a man. But after seeing that snapshot early on, she'd automatically friend-zoned him. She had been quite taken with Ben's compliments, though, when he saw what she looked like for the very first time. It was nice to have a male friend you didn't fancy but who could make you feel attractive. And that's the way it had been—at least, initially.

Hope vividly remembered the first time Ben had phoned her, the first time she'd heard his voice. He had withheld his number, so it was one of those conversations where she racked her brain to recognise the caller's voice yet couldn't. Ben had played on this, knowing full well that she wouldn't realise it was him. He had wound her up no end before finally admitting he'd caught her out, hook, line, and sinker. She'd been on the verge of acting rather rude, too, thinking he was another cold-caller trying to sell her double glazing or such like.

Yet his voice, as silky and warm as a giant mug of hot chocolate on a chill winter's night, had compelled her to stay on the line and bask in its comfort. Then she'd realised it was rather a shame she wasn't physically attracted to him and that maybe she should ask him to send her some more recent photos. But he'd had to go into a meeting just as she was about to bring it up, and the next time they spoke, she'd forgotten all about it.

As the seasons continued to change, Ben and Hope grew ever closer. Their messages lengthened, the content deepened, and barely a day went by when they weren't in touch. As Christmas fast approached, Hope realised they'd been chatting for over a year and suggested they meet up in person to exchange small gifts. They booked a date in the diary.

The day before they were due to meet, Ben left her a voicemail, telling her he had bad news and asking her to ring him. After agonising over her suspicion that he was obviously about to cancel and wondering why she felt so disappointed when she definitely didn't fancy him, she plucked up the courage to call him back. The rascal admitted that the bad news was merely that the weather forecast was for snow, so she'd have to drive carefully. He'd just wanted to tease her into thinking he couldn't make it. She would get him back.

However, they decided at that point to postpone everything until after Christmas, as she was on painkillers for a recent gym injury to her shoulder. So, they set a new date, and once again she'd got all excited, once again without knowing quite why.

This time around, she'd missed a call from him when she was in the shower, and his voicemail had momentarily stopped her in her tracks.

'As much as I don't want to have to cancel, especially this late in the day, I'm afraid I have no choice. Something urgent has come up at work, and I'll have to spend the whole weekend sorting it out. I'll make it up to you, I promise, even if I have to come to you, instead of you coming to Portsmouth. Call me back so I know you've picked this up.'

Well, she wasn't going to fall for the same trick twice. So, she finished packing her bag, applied her makeup, and dried her hair. Only once she was fully dressed and ready to leave the house did she return his call to let him know she was about to set off. But when their brief conversation ended, and she'd hung up the phone, she realised he really had cancelled this time.

They then abandoned all talk of meeting up. Ben was clearly very busy with his business or simply had no intention of ever meeting in person, and she didn't want to get her hopes up again for them to be dashed once more. Their friendship had continued, though, and winter quickly became spring.

One evening, whilst curled up on the sofa watching the sunset leave the sky ablaze with candyfloss clouds, Hope had absentmindedly clicked onto WhatsApp. She did a double-take, noticing that Ben had updated his profile photo. After she tapped on the image to enlarge it, his face popped up on the screen.

That face, not contorted and disfigured as it had been in his previous photo, was breathtakingly handsome. Hope sat bolt upright and peered more closely. She soaked up every little feature and studied each pixel to imprint the vision in her brain. His soft brown hair was tousled on top of his head, and his dark, mysterious green eyes were framed with beautiful, long, black, spider-leg lashes. An intoxicating combination. His delicate pink lips looked almost too fragile to touch, but how she longed to brush her own against them. If this was really Ben, then he truly was one of the most attractive men she had ever laid eyes on. She finally stopped gawping and removed her hand from where she had unwittingly clutched it to her heart. She realised she simply had to meet him, and it wasn't just friendship on her mind now.

Another agonising month or two went by, and in frustration they discarded more plans to meet as their busy lives kept them apart. Finally, they found another weekend when both would be free. The date had been set, and Hope desperately wished that this time nothing would stand in their way. Since discovering his new photo, she had seen him in a whole new light. How had she not known he was so good-looking before? How was he still single? She would soon become acquainted with the man who roamed her dreams at night. She knew how she felt about him in two dimensions. Would she feel the same way when she saw him in the flesh? Her cheeks reddened at the double entendre.

2

Prior to setting off on this little adventure, Hope had spent a few days weighing up the advantages and disadvantages of travelling by train versus car. She had initially favoured taking the train, anticipating the need for a little Dutch courage to steady her nerves along the way. Yet driving had won, hands down, once she realised the train journey involved three changes and added an extra two and a half hours onto the trip. *Not ideal,* she thought, *unless you wanted to look like Worzel Gummidge on arrival.*

Now she desperately wished she hadn't dismissed train travel so quickly. She recalled how alcohol could boost her self-confidence in a matter of minutes, something no amount of carefully applied makeup had ever achieved. Anyhow, stone-cold sober she was, and it was too late to change that. She absentmindedly popped a piece of chewing gum into her mouth and continued daydreaming.

The sound of an aeroplane penetrating the clear blue sky momentarily brought her out of her reverie.

Her thoughts returned to the present and the reason she was here. She flicked her gum out of the window and instantly felt guilty, as though she had just ruined paradise in one quick, clumsy wrist movement. But then again, 'clumsiness' did seem to be her middle name.

She recalled the mealtime when she'd shaken the tomato ketchup bottle before realising the lid wasn't on properly, sloshing red sauce all over the wallpaper and the back of the television. Another memory floated through her mind and then shattered, just as a china plate once had when she'd failed to carry it carefully through to the dining table, depositing spaghetti Bolognese all over the floor.

Hope opened the car door, retrieved the offensive piece of gum from the ground, wrapped it in a tissue, and placed it in the glove compartment to dispose of later. She reached into her handbag for her perfume, then sprayed herself with a delicate spritz while gazing at her reflection in the rear-view mirror.

Her eyes shone like diamonds against her tanned face, almost concealing how desperately nervous she felt. She pulled the crocodile clip out of her chestnut hair and let the locks fall loosely around her shoulders. Her hair looked perfect, in spite of the torture it had endured first thing that morning. Now she gently ran her hands through it, encouraging the grown-out fringe to frame her face.

She'd dreamt about meeting Ben so many times over the last few months. But as she sat here alone in the car now, the enormity of the situation suddenly hit her like a bolt of lightning. She shuddered involuntarily. There was no turning back, though. It was too late for that, and, like it or not, this was the face she had been blessed with. She'd been told she was 'naturally pretty' on countless occasions, but in Hope's vocabulary *natural* meant plain or ordinary, so she never fully appreciated the sincerity of the compliments she'd received over the years.

Hope was unable to shake a feeling of dread—not dissimilar to one she'd experienced an hour into her first day at junior school.

For ages, she had looked forward to going to Upton. She drove her parents crazy with her nonstop ramblings about 'big school'. Little did she know that her first day there would go down in family history, not simply as a significant milestone but as a result of the embarrassing mishap she suffered soon after entering the school building.

To begin with, all had gone well that drizzly September morning. She'd managed not to spill anything on her new uniform whilst having breakfast. They'd arrived at the school in plenty of time for the parent-child assembly without making a mad run-for-it after finding a parking space. Hope felt pleased that she would be in the same class as her 'podgy friend from round the corner'—only her nan referred to Claire that way. Hope had then been even more delighted that they would be in the yellow class, yellow being her favourite colour, alongside pink at the time.

Her elation was short-lived, though, when she realised her knicker elastic had broken. That meant any sudden movement could leave her underwear around her ankles. She would acquire a nickname that would undoubtedly stick with her for at least the next four years or might even accompany her to senior school and beyond. Luckily for Hope, her mum had quickly come to the rescue. With a handbag that rivalled Mary Poppins's carpet bag, she'd found a couple of safety pins. After they made a hasty dash to the toilets together, they were back in the school hall in no time, relief visible on the young girl's face and her embarrassment temporarily forgotten.

Hope grinned at the memory. She had been just seven years old then, yet she could remember it like it was yesterday. Where had the last twenty years gone? The smile dancing across her lips slowly faded, as she sadly acknowledged that her mum was no longer able to offer her any positive reinforcement, in the form of safety pins *or* encouraging words of advice.

Her thoughts shifted again, and she remembered how her dear mum's trusted handbag had always seemed to contain a remedy for every possible crisis. The shape and colour of the bag may have changed with the fashions over the years, but, regardless of its outer appearance, it had always contained an assemblage of random objects that would each somehow, at one time or another, be desperately needed. *If Mum were still alive today, would her handbag contents have evolved as I grew up and now include icy bottles of prosecco?* Hope ran her tongue over her dry lips and salivated at the thought of a nice cold alcoholic drink.

Taking one last look at her reflection, she started to get out of the car.

She faltered and then jumped as her iPhone sang its silly song. Attempting to hide the tremor in her voice, she spoke into the mouthpiece. It was Ben. The joy of mobiles these days was that they at least told you who was calling. Recently, on the landline, she had promised to grab a bite to eat with a caller, yet had no idea who she'd actually been talking to.

Distractedly, she wondered which was ruder: stopping the caller mid-chat to admit she didn't know who the person was or failing to follow up on the lunch arrangement.

'Hope, how near are you now?' the disembodied voice asked, snapping her back to reality.

What kept making her drift off into her daydreams today? Was she simply trying to think of anything other than what she was about to face?

She'd been chatting away to Ben on her hands-free kit for a large part of the journey. But when she'd taken the wrong exit off the motorway, leading to a ridiculously long detour, he'd hung up so she could concentrate on the directions that Google Maps tried to make her focus on. She was sure she detected frustration in the mechanical voice that kept telling her to make a U-turn before it finally admitted defeat and conjured up a new route instead.

'I'm outside, parking the car.' She didn't admit that she'd been sitting there for a good ten minutes now.

He hung up after saying he would come down to meet her. *Ben,* she half-whispered, half-sang his name in her head, sighing inwardly in resignation. *This may not go as I planned, but what a lovely place to spend the weekend.* She closed her eyes and tried to summon up courage to leave the car. Then, slowly and cautiously, she stepped out into the bright sunshine, surrendering to Fate.

3

Knowing Ben was on his way down to meet her, Hope locked the car and took a deep breath. She turned her head towards the apartments once more and spotted a winding path with a delicate handrail leading uphill. *I might need to hold onto that to stop myself from shaking*, she thought.

She took a step forwards, then looked up and smiled at the man charging down the meandering path. He seemed to be whistling with merriment, though somehow made no sound. Her legs suddenly felt as heavy as lead and refused to move, as the realisation hit her that this silent whistler was Ben.

He looked incredible. She blinked, partly because her eyes were still adjusting to the bright sunlight but also to ensure that he wasn't a figment of her imagination. Summoning up her valour, she persuaded her legs to move forwards, left then right, left again, right again, until she was finally walking without concentrating quite so hard. This really was Ben. He really was here. Here in front of her. Solid as a rock and far from being the disappointment everyone had said he would be. Every single square millimetre of her skin tingled with jubilation.

'Hello, Monkey,' he called out. That voice, now free from the distortion of modern technology, seemed to prance around in the silence for an eternity before finally fading away with the wind. Hope tried to respond but nearly ended up choking as he wrapped her in a hug she never wanted to end.

The next few minutes passed by with Hope in a daze. She must have followed him up to the apartment, or maybe she passed out and he carried her up there. She felt intoxicated by lust. She needed to regain control of her brain before he had her down as a blithering idiot.

'Merry belated Christmas,' she spluttered, burying her face in her handbag to hide her embarrassment. She rummaged around in there until she found what she was looking for. Holding the wrapped package out to him, she dared to speak again. 'This is for you. It's something you can hopefully use when you go sailing.'

Ben carefully removed the red ribbon and opened the daintily wrapped parcel. He looked delighted by its contents: a woolly beanie hat with 'Captain' embroidered across the front.

Hope had been mooching around on the Internet, looking for a present for him, way back when they were due to meet up before Christmas the previous year. She'd known all about his fond love of sailing and that he'd wanted to purchase his own boat in the not-too-distant future. Hope had come up with the idea of a captain's hat but knew the traditional style wouldn't be to his taste. Etsy had personalised gifts, so she decided that a beanie hat would better suit the winter season, and had it embroidered to fit the purpose. She hoped he would appreciate the gesture. Ben had finally purchased his boat just a few weeks earlier, but he probably wouldn't wear the beanie until the weather turned cold.

Again, she found herself wrapped in an enormous embrace. Didn't he realise that if he wasn't careful, he would have her fainting in a heap on the floor? Ben said he couldn't thank her enough for the gift. Hope willed her cheeks to return to their normal shade as she moved away from him to get some air back into her lungs.

'Can I have a look around?' she asked, hoping he'd agree so she could take a moment to regain her composure.

'Sure,' Ben replied, 'go have a nosey. It's only small, you won't get lost.'

She noted how tidy, yet homely, the apartment was. Every room was stylishly designed with a contemporary feel, incorporating furniture that created what Hope could only describe as 'snug-as-a-bug chic'. She pictured herself sharing this sort of life with him. A life by the quayside with a man so stunning she was surprised the myriad flowers in his kitchen vase didn't wilt in defeat, unable to compete with his beauty.

Hope wandered back into the lounge towards where Ben stood. His eyes shone brightly as she reappeared. She took a long hard look at his face now, the face that had occupied so many of her dreams. His mouth slightly turned up at one corner in an inquisitive smile as he cocked his head, apparently trying to work out what she was thinking. It was more than she could handle. Her legs buckled beneath her, dropping her neatly into an armchair.

'Drink?' Ben asked, seemingly reading her mind.

After each polishing off a small glass of wine, they fetched her suitcase from the car and stowed it safely in the apartment. They headed back out into the afternoon sun and, in no time at all, were in the thick of civilisation. Despite marvelling at the beauty of the apartment complex earlier, Hope hadn't anticipated the breath-taking quayside. With places to eat around every corner, it had the incongruity of hustle and bustle combined with the total serenity of the waterway. It was certainly nothing like the furore of the city where she spent half of her life these days.

The afternoon sun beat down on their faces, bouncing off the water and lighting up everything as if sprinkled with gold dust. They walked up to a pretty little bar-restaurant with tables shaded by parasols in the front courtyard. After choosing the one closest to the waterfront, Ben pulled out Hope's chair to seat her. He went off to the bar to get them something to drink, and she watched him, studying his body from afar. His shoulders looked so strong and powerful, hidden beneath a white T-shirt that complemented his tan, and his faded blue jeans fit his cute behind perfectly.

Settling into her chair, Hope finally began to relax. It was impossible not to here. She couldn't be tense, lulled by the water singing away as it lapped against the harbour wall. Every now and then, seagulls cried in unison. As Ben returned and placed their drinks down, she noticed him looking at her strangely again. What did he think of her? Was she what he had expected?

Their thoughts turned to their present neighbours, and they began concocting fictitious stories about the lives of the people around them. The man at the next table, dressed in a garish lime-green T-shirt and khaki shorts, was not-so-delicately slurping his beer as though it were hot soup. By day, he worked as a reputed doctor in a crisp white lab coat, but, incognito now behind his sunglasses and casual attire, he had met up for a secret tryst with his new lover whilst his wife was at home cooking dinner. His companion's ample figure was squeezed into more Lycra than any person should wear at any one time. The unpleasant view of her posterior, which those nearby were treated to, made it almost impossible to imagine her in court, putting criminals behind bars, day in and day out.

Hope laughed at their idiocy, realising that she and Ben were probably being observed, too. She hoped people would think the two of them were a couple. In her eyes, they looked great together. Both were happy with who they were, well aware of the flaws in their characters without feeling the need to try to hide them behind a masquerade of false superiority. Both dressed with a casualness that reflected the simplicity with which they lived their lives, and both seemed relaxed and contented in each other's company.

'Oooooh, I know!' Ben leapt up out of his chair and ran around the corner of the screens partitioning this venue from the surrounding establishments.

Hope sat alone, praying that he would return. She wondered if he was just an apparition and whether he would disappear along with the bright sunshine, now that a few clouds had gathered overhead. Thankfully, she didn't have to wait too long before she saw him again. He carried a little pot of plump green olives and popped one into her mouth as he sat back down.

'You do like olives, don't you?' he asked, a little too late.

'No, Ben, allergic!' Hope coughed and spluttered for a few seconds before looking up at his concerned face. He'd jumped up from his chair and was patting her on the back.

'Just joking, I love them,' she continued. She winked and polished off one, then another, helping herself from the plastic container.

Ben laughed and returned to his seat.

Hope stood at the bar a short while later, feeling slightly heady from a combination of love—or, at least, lust—too much sun, and the intoxicating power of alcohol. Nerves had prevented her from eating much today. Whilst waiting to be served, she tried to focus on the premium spirit bottles displayed elegantly on the bar's top shelf. After ordering another bottle of prosecco, she paid with cash and thanked the barman for the change. She'd always appreciated manners. They cost nothing, and she wished more people would adopt them as a way of life. But then again, not everyone was fortunate enough to have had an upbringing like hers.

Hope ventured back out into the bright light of day, blinking to readjust after the darkened bar. She could barely see where she was going but was intent on not drawing attention to herself. She concentrated on getting the bottle to their table without dropping it as she weaved between clusters of patio tables and chairs. Ben leaned back on his perch, his hands linked behind his head, elbows pointing forwards and face raised to soak up the sun's warmth.

She studied his hands as she approached. How she longed to feel his touch, his hand on hers, the brush of his lips on her own. How she yearned to bury herself in the smell of his skin. How—

'Thanks, hun.' Ben halted her thoughts as he dropped his arms and reached for the bottle to top up their glasses. He finally laid it to rest in the ice bucket, which had sat empty for the last half hour, and started to tell her more about his business. Their endless chats during the last eighteen months had somehow never revealed the particulars of his job, and she wondered whether she had always talked about herself too much.

Ben described his job in great depth, and Hope happily listened, fascinated by everything he told her. He had worked for his father ever since turning twenty-one, had then been put in control of the business when his dad considered early retirement five years later, and had taken over entirely the following year.

It was a marketing firm, and Ben's job involved travelling all over the world in search of products being inadequately promoted or not achieving their true sales potential. Sometimes, he would find a new angle and market a product for a totally different end use.

'For example, your key ring'— he reached out and took it in his right hand—'is intended to be an ornament, but it can also open a bottle, like so.' He picked up the discarded Stella bottle on the table beside them to illustrate the point—although, with the lid already removed, Hope had to resort to her imagination.

The talk continued. How it was tough being

responsible for the welfare of his parents, as they still owned a share of the company; how, in order to buy his majority share, Ben had been forced to sell his house and move in with them, taking no salary and surviving on his savings which had depleted at a rate of knots; and how he'd eventually told his father that he needed his independence again, would be taking a substantial salary going forwards, and was looking to buy himself a new home. Not long afterwards, he had fallen in love with these beautiful surroundings. He put a deposit down on an apartment before the construction work had even been completed and finally moved in and away from the family home one last time. He seemed to love talking about his job, but, at the same time, Hope could see a real sadness in his eyes, as if revealing the sacrifices he'd made over the years by being so career orientated. She didn't want him to feel downhearted, so she turned the talk to the idyllic surroundings.

Yet a ruckus at the next table made them turn their heads. Mr Lime Green T-Shirt and Judgey were trying to quiet the children who had recently gathered and started moaning about something. It was difficult to tell exactly what was going on from the inarticulate high-pitched screams emanating from their tiny mouths. Mr Lime's way of dealing with the situation was to shout and swear and make more noise than the children. Hope felt sad to realise that in twenty years' time, Lime Junior would probably behave the very same way when his children got out of hand.

Ben suggested that they move on. He insisted he knew the perfect place to eat and hoped that a table would be free, as his favourite haunt was very popular with the locals. Hope could see why when they entered. How perfect to walk through a doorway, leaving the harbour behind you, to then be greeted with an undercover version of the very same. Pictures of ships adorned the walls, anchors and masts hung everywhere, and even the bar had a nautical feel. People all around them were tucking into huge plates of seafood, accompanied by crusty bread and more ripe green olives.

After they were shown to a vacant table, a young girl with plaited hair talked them through the menu. Ben ordered for them both, and Hope carefully evaluated the significance of this. She wasn't really used to a man assuming charge of any situation. She found she rather liked it. They chatted about everything and nothing as their friendly waitress brought them drinks.

Soon, two huge bowls of king prawns, still in their shells and smelling delightfully garlicky, were placed in front of them. What fun it was to break the prawns open with their hands, letting the garlic butter sauce dribble down their chins before wiping it away with bright white, oversized cotton napkins. How easy it was to spend time in Ben's company now. Hope's nerves had all but disappeared, leaving in their place a heady feeling of contentment.

With the food well and truly finished, a couple approached their table.

'Foxy and Gabby,' exclaimed Ben, 'come join us.' Ben had phoned his friend upon entering the restaurant, suggesting they all meet up for a drink.

Hope had felt her blood run cold when Ben relayed stories of Foxy's younger days as a local gangster. Now, having retired from the game, he was married to a former glamour model. Looking at the man standing in front of her, all Hope saw was a loveable pussycat. She couldn't quite imagine how he had once had people fearing for their lives. *A real live gangster, eh? That will be something to tell Jess when I get home.*

She chatted away to Foxy as Ben became engrossed in a conversation with his wife. Yet Hope's ears pricked up when she heard Ben mention wanting children in the future. The longing in his voice made it apparent just how passionate he felt about being a dad. His yearning stabbed at her heart, and she hastily excused herself from the table, unable to allow herself to hear any more.

As she climbed the spiral staircase to the toilets, Hope couldn't help but compare it to the winding road her life had taken to her current destination. Had the road always intended to bring her here? Where would life take her next? Her mind drifted off into alcohol-induced dreams of baby Bens. She could see them running around the garden, playing with their father as she looked on with love and admiration. *It's time to lay off the alcohol for a while.* She looked at her face in the mirror. Her eyes were alight with a glimmer of mischief, and her cheeks looked rosy against her tan. *What on earth does he think of me? And how will I ever find out?*

When Hope returned to the group, the newcomers were about to be shown to their table. Waving, Foxy shouted, 'See you both at the seafront for the jazz tomorrow.' He ushered his wife in front of him and walked away. Hope didn't fail to notice Gabby turn around, wink at her, and cock her head towards Ben. *What was she suggesting?*

4

Ben chattered away, telling Hope all about his life as they walked along the coastal path towards the green. Had she asked him to? She couldn't remember, yet here he was opening up to her, holding nothing back. He hadn't ever been this open with her before they'd come face-to-face. She could sense his pain as he talked. He'd obviously had a tough childhood. She listened intently to his stories about getting in with the wrong crowd at school; heard how his dad never really had time for him, as he'd always been so busy working; and learned that he'd always worried about his mum, who put up with barely seeing her husband, week in and week out.

He'd been sent away to boarding school at a very young age. Only after telling his granddad how desperately unhappy he was there, was Ben finally allowed to leave. He moved in with his grandparents for a few years, whilst finishing his education at the local secondary. His granddad had been like a father to him, and the older man's death, when Ben was eighteen, had absolutely destroyed him. He hadn't known which way to turn at that point. He'd tumbled into a bout of depression and wandered off the straight and narrow for a few months. In time, he'd finally found the right path again and had since kept his two feet firmly rooted to it.

Hope's heart went out to the little boy she saw walking along beside her. She sensed the obvious emotion he felt at reliving his past. She wanted to pick him up and wrap him in her arms like a baby, giving him all the love he would ever need. Yet all she could muster was to feebly place her hand on his back, then pull it away almost instantly as the electricity that shot through it caught her unawares. Ben looked around at her, smiling sheepishly. Hope thought his smile looked plastered on, for her sake.

'Strange,' Ben confided. 'I don't normally open up like that.' He hung his head.

Their conversation moved to the surroundings. They chuckled together while passing the tacky amusement arcades on the seafront. Hope mentioned how she and her brothers used to love the 2p machines when they were young. Every caravanning holiday during her childhood had involved the family arriving at a beach somewhere in the United Kingdom. Her mum and dad spent each morning setting up all of the seaside paraphernalia and blowing up inflatables, whilst the four siblings gambled away their pocket money at the arcades. Hope sighed as she fondly recalled the old memories.

Finally, the pair neared the park. Their chatter dwindled as music began to drown out their words. Ben fished his mobile phone out of his back pocket and shouted above the din, 'Niki, where are you all?'

'Right near the stage . . . come find us.'

'We'll be with you shortly.'

'I can't really hear you. We'll see you in a bit, I hope.'

It was selfish, Hope knew, but she still really wanted Ben all to herself. She was a little reluctant to meet up with Niki and the gang. The girls appeared to be thick in the throes of the crowd so, fortunately for Hope, Ben suggested that they wait until the music stopped before attempting to locate them. He led her up a steep bank at the far side of the park, then looked down on the throng, trying to identify his pals. Halfway up the slope, he stopped and sat on the cool grass. He placed his jumper behind him so they could rest their heads on it. He lay back, staring up at the sky, and Hope followed his lead as the fireworks began.

The brisk night air was impregnated with the inimitable smell of gunpowder. Whistles and bangs and crackles and booms were accompanied by such bright and beautiful arrays of light above that Hope couldn't help but wonder if there had been an explosion in heaven. People cried out in wonder with 'Oohs' and 'Ahhs' as the magnificent display waltzed through the dark sky. Her arm suddenly brushed against Ben's, and her skin tingled as though it had been touched for the very first time. She felt her whole body shaking. Wrongly sensing that she was cold, Ben took her hands in his and began to warm them. *If only this moment could last forever,* Hope wished. But with an almighty finale, the fireworks, both inside her body and overhead, were clearly coming to an end.

Niki was now walking towards them, clambering

up the embankment and talking to Ben on his mobile as he directed her to their location in the dark. When she finally stood only metres away, he jumped up to grasp her arm and pulled her up the incline. The three of them sat together whilst introductions were made. Then they decided to go back down to where the band was packing up and Ben's other friends sat finishing their drinks.

His friends were a great crowd. The girls, very similar to Hope's best friend, Jess, were definitely people she would have chosen to get well acquainted with if she had met them back in Cheltenham. The few males in the group, not well known by Ben, were the respective partners of these girls. All were clearly eager to find out as much as possible about Hope, fishing for clues about how she and Ben had met and how long she would stay. *So, they don't know about me, and most of his friends seem to be girls*, Hope reflected, *or maybe even his exes.*

Ben gave little away. His friends turned their talk to the crazy man who had hovered around them all night, performing the most peculiar dances. Two of the girls got up to demonstrate and had the others in stitches as they flailed around, ducking and diving, their plastic wine goblets slopping their contents all over the ground. After all six girls had displayed their version of the weird man's dance, Ben decided it was time to move on. He and Hope would head back to his apartment, freshen up, and go clubbing. The others might meet them later on. Hope recalled the contents of her suitcase. She was sure she'd packed clothes for every eventuality, but what would be suitable for clubbing in Portsmouth and also have a chance of knocking him dead?

They took the same route back to the apartment, but the walk seemed a lot longer in the opposite direction. Perhaps it was simply because they had both been so engrossed in conversation on their way to the green. They wandered mostly in silence now, wrapped up in their own thoughts. Hope toyed with her feelings for him.

After arriving back at the complex, they ran up the winding slope and pushed open the heavy front door. They sprinted up the first flight of stairs and fell through the doorway into Ben's entrance hall. Ben gave Hope another huge hug. Then he handed her a towel from the airing cupboard and left her to jump in the bath whilst he switched on the shower in his en suite.

Hope didn't soak for long and was in and out before she'd even finished running the water. She wanted to leave as much time as possible to do a quick fix of her makeup before getting dressed and sorting out her hair. She needed only a couple more minutes to slide her trousers on, do up her bra, and pull on her top, which revealed an expanse of her flat brown stomach. Was it too much? She twisted her hair up into a mass of soft curls on top of her head and stuck her crocodile clip back into it, then pulled at a few stray tendrils to trail down behind her ears. Back in the kitchen, she steadied her nerves with another drink, facing the hallway to await his impending return.

'Do I look okay for the club?' *Please give something away*, she thought.

'You look perfect,' Ben replied. He seemed to approve of her outfit, based on the way he looked her up and down before returning his gaze to her face.

They left the apartment block, and, with a skip in her step, Hope took up the conversation, chatting away as they approached the club. After manoeuvring them to the front of the queue, Ben led her upstairs. They easily found some seats, and he went off to the bar. She giggled about how he lived his life, mingling with the rich and the fabulous. A rope prevented the riffraff from entering this area, with a sign warning that this lounge was for VIPs only. She hoped she didn't look out of place here amongst all the other members. She hadn't known she was going to be a VIP tonight, but one thing she did know was that Ben was already a Very Important Person to her.

The room was quite tasteful. Deep purples and rich creams were mixed in with fuchsia pinks and silvers. The furniture was a mixture of comfy leather and suede chairs and sofas, and the elegant décor gave the room a posh, aristocratic ambience. What's more, the lounge was spacious, unlike the two overcrowded rooms they had fought their way through on the way up here.

Ben returned with a bottle of wine to share and a glass of diet Coke for Hope. She needed some caffeine to wake her up and something to quench her deep thirst. It was time she slowed her drinking down a little. She hoped that if she lingered on the diet Coke, Ben would drink most of the wine himself before noticing she'd hardly touched a drop. She wanted to remember every second she spent with him tonight, and alcohol would only tinker with her emotions and mess with her memory.

Ben leaned forward to refill his glass. She stole another fleeting glance at his striking features, capturing another snapshot of his face to add to the others she stored in her mind's photo album. They talked about their exes, and again her heart went out to him. Pain was etched into his deep dark eyes and furrowed in his brow. He'd been absolutely besotted with his first long-term ex, Laura. He'd provided her with everything she'd ever wanted, and they'd spent eighteen blissful months together.

But it turned out that giving her everything hadn't been enough for Laura. One afternoon, with no sign that anything was wrong in their relationship, Ben had come home to find her in bed with his brother. Ben explained that Laura had walked straight out of their house that day but not out of his life forever. He had forgiven his brother, Cody, in time. After all, he was flesh and blood. But when Laura and Cody had later married and gone on to start a family, Ben had to find a way to tolerate being around the couple.

'Yeah, family occasions are a little stilted, but at least Cody and Laura are happy,' Ben announced in an acerbic tone.

As the conversation continued, Hope wished she could console him. Clearly, the whole experience had left him reluctant to trust women again, in spite of his brother now being off the market. Ben knew he should let go of the past, safe in the knowledge that a repeat performance was highly unlikely. Instead, he'd got into the habit of pushing away any woman who made a romantic advance.

Hope curled up even more in the wingback chair she had snuggled into. It reminded her of a chair that her parents used to have at home. She felt like a young child again as she fixated on Ben's jaw forming words. They seemed to hang in the air above her and finally filter through to her brain. Her head swam in the intoxicating scent of his aftershave, the music so loud now that he had to lean in even closer to speak to her. His face brushed hers, and his lips caressed her ear as he talked. It would be so easy to turn her head and kiss him. Maybe she should lean in just a little farther . . .

'It's like a few months ago,' Ben continued, 'I was on a date with the most gorgeous girl. She was funny, she was intelligent, we had so much in common, but then she tried to kiss me, and I had to push her away.'

Every last fluid ounce of alcohol in Hope's body evaporated, and she stiffened, stone cold sober, realising how foolish she had almost been. To be rejected by Ben must have broken that poor girl's heart. Hope knew she would never want to experience that herself. She was so grateful he'd told her that story before another minute had elapsed, saving her from total embarrassment. Hastily excusing herself, she made her way to the Ladies. She needed to wrap her brain around what had almost happened and ensure she didn't put herself in that situation again. *What a close call. Okay, so no more visions of kissing him, no more dreaming about how this weekend should end, and no more fantasising. I will just have to hold him at arm's length forever and adore him covertly.*

Hope returned to the VIP lounge and saw Ben now standing. He suggested that they venture into one of the other rooms. She was glad the talk of his exes had stopped for a while. It was heart-wrenching to hear about Ben being with other women, knowing that she would never get any closer to him herself. They entered the adjoining upstairs room, but the music being pumped out of the speakers was not really to Hope's taste. She felt as if she were lost at sea and needed to drown herself in some cheesy tunes for a while. That house music threatened to burst her eardrums.

Luckily, Ben sensed this immediately. 'Let's go downstairs. It's seventies and eighties down there.' He must have read her mind.

'Perfect,' she mouthed back at him. This was more like it. Everyone around them was singing and dancing. The crowds had dispersed, too, and Hope felt much more relaxed.

'Would you like another drink?' Ben inclined his head towards the bar.

'No, the queue's too long, honey.' She didn't fancy standing on her own for ages whilst he waited to be served.

'I'll get us some water then. Watch this.' He walked straight up to the crowded bar, leaned over to whisper something in the barman's ear, and was back at her side within seconds, glass of water in hand.

'I'm impressed. So, what's the secret? VIP pass?'

'No. It's easy, though.'

As he told her his trick, she laughed at its sheer simplicity. 'Brilliant!' She took the glass from his hand and gulped down some of the cool liquid.

'Oi, what are you staring at?' Ben's face appeared contorted as he squared up to the man he'd addressed.

Hope thought quickly. She couldn't let him fight and risk ruining his handsome face. No. She had to stop it, and fast.

'Honey, don't.' She stepped in between the two men, reaching up to grab Ben's arms as he raised them above his head. She pulled them down, pinning them at his sides. Why was he now looking at her, a smirk on his lips, not even attempting to free his arms or argue?

'You really thought I was going to hit him, didn't you, babe? It's my old workmate. Karl, meet Hope. Hope, meet Karl.'

Of course, he wasn't going to fight. He was a pacifist. She'd learned that about him, at least, in the many conversations they'd had over the last year or so. She laughed. With the introductions over, she listened to the two of them catch up on old times and joined in the conversation wherever she could.

Karl was clearly wondering about her relationship to Ben. He complimented his friend on the 'little hottie' Ben was fortunate enough to be in the company of tonight. Karl then turned to Hope, falsely implying that Ben was gay and that she was wasting her time with him. He told her she should spend the evening with a 'real man' instead.

Maybe it would be easier on me if Ben really were gay, she reflected silently. 'I know he is, Karl,' she flashed back with a smile. 'I'm gay too, I'm afraid.'

Karl liked her. He admired her comeback. He gave Ben a hefty smack on the back and Hope a kiss on the cheek before retreating into the crowd.

'Your turn to get some water, babe,' Ben challenged, his eyes glinting with mischief.

Hope stepped up to the busy bar and leaned over as Ben had done earlier to shout into the barman's ear, 'Help me, please, my friend's really not feeling very well. Any chance of a glass of water, as I'm worried he's about to be sick?'

It worked a treat. After all, what barman was going to refuse this request and risk having to clean up a pile of vomit later on? *Not a nice image*, Hope surmised as she returned to her partner in crime.

Ben pulled Hope closer, so he could talk into her ear over the music's heavy beat. They stayed that way and danced together whilst the last song played. Just two new friends enjoying the closeness they had shared tonight. She may have been wrong, but she could have sworn he just kissed her neck. Did she imagine it?

5

The lights in the casino reception were brighter than those in a dentist's examination room. Hope's eyes hurt as she tried to get accustomed to the glare. Ben had enrolled here the previous week but now needed to pose for photos to receive his membership card. He stood in front of the hi-tech digital camera and pulled two faces that made Hope's heart skip a beat.

The first portrayed fury, reminding her of a British bulldog, his nostrils flaring and lips forced tightly together, wrinkling over his clenched teeth. His deeply furrowed eyebrows pulled his eyes nearly closed and lifted his cheekbones high up on his face. In a split second, he switched to the second expression, making him look like a little boy, all sweetness and light, head cocked sideways, angelically staring at the camera with blushing cheeks and pouting lips.

Stop it, you're killing me, Hope begged wordlessly.

Ben signed Hope up as a guest, and then it was her turn to stand in front of the camera. She hated having her photo taken at the best of times, so how embarrassing to stand in this harsh lighting with her Adonis watching. She tried to smile sweetly, hating every second of the torturous ordeal.

After filling in their forms, they climbed the stairs to the casino room, then headed straight to the bar. Yet it had closed at two, and the only beverages available until the casino shut at six were orange squash and water. Not really enough to whet an appetite, but certainly not worth dampening their mood over.

They declined the soft drinks and wandered around the various gambling tables, watching people throw away money as if it were waste paper. People won and lost with no flicker of emotion on their faces. They seemingly got little enjoyment whenever they won and didn't allow disappointment to show when their chips were down. She and Ben didn't part with any cash themselves, but they soaked up the atmosphere and chatted some more.

Hope felt quite sober by now. It had been a good idea to lay off the alcohol for the last two hours, but she really longed for something with a bit of a kick to perk her up and stop her from feeling so sleepy. Once again, Ben read her mind, suggesting that they venture back to his apartment where there was more alcohol on tap.

As they ventured out into the early morning air, the friendly doorman bid them goodnight. Ben couldn't resist teasing him by yelling, 'Can't believe how much we won.'

The other man, evidently not realising Ben's jubilation was faked, acted happy for him, cheering and slapping him on the back. Hope half-skipped, half-danced alongside Ben, hoping it wouldn't now simply be home and to bed. The fresh air had woken her up, and she didn't want to face the night drawing to a close, even though nothing romantic was on the cards.

Ben and Hope rounded the corner, and the apartments loomed ahead, silent and still. Most of the inhabitants were likely fast asleep. They crept through the front door and tip-toed upstairs to the first floor. Ben silently swung open the door to apartments five, six, and seven and passed through first. He put his key into the lock of number six, and Hope followed. She hadn't realised the door would swing shut quite so rapidly. It made a terrific bang and no doubt woke up everyone in this and the neighbouring block.

Darting inside, Ben led her straight out onto the balcony. He popped back into the lounge to fill the space with soft melodious notes from his blue-tooth speaker. It was so magical out here. Apart from the tunes inside her head, the only other sound Hope heard was the beating of her heart. Ben sat down beside her and admitted that he'd had to have a couple of drinks before she'd arrived. He'd been nervous about meeting her for the first time.

Why? Hope wondered. *Is this as big to him as it is to me? It can't possibly be.* She scrutinised his face, trying to read his expression. *No, surely it was just a date like any other in his eyes. Maybe not even a date, simply a friendly get-together. Why do I always have to give things labels?*

'You need another drink. I'm far too drunk, and you've sobered up.' His words cut into her train of thought.

Why was he worried about being more intoxicated than her? Were his nerves breaking through again?

Was he uneasy because he wanted to make a move? She silently chastised herself for letting false hope creep back into her mind and taunt her once more.

Hope ventured into the kitchen to pour a small glass of wine. She picked up her mobile phone from the worktop where it had spent all afternoon and all night. She normally never went anywhere without it, yet today she hadn't even noticed its absence. She decided to send a text to Jess, the words spinning before her eyes. Not so much because of the alcohol she'd consumed, but more because the giddiness of yearning had taken her prisoner and wouldn't let her go. It affected her sight and threatened to impede her judgement. She ferociously punched away at the buttons, completed the jumble of words, selected Jess's number from the phone's directory, and sent the message bouncing through the radio waves.

She swallowed her drink and returned to Ben. He was now sitting on the sofa with his head in his hands and elbows on his knees.

'I need to be horizontal, babe. I have to go for a lie down,' he murmured.

What a notion that put into her head. But then she realised that he clearly hadn't been planning to make a move; he'd simply been acknowledging how drunk he was. She took a chance and hedged her bets, still not wanting the night to end.

'Can I come and perch on your bed and chat as you fall asleep, or do you want me to leave you in peace?'

'Come with me. I just need to lie down for a while.' He smiled back at her.

They retired to his bedroom, and Ben pottered around, dimming the lights and putting on more soft music. He undressed down to his boxers and wandered into the en suite to brush his teeth. This left Hope sitting awkwardly on the edge of the bed, chattering away whilst wondering whether to get under the covers with her clothes on or sit on top. By the time he'd returned and climbed in, pulling the duvet around him, she had decided to get under as well. She climbed in fully clothed and waited to see if he protested.

Five minutes passed, and it seemed they were settling in for the night. Then he stirred and pulled her into a hug, enveloping her in his near-naked torso. She didn't dare move. She was so close to him that she could feel his heart beating, see the muscles twitching in his face, and savour the warmth of his soft skin. He opened his eyes and looked deep into hers. And then he kissed her.

A thousand sensations tore through her body, as if someone had just run an electric current through her veins. Desire, passion, and yearning took her brain and her heart hostage and rendered her body paralysed. She'd never before experienced anything like this. Never before felt her heart threaten to jump out of her chest. Never before known how intense one kiss could be.

'No, this isn't right.' Ben's voice pierced her thoughts like a dagger through her heart.

Her lips felt naked without his pressed against them. Her brain needed time to catch up and compute the sudden change of emotion from euphoria to misery. Of course, it wasn't right. He'd warned her that he ran away if women tried to kiss him—although she was pretty sure he had made the first move. The alcohol and the tiredness must have affected his judgement. It was all too much for Hope, and she rolled away from him to hide her disappointment.

'Hope?' Ben pulled her towards him again and held onto her, his chest against her back. 'I can't believe how drunk I still feel. You're not sulking, are you?'

'No, silly, just letting you sleep,' she whispered into the darkness.

'But I don't want to sleep. I just need to sober up a little.' He rubbed his temples.

Hope lay with her eyes open, head groggy, and brain tired, staring into the darkness, while cocooned tightly in his arms. That kiss. How could she ever forget it, how would anything in her life ever compare, and why had he stopped almost as soon as he'd started? If he didn't feel anything for her, then why was he still holding her so tightly?

6

After finally getting home from work, Jess dragged her tired legs up the gravel drive towards the front door. The exterior light sensed her presence and switched itself on to illuminate her way. She turned her key in the lock, then pushed the door open to reveal nothing but silence and darkness inside. The house seemed eerily quiet with Hope not home.

She kicked off her dainty shoes in the hallway and felt her way along the luxuriously thick carpet and into the kitchen. After setting her bags down with one hand and flicking the lights on with the other, she went to the fridge to retrieve last night's left-over wine. She poured a generous glassful, drank a big gulp, and then topped the glass up again. After another glug, she took the weight off her feet and let out an enormous sigh. She was too tired to eat tonight. It had been a long day at work, and all she really wanted was a hot bath and bed. Stretching her arms above her head and letting out an almighty yawn, she rose from her chair. It really was strange to have the house to herself for the weekend.

Hope had purchased this property two years earlier with the inheritance she'd kept in the bank after her mum's death, but it was a large house for one person alone. Jess had moved in less than a year later, when Hope had been looking for a flatmate to help with monthly bills. The two girls had hit it off immediately, becoming best friends. The house was beautiful, a real home set in a tiny cul-de-sac, away from the noise of passing vehicles and the human traffic of society. It had been a five-bedroom semi until Hope had one day decided to knock two of the bedrooms into one.

Jess chuckled as she remembered coming home that day to find a calm Hope, plasterboard dust almost obscuring her from sight. Balancing a beam on one shoulder, she was attempting to free the electric cable hanging precariously from it with the aid of a jigsaw and a lot of determination. The cable, still attached to the light switch but running through a hole in the beam, had prevented this seven-foot piece of timber from dropping to the floor as the rest of them had, but Hope hadn't seemed fazed.

When Jess realised what was going on, she ran to Hope's rescue, only to hear her friend pipe up with, 'Don't worry, honey, I've got it all under control. Just this bugger of a beam to sort out, and I'll be down for tea.' And so, power tool whirring and making it impossible for Jess to argue, she had left Hope to it. The house, having contained five intact but fairly small bedrooms that morning, proudly boasted a massive open space and an impressive pile of rubble by teatime. But that was Hope, headstrong and determined. If she wanted something badly enough, she would make it happen. In the newly created space, she had since completed the master bedroom with en suite. It was nothing short of exquisite. Hope had an eye for interior design and a knack for DIY.

In the bathroom, Jess started filling the tub with hot water. Another of Hope's successes was this perfect getaway, well equipped to cleanse body and mind. Hope had tiled from floor to ceiling herself. Shy of doing the plumbing work—though Jess knew Hope would probably soon acquire this skill—she had single-handedly created this bathroom in less than a week. Jess wandered into her bedroom to get a book. She'd have a quick soak whilst reading a few pages and then head straight for bed.

Lying in the bath, her reflections returned to Hope. She was so glad they had met. After splitting up with her long-term boyfriend and needing somewhere to stay, Jess had spotted Hope's advert for a flatmate at the local gym. A quick phone call to the number listed had culminated in the pair of them meeting up for coffee. They chatted away as if they'd known each other for years, and Hope had asked her to move in that evening. Jess had made a quick dash back to her ex's to gather her belongings but had left behind all of their joint possessions. Well, almost all of them. She took the one thing she treasured: their playful cat, Gizmo, rescued from a supermarket car park in the happy early days of their relationship.

So, here she was now, living with Hope and Gizmo. Like Hope, she was also headstrong and independent, and, looks-wise, many people mistook them for sisters. This delighted them. Jess was the elder of the pair, a year and a half Hope's senior, but she often felt younger, being a few rungs behind Hope on the career ladder, due to her eleventh-hour entry into the retail industry.

Her hair slightly shorter than Hope's and more red than brown, Jess often envied her friend's slightly flatter stomach and sun-kissed skin. She didn't realise Hope coveted her porcelain complexion and beautiful, big, brown puppy dog eyes. There was never any real jealousy between them. They were as thick as thieves and could always solve any problem or disagreement that threatened to come between them. They seemed to understand each other even better than they understood themselves.

Jess often came home to find a glass of wine poured and her tea on the table. Similarly, Hope might find Jess laden with chocolate, sensing that Hope felt hormonal and could do with some pampering. If one of them felt down, the other always supplied the tonic, usually laughter and merriment. They'd end up dancing along to the radio or splitting their sides giggling about something foolish they did that day.

They had built up such a strong friendship during the last year that nothing could divide them. If a man dated one of them, he would sure as hell have to become friends with the other. It was an unwritten but non-negotiable rule. If Hope did end up with Ben, he would have to make room for Jess in his life, too, because wherever Hope went, Jess would no doubt follow.

As she climbed into bed, Jess decided to spend her next day off in town, looking for stylish additions to her wardrobe and any sexy passers-by who caught her eye. Unlike Hope, she wasn't after a relationship. She wanted to focus on her up-and-coming career. But that didn't stop her from window shopping. If she hadn't had to work this weekend, she probably would have joined Hope in Portsmouth. She was keen to meet Ben and see for herself whether he was good enough for Hope. Jess looked at her phone, but there was nothing since Hope had messaged that she'd arrived safely. Was that good news or bad news?

7

Minutes had passed. Hope couldn't tell if it had been five or fifty. She willed all fantasies of Ben to vanish from her head, but they refused to be banished. She thought the alcohol was playing tricks on her as she felt herself being gently rolled over to face him. Then he kissed her again. The kiss stunned her for a moment, making her breathless. His eyes remained open, piercing into hers, staring into her soul and transmitting his unmistakable message of desire.

Such frightening yet incredible sensations rippled through her body, feelings she tried to fight with all her strength but couldn't.

'You're beautiful, Hope,' he whispered in her ear.

She shivered with excitement. The sheer intensity of the moment was almost too much to bear. She felt as if the world had suddenly stopped spinning and now rested motionless on its axis. Time slowed and then stood still.

The early morning sunlight, streaming through the window and across their bodies, was the only indication of how long they'd been pressed together, transported to some other world where only they existed.

'I think you're lovely,' Ben's sleepy voice whispered. He'd already said this twice or three times earlier.

Hope couldn't remember if she'd answered him. She half wondered whether the whole experience had rendered her speechless. What was there to say anyway, without revealing how much he already meant to her?

She still somehow had to execute her plan: not to suffocate him with how she felt, in the hope that he'd fall for her first. Well, not exactly first. But if he wasn't aware of how strongly she felt, then she could pretend she hadn't fallen for him yet. She nestled into the crook of his arm, feeling delirious as he turned and kissed her forehead. He stroked her hair away from her cheeks and let his hand rest loosely on her stomach, exposed entirely now, in spite of her being fully clothed. Their bodies remained entwined, joined from chest to foot, whilst their heartbeats echoed in the silence, pulsating as one. Time once again stood still.

Hope peered over at the man lying by her side. He seemed so contented. A smile was plastered on his beautiful face, and his eyes were now tightly shut. It was the first time she had seen them closed all night. As they drifted off in each other's arms, she wondered what the future had in store for them.

Hope prised open her eyes and looked at the clock on the wall. It was almost midday and time they got up, but Ben wouldn't move. She smiled at him whilst attempting to drag herself out of bed, weak from lack of sleep and the alcohol and oxytocin still in her system. Leaving Ben dozing, she wandered into the bathroom, stretching her arms above her head and yawning loudly. Whilst the bath filled, she pottered into the lounge and put the kettle on, contemplating the recent turn of events.

Ben had said she was beautiful last night, but had he really meant it? What would happen next? And why on earth was she not still in bed with him now? She knew why. She needed some thinking time. She was well aware that the events of this morning's early hours would make it even more difficult to tear herself away from him this evening. She wanted to get used to being on her own again before she had to leave.

She soaked in the bath for a good ten minutes, closing her eyes and lying back in the bubbles. She allowed her body to rest and her heart to recover from pulsating like a big bass drum for hours. After washing her hair and scrubbing her face, she stepped out of the tub and wrapped a towel around her torso. She lavishly applied moisturiser before padding into the kitchen to make a cup of coffee. She considered making Ben a cup, too, but figured she'd wait until she heard him stir.

He had told her, quite a few times during the night, how scared he got whenever women started to like him and how his knee-jerk reaction was always to run away. She vaguely remembered replying on one occasion that he had no need to run from her. She'd tried to play it carefully and not give away how deeply she felt for him. Well, if she had to act ultra-cool, then she would. She wouldn't be standoffish but would make sure she didn't appear to be falling for him. Yes, she could do that. Luckily, she only had to convince him and not herself. Getting out of bed early this morning had been a good start. If she'd stayed there any longer, who knew what might have happened?

After climbing into some fresh clothes, Hope dried her hair and reapplied her makeup: a small amount of foundation, a few strokes of black mascara, and neutral lip gloss. Twenty minutes after getting dressed, she crept into the bedroom and stood by the door.

'Come back to bed,' Ben begged, reaching out towards her but unable to stretch far enough to pull her closer. She climbed under the covers, fully clothed, and snuggled into his arms.

'I want these off.' He pulled at the leg of her jeans.

'And do you always get what you want, Mr Knight?' she asked teasingly. 'I don't think that's a good idea, do you?' He didn't answer either question.

Somewhere inside the building, a clock chimed one.

'Aren't we supposed to meet Foxy and the others on the seafront about now?' Hope muttered, sitting up. The gang would be wondering where they were, but she hoped the tiredness in their faces and the brightness in their eyes wouldn't reveal what she and Ben had been up to earlier.

Ben stepped idly out of bed and bent over to kiss her before wandering off towards the shower in his boxers. She drooled over his near-naked body as he disappeared out of sight, so tanned and muscular, so tantalising. She could picture the soap bubbles running down his chest as he washed away every last trace of their union.

After great hesitation, Hope tore herself away from the sound of cascading water and moved into the kitchen. She turned the kettle back on and made two cups of coffee, then placed the mugs on the lounge table. Ben joined her on the sofa, and the pair sipped their drinks, neither one uttering a word, each grinning lazily at the other. But a phone call from Ben's mother disrupted the silence, and the world once again resumed spinning on its axis. Everything suddenly felt diametrically opposed to how it had been moments earlier. Leaving Ben chatting away to his mum, Hope pulled on her strappy sandals and got ready to leave the apartment.

With the phone call over, Ben ushered Hope out of the door ahead of him and down in the lift to the car park below. They climbed into his silver soft-top and drove off to meet the others. The sun was scorching again today, so speeding along with the roof down and the wind in their hair was a real luxury.

After they'd parked on the seafront, Hope removed her shoes to walk barefoot along the hot paving slabs towards the grandstand. It was almost three o'clock now, and they both felt decidedly peckish, having had no breakfast. The tantalising aroma of fried onions made their stomachs grumble as it coaxed them closer to a burger van and defied them to resist.

'Hot dog, please.' Hope was reminded of the tomato sauce advert in which the male actor orders his hot dog before running up to the roof of an American skyscraper, placing his tomato sauce bottle down on a ledge, and then returning to collect his hot dog just as the sauce has dripped onto it from the bottle above. Ben decided on a cheeseburger, and they wandered over to nearby tables to smother their food with ketchup and mustard.

They walked and ate, looking for the familiar faces of Ben's friends. It didn't take them long to find the group, spread out with a multitude of picnic hampers and blankets as they lay out in the sun.

'Hi, guys,' Ben greeted them, yawning.

'You finally made it, then.' Niki winked, raising an eyebrow at Ben.

A few more introductions were necessary, as Hope didn't recognise everyone from the previous night. Then she and Ben settled down to relax in the afternoon sun. Hope lay on her back and closed her eyes, letting the warm rays beat down on her tired body, recharge her batteries, and allow her to indulge in her fantasies. Ben lay close beside her, their arms brushing. But Hope now felt downhearted, as if they were oceans apart.

They listened as the girls and their respective others recounted amusing stories. Ben and Hope were happy to be the audience, rather than use the little energy they had left to join the conversation. At one point, when everyone else was having a heated debate about where they should go later that night, Ben turned to Hope and told her again how he tended to run away when someone was interested in him.

'I know you do, Ben, you said so last night.' *Many times,* she added silently, turning her face back to the sun and closing her eyes to hide her pain. She didn't need him to tell her again. It wouldn't be easy to hide her true feelings from him, but she knew that being a little detached was the only way she could get him to figure out how he felt about her, instead of pushing her away.

It was late afternoon, with no sign of Foxy, so Ben decided he and Hope should make a move. He was due at his parents' house in a few hours for dinner, and Hope needed to return to Cheltenham before it got too late. She tore herself away from the conversation she was having with a couple of the girls and reluctantly bid them all goodbye. She couldn't help but feel a little miserable, partly at leaving her new friends but mostly because she knew that soon she would be packing her case and leaving Ben, too.

The two of them walked back towards the car, and Ben handed Hope his keys. 'Why don't you drive us home?' he suggested.

'Can I really?' She loved the idea of putting her foot down and couldn't hide her excitement as he nodded. He helped her into the driver's seat and showed her how to adjust it. As Ben jumped into the passenger seat, she looked over and asked, 'But what if I crash it?'

'Oh, it's only a car. They're replaceable,' he replied, smiling.

Only a car! It was worth about ten of her car. She buckled up, let him put the roof down, and started the engine.

Soon after they got back to his apartment, Ben phoned his parents and cancelled on dinner. Instead, he ordered takeaway pizza for the pair of them. Hope secretly loved that he had chosen her over his dinner invitation. She refused to believe it was simply because he was too tired to get ready to go out again and drive all the way over there.

As they finished the pizza and tucked into ice

cream, Ben's phone rang. 'Karl. How are you, mate?' Hope couldn't hear the other side of the conversation but listened to what Ben said. 'Yeah, she's not bad.' His noncommittal tone surprised Hope, and she looked over to see him smiling and winking, teasing her and toying with Karl. 'Well, she's still here now, and you know me, mate, usually scratching at the walls by now, aren't I?' He carried on the conversation, giving little else away, but it was enough to set Hope's mind and heart racing again.

So, he usually craved his own space when in the company of a girl for too long, yet here he was, having cancelled his dinner plans and seemingly in no rush to kick her out. She'd spent more than thirty hours with Ben by now, so she couldn't help but feel a faint glimmer of excitement. Surely, this was a good sign and something she could build on. He clearly liked having her around. She would just have to ensure that she didn't ruin it by outstaying her welcome.

Ben placed his phone in front of him and lay back on the sofa. The television was on, but tiredness had caught up with both of them now. Hope knew it was time to go. She had to be up early to get to Birmingham first thing in the morning for another day's work. *How mundane that will be after such an incredible weekend here.*

'I'd better head off, honey,' she said, turning towards him. It was almost ten now, and she would be asleep on the motorway if she stayed any longer.

'Why don't you stay tonight?' he ventured. 'We'll both need to go straight to sleep, as I have a hectic day tomorrow, and you'll have to get up very early to get back. It would make more sense than driving when you're tired, though.'

She'd not dared entertain such an idea earlier when it had crept into her head, but she'd have been a fool to turn that offer down.

Ben pulled her up off the sofa and left her packing her case for the morning whilst he got ready for bed. After a few minutes, she joined him in the bedroom, and they both climbed under the covers. There was no kissing this time around. He was absolutely shattered, she could tell. *Or did he already regret what happened last night?*

8

Hope battled against the wind as she trudged across the car park. The rain stung her eyes and made her curse aloud. Placing her suitcase in the boot and tugging it down until it latched tightly, she had to acknowledge how the murky morning mirrored her mood. With steely resolve, she gulped back a sob, climbed into the driver's seat, and started the engine.

Mammoth hailstones pounded the windscreen, drowning out the radio. She blinked back tears. Only when she placed her phone in its holder on the windscreen did she realise it hadn't charged properly last night. On top of that, she must have left the charging cable plugged in beside Ben's bed. She was sure she kept a spare in her glove compartment, but no amount of searching would reveal one. Her phone was required for the Google Maps function, yet with only ten percent battery life left, it clearly wouldn't get her far today. Hope sighed, pulling out of the car park and off into the unknown. She felt as if she'd left something else behind, too—yet it wasn't *something* but rather *someone*.

She had dragged herself out of bed at three thirty, a ludicrous hour surely intended to be seen only at the end of a night on the town, not at the beginning of a new day. Having crept around, not wanting to wake Ben, she'd finally taken a few minutes to sit and watch him sleeping once she was ready to leave. His face was set in an adorable sleepy smile with his eyes firmly shut and his body curled in the foetal position. She had kissed him on the forehead, written a quick thank-you message on last night's pizza box, and then forced herself out of the apartment. The large, heavy door had clicked shut behind her with such finality that she'd felt like screaming and begging to be let back in.

After driving for no more than twenty minutes, with her iPhone battery having lasted only fifteen, Hope had a funny feeling that she'd gone wrong somewhere. She'd managed to add an extra hour to the journey on the way to Portsmouth, and she couldn't afford to do that again on the way home. It was half past four already, and in three and a half hours she had to be in Birmingham, opening up the store. If she'd known she would be staying over Sunday night, as well as Saturday, then she would have come prepared and driven straight to the city this morning. *Ah, the beauty of hindsight.*

At least, there weren't many cars on the road at this time of the morning. Most people were sensibly still tucked up in bed. The memory of Ben lying asleep made tears prick her eyes again. *It won't do to cry. The roads are slippery and visibility is poor. Plus, I have to get my brain into work mode.* After two days away from the business, she had a lot to do in the store today.

Seeing a sign to her left, she attempted to read it as she passed by, slowing just enough to make out which motorway she was on and how far away London was. She'd definitely messed up somehow, but now what should she do? Turn back or continue? Turn back towards the man she could see a future with or continue in this direction which might eventually take her home, possibly to never hear from him again?

A bit later, the motorway services loomed ahead of her. She decided to purchase a charging cable so she could fire up her phone again. Whilst there, she also had a quick look at one of the map books on the swirly stand, studying the route and trying to imprint the multicoloured lines into her brain so she could recall the image later. Although purchasing the map seemed like the obvious thing to do, it wasn't an option. Hope was unwilling to waste money and felt that seven pounds was far too much to pay for the solitary page she needed in this atlas whilst waiting for her iPhone to wake up. Especially as she had to shell out almost a fiver for the phone cable.

It seemed that if she continued on for a couple more junctions, she could then leave via an A-road that would take her back to the motorway she was meant to be on. She would only end up taking a short detour. It was mainly dual carriageway, and, after weighing up the odds of following a couple of winding B-roads to cut a corner, she decided to stick to the faster road. She memorised the number of the junction where she would need to exit the motorway, paid for the cable, and ran back out to her car.

Hope sped along, foot to the floor, knowing an extra ten miles an hour on the motorway could be the difference between catching a suitable train from

Cheltenham and having to phone her area manager to explain why she would be late. She didn't tolerate tardiness from her staff, so she was damned if she would be late herself this morning. Come hell or high water, she had to make it to work on time. It was a matter of principle.

After leaving the motorway at the correct junction, she took the first exit off the next roundabout and pulled onto the correct A-road. She smiled, realising she was now back on track. Then she blinked twice and shook her head in disbelief at the sign up ahead, revealing the mileage to Portsmouth. She'd gone and joined this road headed in totally the wrong direction and now was driving back to Ben. Why on earth was she so useless this morning? Was her subconscious taking over, trying to send her back to the place she wanted to be?

Eight minutes later—she timed it because she wanted to know just how long her foolishness at that last roundabout had cost her—she managed to leave the dual carriageway and rejoin the A-road, headed in the right direction this time. It wasn't until she was another half hour into the journey and firmly back on track that she allowed her thoughts to drift to Ben again. Flashes of their kisses crept into her head. She would always have the memories, but that might be all she would ever have.

Hope had intended to be back at the house by six, to spend an hour with Jess before they both left for work, but that plan had gone out of the window. Maybe she could make it back by six thirty and still have time to share some juicy tit-bits with her best friend. She would have to leave for the station at seven at the latest in order to catch her train at twelve minutes past. She usually set off at five minutes to the hour to give her a few spare minutes after parking the car.

At quarter past five, her phone lit up, indicating that it had enough charge to be of use again. *Finally!* She pulled over onto the hard shoulder to launch Google Maps and then set off again, commanding Siri to dial Jess's number.

'Hi, sweetie. I'm having a bit of a nightmare. I hope I haven't woken you.'

'No, hun, you're alright, I've been up for hours. You know I'm a morning person.'

'Yeah, right. I've been getting a little bit lost, but I'm back on track now. Google doesn't seem to think I'll be able to make it back until after seven, so I'm hoping for a small miracle.'

'Fruit loop, what time is it? Have I been snoozing?'

'It's just gone five fifteen.'

'Give me ten minutes to open my eyes. I need a coffee before I can do anything, and then I'll ring you to see how you're doing before I jump in the shower.'

'Okay, honey, thank you.'

Jess reluctantly dragged herself into a sitting position and threw her legs over the side of her bed, aiming her feet into her slippers. She went downstairs to the kitchen and made a cup of coffee strong enough to fuel a whole army of soldiers going into battle. Then she called Hope back.

Hope answered her mobile.

'Hey, how's the traffic? Need me to sort you out a mini miracle?'

'Yes please, it's still not looking good.' She might as well have been running all the way home, she was so breathless. 'I've so much to tell you, but it will have to wait until tonight. I really need to concentrate on driving now. I'm so tired.'

'Okay, hun. Drive safely. Sending mini miracle now.'

The call ended, and Hope peered at the estimated arrival time showing up on her Google Maps screen. *Damn.* She still had ninety-two miles to travel, and, although most of it was on this motorway, it would be touch and go whether she would even be home in time to catch her second train of the morning. That would get her into work half an hour late but still in plenty of time to get everything done before opening the store.

Moments later, the rain began to ease, and the sun ventured out to greet the day. Hope was making inroads now, not daring to look at her speed but keeping track of the miles ticking away on the milometer. Her Google Maps app constantly recalculated her chances of getting back to the house in time for her first or second train. She'd made up quite a few minutes and felt a little less stressed now. Her foot was pressed down on the accelerator, connecting with the floor. Then she watched in horror as her driver's mirror suddenly flew out of its casing and bounced along the road behind her, narrowly missing an approaching car. She'd known it was loose for a few weeks but had never got around to doing anything about it. Well, as long as her car didn't blow up or break down, she didn't mind sacrificing a mirror or two.

Her nonchalance was short-lived, however. An illuminated sign indicated that the road would be closed at some point ahead, due to an earlier accident. The odds were really stacked up against her today. Would grim determination be enough? Google Maps wasn't advising her to take a diversion, so either it hadn't been made aware of the accident, as it had only just happened, or Hope was due to turn off the A417 before it closed. She needed to call Jess again and see if she could figure out exactly where the accident was.

'Jess, there's been an accident. No, not me! I wondered if you could look and see whereabouts it is, please?'

'I don't think I've got time to, honey, sorry. Did my miracle not work?'

Hope laughed. 'No, not yet. Don't worry. I think it will be alright. Keep your fingers crossed for me.'

'I will. I'll ring you when I get to the station. Perhaps the batteries need changing in my magic wand.'

Jess was currently completing a six-week training programme with Next, having recently accepted a job with the company as assistant manager in the Cheltenham store. So, every morning for the last week, she and Hope had set off for the station at around the same time, only to disappear in opposite directions as one went to Bristol and the other to Birmingham. Hope was so proud of Jess, sailing through the interview and following in her retail footsteps. She was sure to become a store manager herself before too long. Hope loved that she could teach her friend a few things about the industry and had helped her prepare for the interview itself. Although, truth be known, Jess had been more than capable of single-handedly selling herself to the area manager.

Jess had to be dying to hear about her weekend at Ben's. Hope was disappointed that she couldn't share all the details until after work. She remembered sending Jess a text on Saturday night, before anything had happened with Ben, and wondered what she had written. She had wanted to save all the juicy bits until they were both sitting in the kitchen together, so she could see Jess's reaction.

The situation with the diversion finally revealed itself. Fewer than one hundred yards of open road lay ahead of Hope, and big signs made her indicate to the left and pull off onto a road that she really didn't want to take. She wasn't in Cheltenham yet, but it was now Google Maps' duty to find her a suitable detour. *What a pain. If I hadn't had to turn off just then, I would have been within minutes of my house.*

Making her way around a roundabout, Hope crunched the gears in her haste. *Whoops. Now I've forgotten how to drive.* At least, this detour apparently wouldn't go too far out of her way. She could see Cheltenham on the signposts now, a mere seven miles and sixteen minutes away, according to Google. But she hadn't anticipated the slow traffic on this single carriageway, and, as sod's law had it, she found herself following a dirty great tractor at snail-miles an hour. *If I can make the 7:12, then Ben will fall in love with me*, she decided. Some people used daisies to find out whether their chosen one loved them, carefully plucking off a petal at a time. Hope was, however, putting her entire love life in the hands of British Rail, an organisation not famed for its reliability. *Anyway, there's no chance. It's far too late now.*

With a final glance at the clock on the dashboard, Hope pulled into the drive and left the engine running. She tore into the house and bounded up the stairs two at a time, then put on a clean top and located the keys to the store. After racing back downstairs and into the kitchen, she grabbed a cereal bar and a can of diet Coke from the cupboard, not even stopping to shut it behind her. She locked the front door and sprinted back to her car to yank her makeup bag from her suitcase in the boot. Then she was off once more, this time heading for the station.

Six minutes past seven—did she have a chance? It should take only two minutes to get there. Time was almost on her side now. But would 'almost' be enough? Parking in her usual spot but without the care and precision she usually employed, she ran across to the platform.

Hope hadn't known what to do when her mobile had rung the moment her train arrived. It had stopped ringing before she'd had a chance to fish for it in her bag. But she had called Jess back shortly afterwards. 'Jess, can you hear me? I'm on it, I made it!'

'I saw you pull into the drive just as I left the close. I found the Duracell batteries. My wand's on fire today!' Jess shouted into her phone.

Hope giggled. 'It certainly is!' she panted into the mouthpiece, before collapsing in a heap in the vestibule end. Too tired to look for a seat, with bags scattered all around her, she'd made it. Ben had to fall for her now.

9

The rain bucketed down as thunder and lightning battled mercilessly in the dark sky. Adam cursed aloud, looking around at the mass of cardboard boxes he'd just unloaded from his hired van. They were stacked in disarray, turning to a pulp and beginning to scatter their cargo all over the sodden floor. The summer storm had appeared from nowhere but threatened to make life really difficult for him this evening. Time pressed on, and he still had to heave all of the boxes up to the flat before finding new homes for their contents—if he managed to salvage anything from this sorry mess.

Adam had once had a highly successful career as a financial advisor, complete with an impressive salary and a company car. He'd loved that job and had climbed the internal ladder, hoping to make managing director by the time he was thirty-five. But his love of fast cars and his reluctance to drive within the national speed limit had cost him his driving licence from a temporary driving ban shortly before his thirtieth birthday, which in turn had cost him his job.

Back then, with bills piling up and his passion for takeaway pizza to feed, he'd had to embrace the first job opportunity that came his way. He took on the role of full-time barman at his local pub, managed by a close friend. He'd only intended the position to be temporary, to tide him over whilst he thought about future career prospects. Within three short months, however, he had learned all there was to know about the trade. He progressed from barman to assistant manager before being offered a pub of his own to manage in London. His fondness for finance had since become a distant memory, thanks to his new-found enthusiasm for pub management.

After he'd spent twelve months running a busy bar in the heart of Soho, though, the novelty of the big city had worn off. He'd had nowhere to properly unwind whenever he wasn't working, and it had been time to move on. When a position within his company came up for manager of a town centre pub in the beautiful spa town of Cheltenham, he'd applied immediately. He'd beaten all of the other candidates for the position, hands down. Just six months later, he was forced to leave when he was made redundant, as the company went into liquidation. Yet he didn't have to wait too long for another suitable management role to come along. Now, two pubs later and having turned thirty-four, he was about to embark on another new adventure, back in Cheltenham.

His ultimate goal was to have his own business, an out-of-town gastro-pub, where people would travel from miles around to sample fine cuisine and soak up the stylish atmosphere. He hoped to have enough money saved within the next year to finally put this plan into action, and he wouldn't let anything get in the way of his dream. He would focus on work and saving money, whilst also keeping his eye on the property market at all times. When the right pub came up for sale, he wanted to know.

Adam had always prioritised work over relationships in the past. Not because he didn't like women. On the contrary, he was the first to spot a pretty face at the bar and wasn't shy with the opposite sex. He had, however, discovered that women seemed to be more of an inconvenience than an asset, a drain on his bank balance and purloiners of his precious time. Whenever he took a woman on a date, he felt that he had to entertain her, keep the conversation flowing, and do all of the heavy lifting. He'd dated plenty of women over the years, but he hadn't ever met one whom he'd felt was his equal or who sparked his interest. All of his encounters with the opposite sex had been based on physical connections, rather than emotional ones. Despite being sure there must be more to relationships, he was yet to be proven right. He was currently seeing someone, but there were no feelings attached. Not on his behalf, at least.

After manhandling the soggy boxes through the pub's back entrance, he opened the door to the flat upstairs. That was the beauty of pub management: his accommodation was usually on-site, not costing him a penny in mortgage or rent. With the company settling all household bills, as well as giving him a hefty discount off his food and drinks, most of his salary was his to dispose of as he wished. Adam's wages went into the bank every month and invariably stayed there, his savings growing at break-neck speed.

He placed a couple of large boxes down to prop the flat door open and decided to take a break. He wandered around the accommodation to familiarise himself with the layout. He already knew the pub itself a little. Although it was tucked away in a residential area of Cheltenham, it was not far away from the town-centre pub he'd previously managed. He'd also visited the premises shortly before his recent interview to do a SWOT analysis, showing what changes he'd make if he were offered the job. The first time he'd seen the manager's flat above the pub, though, was two weeks after confirmation of his job offer had arrived in the post. At that point, he'd driven over to take a proper look around.

There were three generous double bedrooms, a substantial lounge, and a kitchen and a bathroom that were somewhat on the small side but adequate. It was much more space than one man living alone would need, but it meant he could have his friends overnight after a party in the pub or invite his parents over to stay. Who was he kidding? He doubted his parents would visit any time soon. They were still disappointed in him for having to change career paths after receiving a driving ban. They didn't seem to think the pub trade was a good-enough substitute for financial management.

Adam's father, Robert, had instilled self-motivation, determination, and ambition in him, teaching him that he'd need to work hard if he wanted to achieve anything in life. Adam was desperate to make his dad proud; he hadn't yet cottoned onto the fact that it had taken the older man sixty-two years to achieve his success in business. That meant Adam had another twenty-eight years to play with before any comparison was prudent. *It's good to be tough on oneself, though, isn't it? He who snoozes loses, or is it he who dares, wins?* Whichever was right, Adam realised it didn't really matter, as he would never let himself fail. His parents' approval mattered to him, but he was very much his own man.

Adam sat down on the sofa, one of many items of furniture the previous occupant had thankfully left behind. He flicked through the paperwork that his assistant manager had left out for him: a pile of junk mail that had arrived in the post, the manager's handbook, and the pub's profit-and-loss sheets. The bonuses he could earn in this industry were good. Providing his business met certain targets, he could take home up to an extra fifty percent of his salary every year, and Adam's pubs were always very profitable. He worked hard to make a success of everything in his business life, and this pub would be no different.

Turning his attention back to the two boxes he'd dragged upstairs, he realised it wouldn't take him long to unpack. He didn't have a great deal of possessions that were precious to him. His prized Porsche 911, sitting in the car park outside, was the only thing he really valued. He'd bought it as an investment when he'd turned twenty-five, and he loved to take off at speed and disappear to the coast whenever he needed time to himself. Anyone would have thought he'd have learned to slow down since getting his licence back, but he still paid little heed to the speed limit on the open road. The joy of driving was a feeling of pure abandonment as he raced along with the roof down, so he refused to change his habits, on principle. He knew he'd have to sell his car when he was ready to purchase a pub of his own, but he pushed that thought aside for now. In the meantime, he'd need to arrange somewhere safe and secure to house it.

A leaflet in amongst the papers caught his eye. Taking his mobile from his jeans pocket, he punched in the telephone number advertised.

'Hello?' a voice answered.

'Hi,' replied Adam. 'Is your two-large-pizzas-for-fifteen-pounds deal still on?'

'Yes, sir, until the end of this month.'

'And does that include delivery? I'm in Cheltenham.'

'Yes, it includes delivery.'

'Then can I have a spicy chicken and a meat feast, please?' he continued.

'Sorry, sir, we've closed for the night.'

Adam hung up the phone. Why hadn't the voice on the other end led with that, instead of wasting his time? *Imbecile*, he muttered under his breath. He'd stick with Angelo's Pizzeria from now on, the place he'd always ordered from when he'd last lived in Cheltenham. He didn't know why he hadn't rung them in the first place, but by now he'd lost his appetite. Adam didn't consider himself arrogant. He just didn't suffer fools gladly, which was a pain, as he had begun to find incompetence all around him these days. Why couldn't people be more like him?

After making short work of hefting the rest of the boxes upstairs, he left most of the unpacking until morning. The day had been long. He'd begun packing up his rental property at seven o'clock that morning before dropping the keys off with the estate agent. Although he wasn't quite sure of the time now, it had to be well past midnight. He emptied the contents of his holdall into the wardrobe and made his way downstairs to the pub.

It was empty and silent. His assistant manager had locked up not long ago, and everything looked ready for another day's trade. He sank down into one of the leather wingbacks, returning to his childhood when he'd pretended to be his father. He'd sat in his dad's oversized chair at home, puffing away on an imaginary pipe, wearing slippers that swamped his feet, and scrutinising a newspaper. In less than nine hours, he would start his first day as landlord of the White Rose. He didn't feel ready for sleep, despite being worn out. Deciding instead to indulge in a little guilty pleasure, he dialled the number at the top of his contact list and popped open a bottle of red wine.

10

The train finally pulled into Birmingham station, and Hope absentmindedly ran a hand through her hair, then gathered up her bags. She'd managed to freshen up and apply her makeup in the toilet, ready for the working day ahead. All thoughts of Ben would have to be pushed to the back of her mind for the next nine hours, although maybe she'd indulge herself a little at lunchtime.

As the church clock struck the hour, she walked out of the beautiful sunshine and into the shopping centre. She bent down to put her key into the shutter before entering the store. The girls had done well. The shop looked immaculate, and the new clothes from the latest delivery had been merchandised productively in amongst the old. She climbed the stairs to the office and started to complete the weekly paperwork, her mind totally focussed on the job at hand.

The morning went by in a blur. Friendly regulars needed help choosing outfits, and rowdy kids, not really intent on buying anything, whiled away an hour or two trying things on, having broken up from school for the summer. These customers, whether searching for a specific item or just browsing, were all being helped by the knowledgeable staff that Hope was proud to call her team.

Stopping for a quick lunch break at midday, Hope sent a text to Jess. She sat in the sun outside her favourite café, watching the world go by. After finishing the last bite of her sandwich, she threw her napkin deftly into the nearby bin. Then she carried her diet Coke for one or two last gulps during the short walk back to the store.

The remainder of the afternoon was filled with merchandising, selling, training, and one very snotty customer who wanted a refund on a sleeveless top which had clearly been worn. With the sweetest smile and the utmost professionalism, Hope had managed to send the obnoxious customer away without a refund but with less of a grimace on her face. She retained the woman as a loyal future customer by presenting her with a discount voucher for her next three purchases. Hope loved problem solving and always felt a real sense of achievement when she found a way out of a difficult situation. She wondered how easily she could find a solution to falling for someone who wasn't open to being loved. That problem wouldn't be sorted out as quickly as most.

When it eventually turned five o'clock, Hope raced out of the store and tore down the slope to the station, leaving her assistant manager working the late-night shift. A forty-minute train journey, followed by a spin around the corner in her car, was all that now lay between her and a blissful evening of reliving with Jess the magic that happened in Portsmouth. She desperately wanted to catch the first train possible, to avoid a thirty-minute wait for the next one, and thankfully she got to the platform just as one was about to leave.

She arrived back at the house shortly before six and stepped into the kitchen. Imagining that they would both want quite a few mugs of coffee tonight, she filled the kettle all the way up. Fifteen minutes later, while pulling on jeans and a T-shirt in her bedroom, she heard the familiar sound of the front door opening.

'You're home! Come on then,' called Jess's cheery voice. 'Let's hear all about your catfish.'

The girls sat together at the kitchen table, their legs up on a chair to rest their tired feet.

'You know how everyone said I'd built him up in my head and was setting myself up for a huge disappointment?' Hope delayed telling Jess that she'd just had the most amazing weekend ever, then planned to wow her with the details. 'On the way down there, I thought about that and wasn't too nervous. I'd prepared myself. So, after getting extremely lost on the way and adding an hour to the journey time, I finally arrived outside his apartment.'

Jess smiled as the story unfolded.

'He called after I pulled up and said he would come down to meet me,' Hope continued, 'so I got out of the car and suddenly saw him coming down the path in my direction. The second I saw him . . .' Hope put her hand to her chest for a moment's pause, 'I was absolutely blown away. He is the most gorgeous man I have ever laid eyes on in real life. Honestly.' She reddened. 'He wrapped me in the hugest hug, and I didn't know what to do. I think, um . . .' Hope faltered again. 'I think he could possibly be the One!'

To most people, that would have seemed a fairly ludicrous statement. Hope had spent little more than twenty-four hours with Ben and in the last two years had failed to find anyone suitable enough for something as simple as a third date. But Jess knew how strong Hope and Ben's bond had become during the last eighteen months. She was well aware of how much time they'd spent talking on the phone or via WhatsApp, how many stories they'd shared and problems they'd helped each other solve before meeting in person. She also knew that her best friend was a hopeless romantic.

Hope continued with the story as tears welled up in her eyes, her hand remaining on her chest. She spoke about their afternoon in the sun, the meal they'd shared, and the walk along the seafront when Ben had opened up to her. 'I just wanted to hold him and never let him go. He sounded in so much pain as he spoke, I couldn't bear it.'

Jess heard all about Ben's tough upbringing and the serious relationship which had led him to rule out love altogether.

'You know when someone leans in really close to talk to you and all you can do is imagine kissing them?' Hope continued. 'I was so near to kissing him in the nightclub, but right then he told me about a girl who'd made a move to kiss him a while ago and how he'd had to push her away. I would have died if I'd made the same mistake.'

'I got your text Saturday night. I'd hoped you were going to tell me you *had* kissed him,' Jess admitted, 'and give me all the gory details.'

'I can't even remember what I wrote. I just remember sending it when I realised I was totally besotted with him, yet nothing was going to happen.'

'So, nothing happened at all?'

'Well . . .' Hope's eyes gleamed.

'Come on, Hope, tell me.' Jess was so close to the edge of her seat that she almost fell off it.

After racing through the sausage casserole which had kindly taken care of itself in the slow-cooker all day, they chatted for another hour or two. Well, Hope chatted and Jess listened attentively.

'I'm so happy you found what you're looking for,' Jess said. 'But is this a beginning or an end of any relationship potential?'

'I don't know,' Hope replied. 'He kept saying that he runs when women are interested in him. But when he said it in the park on Sunday, I wondered if maybe he was trying to tell me how to play it. You know, letting me know that if I wanted him, I had to play it cool so as not to frighten him off. I don't know, maybe that's just wishful thinking. But you know what? It's taken me a year and a half to meet him, so if it takes me another year and a half to get him to fall for me, then that's fine by me. I'm not even interested in looking at another guy anymore. I know what I want, and I simply have to be patient.'

Jess smiled but stayed quiet.

Hope blinked back tears again, not wanting to acknowledge how hard it would be to hide her true feelings from Ben. 'Oh, Jess, I can't begin to explain how I felt when he kissed me. Since Mum died, I've always felt incomplete. It's as if part of me went with her, as though I've been wandering around like a jigsaw with a missing piece for years. When Ben kissed me . . .' She hesitated once more and then added, 'I finally felt whole again. I didn't want that feeling to end. I never told you my recurring dream about him, did I?'

'No, I don't think so,' Jess replied.

Hope relayed the dream she'd had many nights before meeting Ben. It had so many similarities to the way her actual weekend had just played out. 'And I'm sure he kissed my neck in the nightclub, like in my dream. We were dancing so close, and I could swear he kissed it. Lying next to him later, being so close to him that I could feel his heart beating, was more powerful than anything I've ever . . .' Her voice trailed off in a poorly disguised sob. She wrapped her arms around herself. 'I think it was even more intense than if we had taken things further. I guess there was something quite tantric about it.' Hope stopped, unable to find words to convey how wonderful her night with Ben had been. She struggled to control the emotions playing games with her head and her heart.

Powerless to suppress their yawns any longer, the two girls gave each other a huge hug and then got ready for bed. Tomorrow was another day, and they had money to earn and customers to keep happy.

'Oh, but it's all okay,' Hope said, wandering into Jess's room in her pyjamas. 'He *has* to fall in love with me now. I made a bet with myself that if I caught my 7:12 this morning, then he would. And there is no way on earth I should have managed to catch that train. I still don't know how I did.'

Jess laughed. 'You're right. There was no way you should have made it onto that train this morning. It must have been the Duracells! Goodnight, honey. I hope you get your Ben.'

'Night, Jess. I do think I might love him a little bit already. Is that silly?'

'Not really,' replied her friend matter-of-factly.

Hope set her alarm and climbed into bed. It was good to be home with Jess, but her heart, along with her entire body, longed to be back with Ben.

11

Three weeks had passed since Hope's eventful weekend at Ben's. The first time she had heard from him was via a message when she'd got home from work the day she'd left Portsmouth. He told her that she'd left her black boots at his apartment and asked if she would like him to put them in the Snail Mail. Later that evening, he sent her a text saying how much he'd enjoyed the weekend. They exchanged many more messages over the following weeks. Well, at least he hadn't totally disappeared. And as long as he stayed in touch, she could continue to lie low until he fell for her. Only then would she admit her true feelings for him.

Hope stepped onto the train in Birmingham and was pleased to find a seat at an empty table. It was Friday afternoon. She had just finished nine days in a row at work, and she looked forward to having a glorious weekend off. As she fished around in her handbag to get her ticket ready for inspection, her mobile vibrated and chirped away. It was Jess, with a text message to say she was on her way home, too, and wondering if Hope might fancy anything special for tea.

Yes, Hope had an idea. Why didn't they push the boat out for once and go out for a meal? Nothing too extravagant, but they both worked so hard that they surely deserved to spoil themselves now and again. Jess loved the suggestion, and they arranged to meet back at the house before wandering around to the local pub for a bite to eat and a few drinks. They would soak up the atmosphere of pub life whilst putting the world to rights once again.

The girls loved their little local. It wasn't the closest pub to them; they had three to choose from, all within walking distance. Yet they'd always favoured the White Rose because it was so homely. With its subdued lighting, leather sofas, and log fires that roared in the winter months, as well as its green outdoor area dotted with parasols in the summertime, the pub was always so cosy and inviting. And the music was kept to a level that didn't stop them from having a conversation, yet added to the overall ambience.

Hope was on first-name terms with a couple of the bar staff nowadays. She and her date had kept them late one night by failing to drink up as quickly as they should have, lingering long after all the other punters had departed. She had promised a pint to the two barmen they'd delayed, but, until tonight, work and sleep had prevented her from returning to fulfil this agreement.

Jess locked the front door behind them, and they set off at a brisk pace, wishing they'd taken their coats. The September air had become nippy now that the sun had set.

They arrived at the pub fifteen minutes later and walked up to the bar. Hope ordered their drinks whilst Jess scrutinised the food menu. Hope already knew what she wanted without taking a peep. It had to be the chicken-and-bacon club sandwich. Served up as a triple-decker and needing skewers to hold it together, it really was the only choice when she wanted something satiating. It was rather satisfying to peel the layers apart and destroy the masterpiece before she tucked in to devour it. She wasn't sure what she'd do if they ever took it off the menu.

As the familiar faces of the barmen came into view, one of them caught Hope's eye. She gesticulated to him with wild hand movements, trying to signal that she was buying him the pint she owed him but confusing him so much that he had to come over and ask what she was trying to say.

A new face was serving them tonight, though. In fact, there were a couple of new faces behind the bar. The black shirts of the barmen made it clear that the blond in blue stripes, tending to the optics, must be the landlord. Assuming he hadn't been in hiding since she'd been a local because Hope certainly would have remembered his face, she could only imagine that he must be new to the pub. Jess had clearly been eyeing him up, too. She now raised her eyebrows in a not-too-subtle manner and nudged Hope in the ribs with more force than she intended. Her friend doubled over in pain.

'Not too obvious, Jess,' shot Hope with a withering look.

They paid for their food and drinks and added four extra pints to the total. Hope couldn't leave out the new barman who'd served them, when buying a drink for the other two. She also wanted a reason for the new landlord to talk to them, even if only to say thank you for his pint. He did and then, to her disappointment, moved on. Hope had intended to do a little matchmaking, but she would clearly have to find another way to get this landlord and Jess to start a conversation.

The girls sat on their usual sofa in a secluded area of the pub. In their opinion, it was the cosiest area, but, for some reason, nobody else ever seemed to share their affinity for it. Not that Hope and Jess minded because their favourite perch was always vacant. The landlord himself brought them their food and asked if they were staying for the quiz. He disappeared again almost before they had a chance to answer. *Surely, he's not shy*, Hope pondered.

There was something intriguing about him. He was rugged and unshaven—un-ironed, too, by the look of it. He appeared masterful, yet at the same time seemed in need of being looked after. It was an intoxicating combination of masculinity and vulnerability, but Hope wasn't looking for a man. She had already found the one she wanted. All she had to do now was get him to feel the same way she did. This landlord would be great for Jess, though.

A few drinks later, the girls found themselves in the throes of the pub quiz, a slightly rowdy affair. Fuelled with alcohol, they engaged in a little cheating. They ran up to the bar every now and then to try to get answers from their new barmen friends and sneaked a peak at other answer papers on the way back to their seats.

The landlord was conducting the quiz. He sat by

the bar with his microphone, reading out from the question paper, then wandered through the pub to give people clues. He stopped at their table a few times but didn't seem to know how to handle their forwardness. He tried to deliver witty retorts and returned to the safety of his perch by the bar when he failed. Jess and Hope found nothing wrong with a bit of harmless flirting, and they were on top form, playing off each other.

The evening drew to a close, and the girls said goodbye to their hosts. They set off into the cool night air, giggling away.

'How scared was Adam?' They'd finally found out his name from one of the barmen and could now stop calling him 'the landlord'.

'I'm not surprised, poor guy,' Hope replied. 'I can't believe he didn't disqualify us for all the cheating. Not that it helped. Didn't we used to score a lot more than thirty-four when we *didn't* cheat?'

'I've *always* cheated!' Jess replied. 'You probably just scored a lot more before I moved in and started going along.' Hope laughed. Jess was probably right.

They collapsed through the front door and staggered into the kitchen, with time for one more drink before bed. Hope looked at Jess, grinning. 'So, what do you think of Adam, then?'

'Hey, no, Hope! You know I'm not looking for a man at the moment. I just figured he might be a good distraction for you, to take your mind off Ben whilst you give him the space you think he needs. He's very good-looking, but I'm not interested at all.'

Hope considered Jess's proposition. It wouldn't hurt to have a distraction from Ben, but she didn't think she'd be able to stay distracted for long.

12

Jess's idea of Adam being a distraction had flitted around in Hope's head ever since the night they'd met him. She returned to the pub alone the following week, attempting to put that plan into action. Hope had never been troubled by other people's opinions, and she certainly didn't worry about how she appeared sitting in a pub with just a book for company.

The friendly bar staff greeted her on arrival, and, as the night drew to a close, invited her to stay behind after they locked up. Hope listened to their stories about life behind the bar and felt as though she had been welcomed into a whole new family.

Adam regaled her with countless stories and was clearly as passionate about his job as she was about her own. She finally had to leave, and Dillan, the young barman, walked her all the way home. He stepped into her kitchen for a quick cheese-and-tomato sandwich and gave her Adam's mobile number when she admitted he intrigued her. Hope added it to her phone directory, wondering whether she would have the courage or inclination to contact him.

A couple of nights later, she ventured to the pub again, with her friend Tomasz this time. She decided she would have to be a little more obvious. If Adam hadn't yet realised she was somewhat interested in him, she would have to try harder to get him to notice.

It wasn't that she had forgotten Ben. On the contrary, her feelings seemed to grow stronger each day. But if she didn't find a suitable distraction from Ben very soon, she would blurt out to him how she really felt, especially if she had a drink or two too many one night.

She and Ben were still in contact pretty much daily. Most of her messages ended with 'Mwah', followed by three kisses That would generate the reply 'Mwah backatcha' from him. It always made her smile, as it reminded her of those precious almost-never-ending kisses they had shared when time stood still in Portsmouth. But how long should she wait before she mentioned meeting up with him again? She would have to bite the bullet at some point. She had told him to look after her boots until they next met, and he hadn't insisted on posting them to her, so he must have assumed they would see each other again.

Hope, chewing at her lip as she ruminated on this, grinned inanely. Ben had joked that her knee-length boots looked good on him and that he might want to keep them for himself. He always made her laugh. So, here she was, trying to focus on another man but only to take her mind off Ben for a while, giving him a chance to gravitate towards her at his own pace.

Still grinning, she stepped up to the bar with Tomasz. He had become a close friend during the previous few months, ever since the day they had both reached for the last bag of freshly baked chocolate chip cookies in the local supermarket. He had come up with the solution of buying them and giving her two of the four, provided they go out for a drink together the following evening. She had hesitated until he assured her he wasn't hitting on her, as he was gay. He simply wanted to increase his circle of friends, having recently moved to Cheltenham. At that point, she had accepted his offer. After all, it takes a lot to hand over two deliciously warm and chewy chocolate chip cookies to a total stranger.

Hope had begged Tomasz to go to the White Rose with her tonight, but he'd declined at first, as he had other plans. They finally compromised on him picking her up and taking her there but leaving after an hour or so, once she was settled in. Hope felt energetic. She was off work the next day, so she fancied letting her hair down a little tonight. She felt bad that Jess, unlike her, couldn't relax this evening. By the time Tomasz was ready to leave Hope to it, they had already mingled with the group of pensioners from whom she and Jess had stolen many, albeit wrong, answers on quiz night.

Hugging Tomasz goodbye, Hope returned to her conversation with the two Tony's and Tom. Adam wandered over every now and then, never staying long enough for her to strike up a conversation. Yet it was always sufficient time for her gaze to trail after him when he left their table. The three T's had clearly picked up on this. They ribbed her about it once, asking what her boyfriend would think about such blatant, disgraceful behaviour. She explained that Tomasz was just a friend and foolishly admitted that she did think Adam was very good-looking. The old men apparently conveyed this information to the landlord in double-quick time. When she returned from a trip to the bar, she found Adam sitting in her seat, asking them if she was indeed single.

Adam stayed there for a while this time. He pulled up another stool for Hope to perch on and listened as she talked about her job and the travelling she did every morning on the train. It just so happened that on the following Tuesday, he would also be catching a train to Birmingham first thing in the morning, for a two-day course at his company's head office.

As the bell rang for last orders, Adam suggested that he and Hope travel to Birmingham together on Tuesday. He gleefully recounted a funny story about the last time he had travelled by train, when a lady with a bad stomach had been having trouble with the new-fangled, space-age toilet.

Adam and his fellow travellers, stuck in the vestibule end as all the seats were occupied, had been treated to the not-so-pleasant sight of her crouching over the toilet. She clutched her skirt tightly around her legs, attempting to maintain as much dignity as possible whilst trying to empty her bowels as the automatic door swished open and closed with a mind of its own.

'It was so funny,' he recalled, tears staining his face at the memory. 'She just kept saying, "Oooh, I'm so, so sorry about this", whilst we tried desperately not to laugh.'

The oldies got up and left shortly afterwards, and

Hope made to do the same. 'So, Tuesday, Hope?' Adam's eyes searched hers, and she didn't want to see his look of disappointment if she said 'no'.

'Tuesday it is, then. The seven twelve train. I'll meet you on platform two.'

'It's a date,' he replied, jumping up from his seat.

'It's not a date; it's a shared commute.'

'Shared commute,' he acknowledged, nodding sombrely, having been firmly corrected.

Then he broke into a big grin, and Ben's face popped right out of Hope's mind, just for a few seconds, before jumping straight back into it again. *So, they were to have a train date . . . shared commute,* she corrected herself. Hope always liked the unusual and had to admit that it sounded like fun.

After locking up the pub for the night, Adam pottered around his flat, still thinking about Hope. She'd seemed keen that they didn't label Tuesday a date, even though she'd told his regulars she was single. She was certainly a bit of an enigma at the moment.

Finally clearing all thoughts of Hope and their impending commute from his mind, Adam picked up his mobile and accessed his contact list. He dialled the first entry alphabetically, waited for the familiar voice to answer the call, and then plodded downstairs to unlock the back door to his flat.

***

Angelisa tried to settle into an armchair across from Adam and quietly watched him. He seemed self-absorbed and uncommunicative, staring out of the window and ignoring her presence. Now that she knew he and Hope planned to meet up on Tuesday, she wanted more details. Should she be worried?

13

Hope woke with a start as the alarm went off. The vibrations on the bedside table sent shockwaves through her body, warning that it was half past five and time to rise and shine. She sat up and had a good stretch, feeling every limb slowly come alive and every muscle groan in despair at starting the day at such a ridiculous hour.

Maybe she could snooze for half an hour and not worry about washing her hair this morning, just twist it up into her crocodile clip and make do. No, there was a reason for washing and drying it, getting her makeup perfect, and selecting a sexy outfit for work. She wouldn't be invisible on the train this morning, hiding from the world with her head against the window and her eyes closed, enjoying some time to herself. No, today was Tuesday, and she had an early morning train date . . . shared commute with an eligible landlord. Today there was no time to snooze.

She giggled at how silly she was being. Yes, Adam seemed like a nice guy, and he was good-looking, ambitious, and beguiling, so, of course, she wanted to look her best this morning. But it was only a train journey. Not exactly the most romantic liaison of the century. Also, hadn't she totally fallen for someone else? Still, Adam had suggested she meet up with him again after work today, too, because his course would finish in the afternoon before continuing the following day. He and some others would enjoy a meal and drinks in Birmingham tonight, all paid for by his company, and she was invited to join them. She hadn't promised to tag along but had packed a change of clothes in her bag the previous night, just in case she decided to. Well, she didn't have work the next day. She could afford to get a little inebriated, catch the last train home, and worry about the hangover on her day off.

Hope took a quick shower and plodded downstairs in her dressing gown and slippers. She stuck two pieces of wholemeal in the toaster and flicked on the kettle. At the kitchen table, she looked out on the world through the patio doors. Yes, she'd probably meet up with Adam after work. After all, she hadn't been out in Birmingham at night yet.

Adam arrived at the station and queued to buy his ticket. He looked forward to spending time with Hope and suspected that she would see him again that evening. He was just about to cross the bridge leading to platform two when his phone beeped. He stopped walking and pulled it out of his pocket.

I'm on the platform, where are you? Hope Xxx

He'd always found it funny that phones were

supposed to be mobile these days, yet people invariably found it too difficult to use them whilst walking. And here he was, true to form, standing motionless to read this text. He sent her a quick reply to say he was right behind her and made his way downstairs to where she stood.

Adam suddenly felt nervous now that they were alone together.

Hope looked over at him. In the cold light of the morning, he still looked quite handsome, but he didn't make her heart race. Then again, she hadn't exactly expected him to. She really wanted Ben, and no one would ever come a close second to him.

The train was crowded, but they somehow found two seats together. Hope squashed herself against the window, not really liking the fact that another person sat on the seat next to her, rather than just her handbag.

Adam reached into his jacket pocket before saying, 'Remember my text last night when I asked if you were sure you'd recognise me today?'

She'd joked that he'd have to buy a single red rose to carry, but it had been nearly midnight. He'd said no place would be open to sell him one that late.

'Mr Jones, my regular from the pub, brought me here in his taxi this morning. He had this on his dashboard.' Adam paused. 'It isn't a real one, but it's the thought that counts, isn't it?'

He presented Hope with a decidedly ugly, artificial-looking red rose with huge unsightly petals. She wished he had *left* it on the dashboard of Mr Jones's taxi. Looking around sheepishly, she wondered what on earth to do with it and, more importantly, who in the train had seen Adam hand it over and was now sniggering away.

'It's, um . . . it's lovely, thank you,' she finally managed politely. Then she felt bad for not being more appreciative and set about pulling off the larger petals to leave a delicate rosebud, still imitation but really quite pretty.

'There, perfect,' she added, looking at him and smiling. 'Thank you, kind sir.'

Something troubled her, but she wasn't quite sure what. Then she realised. Adam seemed very keen, too keen, and it was quite unsettling. She didn't want a relationship with anyone other than Ben and didn't want to lead Adam on. She hoped he wouldn't start liking her too much. He would be a good friend, a good distraction from Ben, but romance was definitely a no-go.

The train soon pulled into Birmingham station, where they made their way up the stairs and out into the fresh air. The sun was shining in a sky of such intense blue that it looked as if it had been touched up with a giant paint roller. Adam made a move towards the taxi rank, and Hope said goodbye, ready to walk up the slope towards the shopping centre.

'You will come out tonight, won't you?' he asked, but it was more of a statement than a question.

'I'll see what time I get out of work, but probably.' Hope hadn't yet decided. She would make up her mind later and call him when she finished work.

'Please!' Again, the overenthusiasm was apparent in his voice.

'I'll call you when I finish.'

'Promise?'

'Yes, enjoy the course.'

'Bye, then.'

Hope wandered towards the shop, smiling inwardly and making her decision there and then. She would go. It would be nice to be treated to a meal and some drinks for a change, so why not?

At five o'clock, Hope ran up to the staffroom and fished her bags out of her locker. She jumped into her cropped jeans and halter-neck top, kicked off her shoes, and pulled off her socks before placing her bare feet into her mules. After tugging the clip out of her hair, she shook her head upside down, messing up her chestnut locks. Then she stood upright in front of the mirror to smooth her hair with her hands. *Perfect.* She redid her makeup, spritzed herself with perfume, and popped a piece of chewing gum in her mouth. Cramming her work clothes back into her locker and grabbing a few essentials, she set off into the sunshine.

Only, the sun had now decided to hide behind the clouds, and they in turn bawled inconsolably in disapproval.

Damn, I don't want to turn up looking like a drowned rat.

'Adam, I'm just leaving work. Where are you all?'

'Jump into a taxi and ask the driver to take you to the theatre. We'll meet you there.'

'Ooh, we're going to the theatre?' she teased him over the phone.

'No, but we're going nearby for a meal. See you shortly. I'll pay the taxi when you get here.'

She found a cab at the rank and hopped in. Five minutes later, it pulled up in front of the theatre. Adam ran up with an umbrella to pay the driver and help her out of the car.

Adam's friends were lovely, a couple in their late

thirties who were starting out in the industry. They were currently completing a ten-week training programme which would teach them all they needed to know before managing their first pub together. Adam had met them on a previous course and had been drawn to them instantly. Hope clearly saw why. They were easy to chat with, and, as they all entered the restaurant and sat at a table, Hope was pleased she'd decided to tag along.

The waitress brought them the wine they had requested and took down their food orders on a notepad.

Hope nudged Adam and whispered in his ear, 'Oh, no, a silver wine bucket is no good. I have a phobia of silver wine buckets.' She was in a silly mood today. The first two sips of wine had already gone to her head, and she felt like having fun after an intense day at work.

Adam looked at her quizzically and smiled. 'You really are a crazy girl, aren't you? You're more of a handful than the girls I usually date. But I'm not allowed to call this a date, am I?'

Their meals were delicious, and the wine continued to flow. Hope listened to Jane and Edward talk about how they gave up their high-powered jobs to enter the pub trade. They felt so excited about the journey they were setting out on. Adam joined in with stories from pubs he'd managed, and Hope found herself chattering away as well. She asked them questions and told them a little about her own job. It really was fascinating hearing the three of them talk about the industry, and Hope wondered why she'd never considered such a career. She loved socialising, so what better way to earn a living than to provide people with an enjoyable social experience every day and night of the week?

The waitress returned to check that their meals were okay and reached to retrieve the empty wine bottles from the table.

Hope whispered to Adam again, 'No, we need to keep the empty bottles on the table. It's bad luck for twelve years, otherwise.'

'Would you mind if we keep the empties on the table until we leave, please? And I don't suppose you have a wine bucket that's not silver, do you?' Adam looked up at the waitress and flashed his sweetest smile.

Hope was impressed. Here she was, playing up and being silly, perhaps testing him to see how he would behave if she were a little odd, in a far-ditch attempt to put him off her. Yet he played along. Even the waitress joined in, returning to the table a few minutes later with the silver wine bucket now all covered in blue tissue. She appeared highly amused at the request but was willing to go that extra mile for these diners.

The evening continued with more conversation, divine desserts, and too much alcohol, leaving Hope lightheaded. She and Jane made their way to the Ladies. Hope took a while to steady herself as she sat down to answer the call of nature, whacking her head against the side of the cubicle. 'Ouch.'

'Are you okay, Hope?'

'I'm fine, Jane, be out in a minute.' *No more alcohol*, she thought.

As they washed their hands at the sink, Jane told Hope that she really shouldn't go back to the station on her own later. She was welcome to stay on the sofa bed in Jane's room, leaving Edward to bunk in with Adam. Hope thanked Jane. She truly was a lovely lady, taking Hope under her wing and looking out for her. But as long as Adam slept on the sofa bed and let her have the bed, Hope was comfortable staying the night in his room. She felt she knew him enough by now to trust him. She'd always been a good judge of character.

The women returned to the table as the men were settling the bill. The company would end up paying once the men claimed the expenses later. That reinforced Hope's insistence that this was not a date. They moved onto a bar for a few more drinks afterwards, but it was soon time to retire. Hope and Adam bid Jane and Edward goodnight and wandered off on their own, at a much slower pace than the other couple.

The hotel was only a fifteen-minute walk away, but it had started to rain. Hope felt decidedly the worse for wear and figured that if Adam had started to like her, he would certainly be put off by now. Every couple of minutes, she kept asking if they could get a taxi and how much farther they had to walk. *Good. I can't have him falling for me when I've already fallen for someone else.* They finally arrived at their destination and staggered into the lift to go up to his room.

Hours later, Hope opened her eyes. She tried to focus on the shirts hanging in what looked like a kitchen dresser. *Where on earth am I? This isn't my bedroom.* Flashes of memory, contorted by the pain throbbing in her head, crept into her cerebellum as she attempted to fully open her eyes. She looked down at her body, still clothed, and then over to her left to see a sleeping lump on the sofa bed across the room. She began to remember the previous night.

She had been out with Adam and his friends, they had plied her with far too much alcohol, and she had decided to stay the night, provided he slept on the sofa bed. Well, he had clearly kept his side of the bargain, which she was grateful for, but couldn't she remember having kissed him last night? No, surely not. She must have managed to put him off her by the way she'd behaved. She was mortified to realise how inebriated she'd been and how silly. *If Adam has any sense at all, then he won't want to see me again—not romantically, at least. Mission accomplished*, she thought, pleased with herself.

Adam stirred, and Hope sat up in bed.

'How are you feeling?' he asked, grinning. She had been so funny all night. They'd ordered flaming sambuca shots at a bar after the meal, to play a drinking game. But each time they'd tried to set the game up, with one shot glass in front of each person, Hope had mindlessly downed whatever was put in front of her. They'd had to give up after two failed attempts.

She had been rather inebriated. Then, on the way home, she had flung her arms around his neck and kissed him, and he hadn't been able to resist her. She was stunning, entertaining, and intoxicating—somewhat kooky but in a good way. She clearly had real intelligence that she seemed to feel the need to hide by playing the fool. He liked her a lot already. She was still a bit of an enigma, but he knew he wanted to see her again soon. The realisation surprised him.

Hope groaned aloud and put her hand to her head. 'I'm sorry. I was a nightmare last night, wasn't I? I only ever drink wine these days. It's years since I've done shots.'

She seems sheepish. Does she regret kissing me? he wondered. *Does she even remember kissing me? How can I broach the subject?* 'You were funny. I hope you enjoyed yourself. I did.'

'Um, I seem to remember kissing you. I hope I didn't throw myself at you. I'm really sorry.' Hope was always one to speak openly.

'You did kiss me, yes, but I will forgive you on one condition.'

'Um, okay . . .' Hope looked over at him with a worried expression.

'That you promise to see me again. I deserve a second date for putting up with you.' He laughed, enjoying teasing her.

Is he serious? Does he really want to see me again after the way I conducted myself? Not that I can remember exactly how I behaved, but I know I drank far more than I should have on a first date, not that it was a date, and I was probably really embarrassing. I can't believe I kissed him. Now I really am in trouble. I'm besotted with Ben. Yet here I am getting drunk and kissing a random landlord, a landlord who doesn't even know Ben exists and who, strangely enough, wants to take me out again.

Okay. Maybe I'll give him a second date, but I'll stay sober next time. I feel I owe him something to make up for my intoxicated behaviour and stolen kisses, but my heart isn't really into seeing him again. He isn't the one I want. He isn't Ben. 'You're on. But to be honest, Adam, I thought you wouldn't want to see me again. I shouldn't have drunk so much last night.'

'You were good fun. We were all a little

intoxicated, and that was the plan for last night anyway.'

After taking some painkillers and a hot shower each, they went down to breakfast in the dining room. There, they gorged on croissants and pastries and soaked up all of the alcohol they had poured down their throats the previous night—or at least a good proportion of what still remained in their systems. Once they finished eating, and after their third cups of strong coffee, they went back up to the room to fetch their belongings. The hotel was just a short walk around the corner from Adam's company's head office, where he ordered Hope a taxi. He gave her a kiss goodbye and told her he'd call her when he got back to Cheltenham that night.

Hope contemplated long and hard on the train journey home. She had been impressed by Adam's request to the waitress about the wine bucket and the empty bottles, and she had thoroughly enjoyed the conversation and his company all night. But she couldn't remember much about the walk home and how she'd come to kiss him. She didn't know exactly what happened when they got into the room, either, but she had most likely passed out the second she had lain horizontal. How utterly embarrassing. Yet he was desperate to see her again. *What could be the harm in seeing him once more?*

14

The train finally arrived back in Cheltenham, where Hope was thankful to be only a few minutes' drive away from home, her comfy bed, and more painkillers. She was now really suffering from the morning after the night before. From the minute she'd boarded the train in Birmingham, she had felt as sick as a dog. She willed herself not to throw up and cursed herself for not sticking to wine. Why didn't she realise that pub landlords would drink her under the table?

As she got back to her car, parked neatly in her usual space at the station, her mobile beeped. It was a message from Ben. Worn out and with heavy eyes and clumsy fingers, she summoned up all the energy she could to navigate her phone's menu. She discovered that she'd sent him a text the previous night.

Ben . . . Xxx

He had later replied:

Oui, c'est moi, methinks. X

Thankfully, she apparently didn't continue texting past that. *Jesus, Hope*, she reprimanded herself, *what on earth did you almost tell him last night*? In one drunken text, she might have been close to admitting how she really felt about him.

Hope read Ben's new message, asking how she was and what she'd been up to lately. She sighed, remembering the time she'd spent with him in Portsmouth. That night with Ben seemed like aeons ago, yet it was exactly a month to the day since they had kissed. She'd calculated it at one point in the early hours, she realised. Had she sullied the memory of that time with Ben by inadvertently kissing Adam? She hadn't yet told Ben about Adam, but maybe it was time to do so. Perhaps a bit of competition might make Ben realise he didn't want someone else to sweep her off her feet whilst he remained chicken-hearted.

As she swung her car into the driveway and turned off the engine, Hope took a minute for long hard reflection. Here she was thinking about Ben yet again, when she'd only just got home from a night out with another man. A man she'd been happy to spend time with at the White Rose and an evening with in Birmingham. Was she only seeing Adam to keep her mind off Ben, or was she now a little confused about both men? In which case, why were two eligible bachelors in her life at the same time, after no one suitable being on the horizon for years? One of these men had to be held at arm's length, but the other man wanted to take her out again. One wanted to take things further, but the other was the real object of her affections. This sobering thought brought her back to her senses, and she realised she would have to talk to Adam before things got messy.

Right on cue, a message from the landlord himself danced onto the screen of her mobile. He said he would love it if she could meet him at the pub later that evening and thanked her for a wonderful night in Birmingham. Okay, so this gave her the perfect chance to tell him the score. To let him know that her heart belonged to someone else, someone who was out of reach right now but whom she might never get over. She would tell Adam and hope that he'd still be happy to be friends. After all, they did both love to chat. It would be a shame to see no more of this man who had temporarily and quite effortlessly distracted her from thoughts of Ben. She was powerless to change the way she felt about Ben, but something about Adam appealed to her more, now that her hangover had finally started to abate. What disaster was waiting to happen?

Hope's bed called her the second she stepped into the house. After dropping her handbag on the kitchen table and making a meal of clambering up the steeper-than-usual stairs, she fell onto the bed, still wearing her clothes from the previous night. She pulled the covers tightly around her and surrendered to exhaustion. Whilst others were hard at work, Hope slept a dreamless deep slumber that allowed her body to recuperate and her head to clear.

It was just gone five in the afternoon when she awoke, still drowsy but not hungover anymore. A bath would repair the last of the damage, and then she could get ready to see Adam again. Looking around for her iPhone but finding instead a photo of Ben she had printed off the PC a few days earlier, she groaned inwardly. *Why is everything so complicated all of a sudden? And where on earth is my mobile hiding?*

She didn't look forward to putting Adam in the picture, but she couldn't put it off any longer. He deserved to know the truth. Honesty was always so important to Hope. She couldn't let him take her out again if he didn't know what he was getting into. Not that *she* really knew. There was a chance Adam could in fact be her Mr Right, but, then again, he might always play second fiddle to Ben. She hoped Adam wouldn't hate her for leading him on with that unintentional but enjoyable kiss the previous night.

An hour or so later, Hope appeared much less like she'd had a heavy night. Her hair was freshly washed, her face was delicately made up, and she looked and felt fine in a pair of jeans and a white top. She found her phone on the kitchen table and sent Adam a text message, telling him that he needed to know something important about her and that she really had to talk to him alone tonight.

It was past midnight by the time the pub was eventually cleared of all but the bar staff, and Hope finally got a chance to sit down with Adam. He hadn't been scheduled to work this evening, but one of the team had called in sick. It had been down to him, as landlord, to step in and cover the shift. Hope hadn't minded. She hadn't got to the pub until just after nine, having spent a few hours catching up with Jess first about her big night out.

Adam hadn't neglected Hope from the second she'd walked into the White Rose, even though he'd been on duty. He'd brought her drinks over and sat and chatted for a few minutes whenever he'd got a chance. Then he'd even sent one of the many regulars over to keep her company whilst he and the staff finished wiping down tables and bottling up at the end of the night.

Now, the two of them sat on the sofa that Hope normally shared with Jess, waiting for the staff to go home. Adam looked concerned.

He had been worried ever since receiving Hope's text that afternoon. He dreaded what she had to tell him and hoped she would change her mind and decide she had nothing to say. Nothing, at least, that might threaten the chancc of exploring the attraction they clearly both felt.

'Adam.' Hope's voice was a delicate whisper and the look in her eyes said she really did need to talk to him before going home. He suggested that they leave the clan to seek privacy up in his flat for a few minutes. That turned out to be a really bad idea. The cheeky twenty-somethings relaxing over a pint after work ribbed them about what exactly they were going upstairs for. Hope sat firmly back on the sofa, pulling Adam down beside her.

Time was ticking on, and Hope had work early in the morning. She would have to talk to him shortly, yet the staff didn't look like they would make a move any time soon. Seeing the anxious look in her eyes, Adam realised that he couldn't put this off any longer and looked imploringly at the staff.

'Come on, guys, it's time you were heading off,' he murmured. Without much further ado, they were gone.

'Adam . . .' Hope started but went no further.

'What is it, Blossom? You've got me really worried. I've been imagining all sorts of terrible things.'

'Um . . .' she tried again. 'I need to tell you something, and I feel bad that I haven't told you before now . . . I am totally single, but . . .'

His eyes searched hers, but they gave nothing away. He would just have to wait for her to reveal everything, which at this rate could take until opening time tomorrow. He tried to pull her into a hug, but she backed away from it. Her cold response unsettled him, and he turned on the sofa to face directly towards her.

'There's someone I really like. I can't tell him, and I know I have to get over him, but it wouldn't be fair to start something with you whilst I'm still crazy about him. I didn't intend to meet someone like you at all right now. I had planned to stay single whilst I work out these feelings, but then you came along, and there's definitely something about you that I really like, too.'

She was rambling, but Adam let her continue. She was finally telling him what she'd needed to say, and it certainly wasn't good news for him. She was single but only in one sense of the word; her heart and soul seemed to be someone else's. Yet at the same time she seemed torn, as if she wished it weren't the case.

Hope told him about getting to know Ben online for eighteen months; how he had more than lived up to her expectations when she'd met him; the weekend she had spent with him in Portsmouth; and why she couldn't simply tell him how she felt and might never be able to do so.

Adam weighed everything up. She was now asking

him what he wanted to do, putting the ball in his court and suggesting that if he could bear with her whilst she tried to quash her feelings for this other guy, then there might be a chance of them going out for that second date, sometime soon if he still really wanted to.

Hope sat back in silence, and Adam waited.

'I understand if you want me to go now,' she piped up. 'I just wanted to be honest with you. It's a bizarre situation I find myself in. Maybe I should leave you to think about it overnight. The last thing I want to do is lead you on or hurt you.'

Adam realised that at any minute, this beautiful, honest, incredible girl could run into the arms of someone else, a person she clearly had strong feelings for. He understood that if he continued to see her, he might set himself up for a nasty fall. Yet he also quite fancied his chances because he didn't see how Ben could be any more of a catch than he was. Maybe in time he could make her forget about Ben altogether. Adam didn't need tonight to think about it. He knew he was up for the challenge, and he told her so without wasting any more time. 'I still want that second date you owe me, Blossom.'

'Okay. Wow,' Hope said. 'But I'd need to take things really slowly whilst I figure out how I truly feel about Ben. Would that be alright?'

'You dictate the pace that you're comfortable with. I'm guessing sex is off the table then?' he joked. 'But what about kissing?'

'Kissing is fine.' She laughed as he took her face in his hands and pulled her into an embrace.

She hoped she was doing the right thing. Only time

would tell. Maybe she was being greedy, not willing to let go of Ben until she was sure he wouldn't fall for her, yet at the same time happy to indulge in the affections of this sexy landlord. She'd been up front, though—had told Adam everything and was delighted that he still wanted to take her out again. She knew she'd changed her tune in a short space of time, one minute holding him at arm's length and the next wanting to pull him close, but there was something about the man at her side, resting his weary head on her shoulder. Every minute that she spent with him, she found herself being more and more drawn to him. She loved the way he told the stories of his life, the way he was with his staff and his customers, the way he looked at her with his eyes always twinkling. And although she had no idea why he'd recently started calling her 'Blossom', she rather liked it. Yes, she really was glad he had risen to the challenge she had presented him with. But now it was time to head home, as tomorrow would no doubt be another hectic day.

Adam escorted her out of the pub and into her car. He gave her a lingering kiss and then shut the door behind her once she was safely inside. He bent down to talk to her through her open window, his palms resting against the cold silver paintwork. 'How about I take you out for dinner next week?'

'I'd like that. I'd like that a lot.' She might end up regretting this, but right now she was too tired to think about it. As she drove back around the corner to the place she called home, she sang silently along to the radio. Now, did she have any clean clothes ready and ironed for work in the morning, and where had she put the keys for the store?

Adam had something important to do. If he was going to pursue Hope, then he would have to end things with the woman he'd been seeing for the last few months. He didn't have any feelings for this other woman; it had only been casual. But he had always hated ending relationships. He preferred to distance himself from prospective girlfriends when he wanted things to be over, hoping they'd take the hint and save him the job of having to spell it out. He could do this. He had to do this. If he was going to date Hope, then it wouldn't be right to carry on seeing someone else behind her back. Hope needn't know about the other woman. He'd just put an end to things, right now.

He picked up his phone, accessed his contacts, and pressed the call button. *It's the right thing to do . . . yet . . . Hope is still kind of involved with Ben,* he thought, reaching for a bottle of wine.

***

Angelisa slipped out of Adam's flat in the early hours, convinced that no one had seen her. Adam and Hope had clearly hit it off, but there was evidently someone else still firmly wedged inside Hope's heart.

15

As Hope approached her front door the following Monday, she noticed a beautiful bouquet of flowers propped up against it. The small attached envelope was addressed to her, and she opened it to read the card inside.

Be ready at 8, dear. X

She remembered teasing Adam when he'd called her 'dear' in Birmingham, saying that when she reached the age of sixty, it might be appropriate, but she wasn't that old yet. In fact, she now recalled that he had only started calling her 'Blossom' after she had ridiculed him about it on many occasions. She grinned at his smart revenge with these flowers. After all, how could she reprimand him for using such an old-fashioned term when it was accompanied by this perfect romantic gesture?

Jess shrieked in delight as Hope stepped through the door, even though they had seen each other mere hours earlier.

'Hi, honey, just time for a quick cuppa, and then I must jump in the shower. Look what Adam got me.' Hope held up the flowers, beaming as she walked into the kitchen.

'Hope, they're beautiful. Let me put them in some water for you whilst you get ready. Now, do you want my standard arranging fees, at £1 per flowerhead, or my super-duper deluxe for £1.50?'

Hope smiled at her. 'Your freebie-for-a-friend service, as per usual, please.'

Jess's talent as a full-fledged florist had not been lost since she'd moved into retail management. Her fingers deftly set to work on the budding lilies and roses, as Hope marvelled at the masterpiece taking shape.

By five to eight, Hope was washed, dressed and ready, thankful Adam still hadn't arrived. The doorbell rang just as she and Jess sat down for a chat, meaning the day's catch-up would have to wait until after Hope's date. She hugged Jess tightly, then rushed along the hallway to answer the door. Adam grinned at her, and she smiled back, all thoughts of Ben temporarily abandoned. Shouting goodbye to Jess, they hustled out to the waiting taxi.

Hope recalled the seafood meal Ben had taken her for in Portsmouth, but she pushed the memory away, not wanting him on her mind this evening. *Maybe Ben isn't the one for me simply because he isn't open to being loved now. Adam, though, is another story.*

The Italian restaurant Adam chose was the perfect setting for their first real date. Hope marvelled at the beautiful ornate ceiling and the spiral staircase that swam in front of her eyes, seemingly taking its travellers to the top of the world. *I must have a spiral staircase in my house one day*, she decided, having been fascinated with them since childhood.

'Hope?' Adam's voice jolted her into the present. She turned to face him, waiting for him to repeat what he had said. 'I used to work here before it was turned into an Italian restaurant. I ran it when it was a pub. It was such a great pub. I wish you could have seen it back then.' He pointed out all the changes that had been made to the décor, the structure, and the original bar set-up, painting a picture of the interior in the days when he'd been in charge. 'The company I worked for had to sell the premises, and I was made redundant. I had hoped to buy the place myself, but the price was too high.'

She reached out and took his hands in hers, sensing his shoulders drop and the sadness in his tone. On top of his offer being turned down, there had been an extra sting in the tale. He had found out, a few months too late, that the asking price was later reduced substantially for a quick sale—in fact, lowered to such an extent that he would have been able to afford the place after all.

'Let's order, honey. What's good?' she asked. Hope never liked to see anyone miserable and always did whatever she could to make people happy, often at her own expense.

Having decided on starters and mains, they sat chatting whilst sipping the champagne Adam had insisted on ordering, to her protests. She'd worried about the expense and that they weren't celebrating anything, thus had no excuse to order bubbly. Yet Adam had begged to differ.

'We are celebrating the fact that I now have a

girlfriend,' he'd announced, smiling broadly. 'I think that's definitely worthy of champagne.'

She'd also planned to stay sober, especially since she'd skipped lunch to save her appetite. But he had once again made her feel very special. Perhaps that was what she liked about Adam. In his presence, she felt smart, sexy, and desirable, as if the two of them were the only people in the room. He gave her his undivided attention. But . . . *girlfriend*? That term implied she had swiftly been taken off the market. Where did that leave her and Ben?

Once their starters had been cleared and they were waiting for their mains, Hope walked up the spiral staircase to the toilet. Now she remembered why the staircase had made such an impression on her. It wasn't a memory from her youth but instead from the restaurant in Portsmouth she had visited with Ben. That had only been a little over a month ago. Did it really seem like an ancient childhood memory? Was this a cruel realisation that, by her spending time with Adam, Ben was slipping further away and becoming a dim, distant memory?

Just as on that day in Portsmouth, she once again stood at the top of a spiral staircase, feeling lightheaded as she approached the toilets. On returning to the restaurant, she couldn't figure out where the spiral had gone and why she was no longer descending in circles but was instead heading straight down two flights of very narrow, very regular stairs. Seeing someone ahead of her, she moved to her left so he could pass but then realised there would not be room. The young man waited for her to get to the bottom of the stairs, looking bemused. Yet Hope felt even more baffled when she cast her eyes around to discover that Adam was nowhere to be seen. Their table was gone, and the décor was not as beautiful as she had first believed.

'Um, I think I'm a little lost.' Hope smiled awkwardly, addressing the twins swimming in front of her eyes. 'Am I in a *kitchen*?'

The young men, although there was actually only one of them, led her back up one flight of stairs to the restaurant. He pointed out that she must have failed to see the Staff Only sign after leaving the toilet, but he told her not to worry. With as much champagne-fuelled dignity as she could muster, she smiled sweetly, nodded, and half-walked, half-stumbled back to their table. Then she collapsed in a fit of such contagious giggles that Adam couldn't help but join in, though he had no idea what she was laughing about.

Once Hope had revealed her embarrassing mistake and they'd started to tuck into their mains, Adam took over the conversation. He talked animatedly about love, work, life, and his upbringing, seemingly leaving no stone unturned. It was so refreshing for Hope to have met someone else who talked so openly. She interjected occasionally, asking him to tell her more about his exes and more about his childhood, but was most interested in hearing about his job. All the while, his eyes were fixed on hers, searching for something, possibly trying to find out what she truly thought about him and whether her head was still filled with fantasies of Ben.

Hope decided it was time to put Adam fully in the picture. She felt pretty sure by now that he would still stick around to try to eliminate Ben from the equation, but she needed to give him all the facts and figures so that he could do the maths. She described her weekend in Portsmouth in more detail. She could see the pain or fear or regret in Adam's eyes, but it didn't stop her from talking. He needed to know what a tough job he had let himself in for, and she had to find out whether he could handle it.

She played down the night in Ben's bedroom, letting Adam know they'd gone no further than kissing but not revealing just how breath-taking that experience had been. She didn't want him to realise her physical encounter with Ben had been so utterly perfect that no other romantic liaison could ever compare. Adam remained seated at the table, listening intently and not interrupting.

Having talked through their main courses being cleared and replaced with delicious desserts, through all of the champagne, and through coffee and mints, Hope finally fell silent. She stopped staring into her coffee cup and looked up, daring to search his face for clues on what he was thinking.

Moments dragged by as she watched him for a reaction. She wondered whether she had been too honest and tried to figure out what she expected him to say.

Then, uttering not a word, Adam pushed his chair back from the table, breaking the silence as it scraped the floor. Discarding his napkin, he gripped the sides of the table with both hands and leaned over the remnants of their meal to kiss her hard on the mouth.

'I don't think I've ever been in love before, Blossom, not properly, but I think I could fall in love with you,' he confessed. With that, he sat back down and summoned the bill from the passing waiter.

Wow. Hope had not expected that. He thought he

could fall in love with her. Had she finally found a strong but sensitive man who could love her back if she dared to fall for him? So, why couldn't she help but compare his kisses to the ones she'd shared with Ben?

When Hope got home to Jess, she was giddy and giggling again. The taxi had dropped her off before taking Adam the rest of the way back to the pub, and his lingering kisses had made getting out of the cab a real wrench. Climbing into her pyjamas before heading back downstairs, she felt pleased to have some thinking time alone with no further distractions from either object of her affection. Was she ready to admit that Adam was really growing on her—and fast?

Feeling sleepy and slightly tipsy from the alcohol, Hope sat at the kitchen table across from Jess. 'I know how I feel about Ben,' she began, 'but Adam thinks he could fall in love with me. Wouldn't it make more sense to fall for someone who is capable of loving me back?'

Jess didn't know how to reply. Logic was Hope's middle name, or at least one of them, as 'clumsy' and 'impatient' had to fit in there somewhere. But was logic the right standard to apply in the case of love? A few months ago, Hope had been Miss Difficult to Please. Could there really be something so special about both of these guys, or was alcohol simply affecting her judgement?

16

At work the next morning, Hope's mind was only half on the job. She'd had such a fun night with Adam that she couldn't wait until her lunch break to see if he'd been in touch. She'd considered texting him first thing that morning to thank him again for their meal but had decided against it, not wanting to appear too enamoured. Instead, she'd distracted herself by messaging Ben and then chuckled at the irony. Had she forgotten who was supposed to be distracting her from whom?

When eleven thirty finally came around, she took the bag from her locker and eagerly checked her mobile phone. Ben had sent a message with details about an exciting new client he'd landed who would be really good for business. She sent him a congratulatory reply, letting him know how pleased she was for him. Yet she realised it would probably mean he'd now be even busier than usual. *Will I ever get back to Portsmouth to see if my heart still resides there, along with my black boots?*

Feeling decidedly hungry, despite having eaten a ridiculous amount at dinner the previous night, Hope fancied a cheese baguette from the nearby bakery. She would wander while she ate today. It had only stopped raining a short while ago so was too wet for her to sit on a bench in the high street. She didn't want to go back to the staffroom or eat in one of the cafés, though, because she wanted some time alone with her thoughts. She was surprised at her disappointment over Adam not messaging her yet. He was becoming more than just a distraction. But what did she find so appealing about him? And where did that leave Ben?

Whilst she tried to figure that out, a message jumped onto her phone screen.

> Hope, I really enjoyed our date. I'm working tonight but would love to see you again. Why don't you and Jess come to the pub after you get home from work, and I'll treat you both to something to eat and a bottle of wine? Let me know. Adam X

It sounded like a fantastic idea. Adam was scoring major brownie points already by factoring Jess into the equation. Hope messaged her best friend, then paid for her baguette and sent Adam a reply.

> I really enjoyed it, too. Thank you again for the meal. I've messaged Jess, and I'll let you know for sure later, but we'll hopefully be there tonight. Hope Xxx

> Great, bring a copy of your rotas so we can

work out when we next have some time off together. Adam X

Luckily, the afternoon went by a lot more quickly than the morning had. The shop had been extremely busy with customers, all keen to spend. Before Hope knew it, she was finishing for the day and locking up the store. In spite of getting soaked on the way to the station in the downpour that started the moment she'd left the building, she wasn't deterred by the turn in the weather. Jess had replied to her earlier message, agreeing that a meal at the pub sounded lovely, and Hope was in high spirits, trying to work out what to wear.

When the girls arrived at the White Rose a little after eight, they were pleased to see their favourite sofa once again free. Adam greeted them as they approached the bar, helped them choose a wine, and sent them away with menus. He said he would deliver the wine to their table and take their orders shortly. The pub didn't normally offer table service. All of the other customers had to order their food at the bar as usual, but Jess and Hope were being treated like VIPs tonight. Once again, Hope's mind started to wander as she remembered her weekend with Ben. Willing him out of her head for at least the next few hours, she tried to concentrate on the menu.

The girls made short work of their meal and most of the wine, chatting whilst they ate and drank. Both agreed they wouldn't stay at the pub too late because they felt decidedly tired already. Adam was able to take a break a short while later. When he joined them at their table, they thanked him for his treat.

'My pleasure,' he replied, smiling. 'Did you bring a

copy of your rotas, Hope?'

'I took a photo of this week's and the next four. I'll airdrop them to you now. Can you turn it on?' she requested, fishing her phone out of her pocket and tapping away at the screen.

'Done? Mine are all pinned up in the staffroom. Give me a minute or two, and I'll see when we're both free next.' He got up and kissed Hope's neck before disappearing out the back.

Adam wasn't exactly at home with modern technology. He would have preferred Hope giving him hard copies of her rotas rather than sending minute photos of them to his phone. He liked his paperwork in A4 size and on actual paper, not held in a device that would only cooperate if you handled it delicately and knew how to coax what you wanted out of hiding. He wasn't a fan of all the gimmicky things phones did these days and was proud that he didn't have a single social media account. Eventually, after a great deal of help from Dillan, he was able to review Hope's rotas alongside his own and see when their time off coincided.

Returning to the girls' table twenty minutes or so later, Adam smiled wanly. 'Well, there's good news and there's bad news,' he advised, sitting down just as Jess jumped up to head to the Ladies.

'It's alright, I've heard this one before. The bad news is, he's spilled coffee all over his computer keyboard. The good news is that it's all under control.' Jess giggled, and then she was gone.

Hope laughed. 'What's the bad news, Adam?' she enquired.

'We don't have a day off together until the twenty-fifth.' Disappointment showed all over his face.

'Of October? But it's still September until Friday!' Hope frowned.

'I know. I know.' Adam took her hands in his. 'But in the meantime, I have early finishes on a couple of your days off, and when I'm off we can see each other once you're back from work. So, we'll have five or six evenings when we can do something together before then.'

'That's sounding a bit better,' Hope noted, managing half a smile.

'And on the nights I'm working, I'll still be able to spend some time with you when it's not too busy here, whenever you fancy coming to the pub after work.'

'Okay,' Hope agreed. 'And what shall we do on the twenty-fifth to make the most of finally having a whole day off together? Have you got any ideas?'

'Let me surprise you.' He winked at her cheekily. 'I might have a thing or two up my sleeve. Just leave it with me.'

She couldn't help but feel a little excited at the prospect of Adam planning a surprise. She had no recollection of any man ever going out of his way to arrange something special for a day off. 'Okay, surprise me,' she replied, smiling.

Not long afterwards, the girls made a move to leave. Adam walked them to the door of the pub, gave Hope a big cuddle and a kiss on the lips, and said goodnight.

'What do you honestly think of Adam?' Hope asked as soon as they'd set off.

'Well, he definitely seems besotted with you already,' Jess exclaimed, 'not that I blame him, of course. But more importantly, how do you feel about him, and is he helping you to forget Ben?'

'He's certainly giving Ben a run for his money,' was all Hope said in return before turning the conversation to her friend's training with Next.

Jess had enjoyed the course but also found it exhausting. Soaking up vast loads of vital information and then digesting it, on top of the long commute to and from Bristol every day, had taken its toll. She was pleased she'd finally completed the training and could now begin her role as assistant manager in the Cheltenham branch.

As soon as they entered the house, Jess said goodnight to Hope. The younger girl remained alone in the kitchen accompanied only by her thoughts. Ben and Adam both swam through her head, a question mark hanging over each of them.

A few days later, Hope was strolling around town on her lunch hour and wondering whether to see Adam after work. She marvelled at the magnificent store windows displaying all things Christmassy. Jess had just messaged that she was shattered and would be having an early night, and Hope realised she should probably give the pub a miss, too. She'd seen Adam the previous night, and they already had plans to spend the following evening together, bowling. So, if she didn't see him tonight, whilst he was working, it wouldn't really hurt. But then the chocolate-filled advent calendars inside the next store caught her eye, conjuring up an idea that gave her the perfect excuse to see Adam again.

After arriving back at the station that evening, Hope jumped into her car, checked her appearance in the rear-view mirror, and drove straight to the White Rose. When she caught sight of Adam, she rushed towards him and then faltered, unsure of how to greet him in front of his staff and customers.

He grabbed her into a hug and gave her a kiss, shouting, 'You came! I didn't think you were coming tonight. I hoped you would, though.'

'I'm not staying,' Hope replied. 'I just wanted to give you this.' She handed him the advent calendar.

'Thank you, Blossom, but Christmas is still months away. Why the great rush?'

'I'm crazy about Christmas. But that's beside the point, as this advent calendar is for a different countdown. Open up door one now and then open up another door each day. When you finally get to number twenty-five, we'll be spending the whole day off together. I'll get you another one to open in December.'

'That's so sweet, thank you.' Adam opened door one and took out the chocolate concealed within. It was heart-shaped, so he handed it over to her and kissed her again. 'And when you say you're crazy about Christmas, just how crazy are we talking?' he probed.

'My mum died suddenly when I was seventeen, a couple of weeks before Christmas—'

'Oh, Hope, I'm really sorry to hear that—'

'No, it's okay. It's been over ten years now, so these days I can talk about her without crying or choking on my words. But Christmas was always utterly amazing when my brothers and I were young because Mum always did so many wonderful things to plan the most magical time. Ever since she died, I can't get enough of Christmas. I'm trying to hold onto the memories, perhaps. So, if you're at all "Bah, humbug", then you'd better come clean now.'

'Ha, I'm no Scrooge,' Adam reassured her. 'Being in the pub trade means I don't really get to stop and properly enjoy the big day itself, as I'm always working on the twenty-fifth. That's the one downside to this job. But I'm a big fan of all things Christmassy and love the build-up, too, so don't worry about that.'

Hope smiled adoringly at him.

The following weeks went by a lot faster than Hope had anticipated as, one by one, Adam opened the calendar doors and they devoured the chocolates. On a few evenings, she went to the pub shortly after arriving home from work, then often stayed until after it closed. That way, she could join Adam and the staff as they wound down after a late shift. Jess sometimes accompanied Hope, at least for the early part of the evening, and the girls swapped their kitchen table catch-ups for a meal together or some drinks.

On nights when Adam wasn't working, he and Hope made the most of their time together. It was a treat for her to have him all to herself, instead of sharing him with his customers and staff. The pair had recently laughed through a couple of comedies at the local cinema, spent a good few fiercely competitive hours at the bowling alley, and played umpteen games of Scrabble in Adam's lounge, often ordering food to be sent up from the pub.

Tonight, they were once again up in his flat but this time in the kitchen, reminiscing about childhood whilst he cooked a meal. As Adam chopped and whisked and stirred, Hope chattered about everything her mum had done to make Christmases special when she was young. Adam listened attentively, eager to gain insight into making this Christmas incredible for her. They always found plenty to talk about. Ben had started to drift from the forefront of Hope's mind, and Adam had proved to be far more than just a distraction, creeping into her heart, slowly but surely, and staking his claim.

When their mutual day off eventually dawned, Hope was up and ready, bright and early. Adam had said to be at the pub by ten. Dressed in jeans and a thick jumper, she put on her winter coat and scarf to walk to the White Rose.

Adam's assistant manager sent her straight up to his flat. There, Hope saw Adam busy knocking up eggs Benedict for breakfast. She'd recently admitted that she'd never tried the dish but had always been desperate to. *How sweet of him to go to the trouble of making it for me,* Hope thought. *He really is kind and considerate.*

As they tucked into their food, Hope marvelled at the flavour combinations, and Adam finally revealed his plan for the day. After breakfast they would be going to the local funfair that had just been set up on the other side of Cheltenham and would stay until it closed late that night. She couldn't wait.

They arrived at the fairground before midday, then followed the throng and the intoxicating scent of caramelised candyfloss across the car park to a ticket kiosk. Adam purchased two wristbands, giving them unlimited access to all of the rides. They looked around, wondering what to go on first. Hope suggested the ghost train. They didn't expect much of a scare, but it was one of the few rides with no queue.

'Where next?' Adam asked as the ride came to a stop a few minutes later.

'Something fast and actually scary?' Hope

suggested. 'How about that one?' The roller coaster she indicated whooshed past them and disappeared out of sight.

'Okay,' Adam agreed. He grabbed her hand and led her across the fairground towards the end of the queue.

They spent all afternoon on the rides. The thrill of the faster ones sent their endorphins into a frenzy and made them feel like teenagers again, racing around together. After they had been on most of the big ones, Hope insisted that they go on a children's ride, too. They squeezed into the tiny seats of the banana boat, pretending to people around them that they were genuinely afraid and wanted to get off before it even started. They got some funny looks from the toddlers accompanying them.

One sitting opposite Hope even piped up with, 'Don't worry, lady, it's not scary. I've done it seventy-eleven times already. Even my little sister doesn't think it's scary, and she still wears nappies!'

At this point, Hope and Adam could no longer keep up their pretence, collapsing into fits of giggles as the children around them burst into hysterics, too.

As the day turned to early evening, the pair realised they were ravenous. They stepped up to a food van to order giant pulled-pork burgers and chips. They sat on a picnic bench nearby, the delicious food filling their stomachs and warming their hands as they soaked up the atmosphere. Dusk had started to settle when Adam spotted a passing vendor selling light-up toys. Calling him over to their table, he said to Hope, 'Shall we have a princess wand, a crown, a dagger, a light sabre, a whirly thingy, or a . . . nope, I don't know what that last one is at all, do you?'

'A majorette's baton?' Hope ventured, then she turned to the seller. 'Does the whirly thing spin around?'

'Yes, and it has three different light-up options, like so.' He handed her one to play with whilst demonstrating the different modes.

'I really like this one. What do you think?' Hope asked Adam.

'I think I really like *you*, Hope,' he whispered back, paying for the toy.

Hope placed it on their table, and the spinning multicoloured light allowed them to finally see each other's face. 'I really like you, too,' she assured him, smiling.

'And how about Ben? Do you still really like him?' Adam wiped a dribble of sauce away from the side of her mouth, but before she had time to answer, he'd jumped up and run off. She had no option but to race after him.

'We can't leave the funfair until I've won you a teddy bear!' he shouted as they joined the masses. A number of stalls dotted the fairground where people could show off their skills to win a cuddly toy for the object of their affection.

'I have to prove myself worthy of you, milady.' Adam took a quick look around to assess his options. He didn't fancy his chances with the sledgehammer bell game and wasn't too great at darts, despite working in the pub trade. Rejecting the basketball stall, too, he settled on the beanbag tin-can alley. He paid the vendor for two goes so as not to look arrogant. On his first attempt, he managed to knock over a couple of cans, but unfortunately not all of them.

As the stallholder restacked them and Adam prepared for his second go, Hope's phone warbled with an incoming message. She looked to see who it was from and then placed it back in her pocket. 'It's alright, just a message from Ben. Nothing I need to reply to. You've got this,' she said, adding, 'Oh, no, so close,' as Adam's second throw left one solitary can on the shelf.

'So, my competitor wants in on the action, does he? Well, faint heart never won fair lady. Now I *must* win you that teddy!' Adam declared. He pulled another note from his wallet and grasped Hope's arm, spinning her around and over to the stall behind them. Before she knew it, he had paid the vendor, procured a rod, and hooked a duck with the highest score. Now he was presenting her with the biggest stuffed toy on the stall.

She giggled and beamed at him. 'Why thank you, kind sir.'

'At your service, ma'am.' He pretended to remove a hat from his head and bowed to her.

All too soon, the fair began shutting down for the night, and it was time for them to go home. Adam drove back across Cheltenham.

'I still can't believe how quickly the time went,' Hope moaned, a little dismal.

'At least, we won't have to wait so long for our next day off together, now that we've synchronised our rotas going forwards.' Adam patted her knee.

'True.'

They always consulted each other before drawing up any weekly staff rotas these days. Some weeks proved harder to synchronise than others, if any of their team couldn't work certain shifts, if either of them had training, or if something out of the ordinary happened at the store or the pub. But things looked far more promising than when they'd first compared respective days off.

Adam pulled up quietly in Hope's close and turned off his engine so as not to disturb the neighbours. 'I wish you didn't have to go,' he said, kissing her longingly.

'I have such an early start again tomorrow,' Hope grumbled when he finally let her up for air. 'Maybe another night, when we both don't have work the next morning, I could stay over at yours or you could stay at mine?' They were still taking things slowly on the physical front, but it would have been nice to end such a perfect day by falling asleep in each other's arms.

'Yes, you must stay at mine next time we have a night out,' he agreed before kissing her again.

As their kisses intensified, Hope realised she was in danger of letting him whisk her off to his flat now, if she didn't head indoors soon. 'I really must go, but I had such an amazing day, thank you.'

'Night, Blossom.' He reluctantly let her out of the car.

'I'll see you soon,' she promised.

'Tomorrow, hopefully,' he said, waving and blowing her a kiss goodnight.

When Hope climbed into bed, still thinking of all the fun she'd had at the fair, she was unable to resist the urge to pull up Ben's earlier text message and send him a quick reply.

> Ben, I've just got home from a day at the fair with Adam. It was great fun! Mwah Xxx

Adam was also unable to resist temptation.

***

Angelisa was aware that Adam and Hope had been dating for a while now, but it gave her no real cause for concern. It seemed that Hope was still torn between Ben and Adam, so she'd just have to wait patiently to see how things played out. Would Hope keep pursuing Adam in the long run?

17

During the following fortnight, Adam and Hope saw each other almost every evening and spent their days off together whenever these coincided. Hope had begun to stay later and later at the pub when Adam worked nights. She struggled to tear herself away from him and often got home with little time to sleep before work the next day. On two occasions, she stayed behind after the staff eventually went home. She had time alone with Adam in the early morning hours and later spent the night in his bed, but they still took things no further than kissing.

On Bonfire Night, the pair arranged to go to a fireworks display that one of Adam's regulars put on in his garden. While walking the short distance to the venue, Hope bubbled over with excitement.

'When we were younger, my brothers and I always spent hours making a guy, using Dad's old clothes, some newspapers, and a Halloween mask,' she gushed. 'We'd push him up to the local shop in my little brother's pushchair, on the Saturday before Guy

Fawkes Night, and stand there for hours shouting, "Penny for the guy". Then we'd spend any money we collected on sweets and comics before making our way home.'

Adam smiled at her. He loved hearing about her childhood and seeing her eyes light up when she reminisced. 'I bet that was great fun.'

'It really was. When Dad came home from work on November the fifth, he'd build a bonfire with my older brothers whilst my little brother and I helped Mum wrap jacket potatoes in foil, ready to bake in the oven. We'd all sit down together for a picnic-style tea, followed by two homemade birthday cakes because it was Mum's birthday that day and my eldest brother's. Finally, it would be time for Dad to light the bonfire and burn the guy. Then we'd all roast marshmallows in the embers before being ushered indoors so Mum could keep us all safe whilst Dad set off the fireworks. I was always enchanted by them. We watched with our noses pressed up so tightly against the patio door that the glass steamed up . . .' Hope trailed off, her eyes bright with passion.

'Sounds magical.' Adam noticed a solitary tear running down her cheek. He wiped it away with his thumb and waited for her to continue.

'The Catherine wheel was always my favourite—not that it ever worked, mind. We had one every year, and we'd all place bets on how it would behave. Dad would nail it onto a piece of wood and light it. But it would either not spin at all; spin once or twice and then stop, with Dad racing back to coax it to continue; or jump right off the post and roll around the garden, with Dad chasing after it.'

Adam smiled but said nothing.

'It was always hilarious. He wasn't afraid of getting burnt. I think that's why Mum always made sure my brothers and I were never outside at the time, so that we didn't follow in his recklessness. We were allowed to go out at the end for sparklers, though, provided we had at least two pairs of gloves on.' Hope giggled at the memory.

'We didn't really ever do much for Guy Fawkes Night,' Adam admitted. 'I think we went to big displays some years, but I don't remember them all that well.'

'I guess it was always a special day for our family because of Mum's and James's birthdays being on the fifth.'

After arriving at their destination, Adam opened the gate and led Hope through to the back garden. He made the necessary introductions and then got them both something to drink. Not long afterwards, the fireworks started. They took Hope back to her childhood but then transported her to a far more recent time, the fireworks display in Portsmouth. Why was it that every time she and Adam were together, something ended up reminding her of Ben?

After getting home from work the next day, Hope headed straight for the bathroom. She planned a long hot soak before going to see Adam at the pub. She loved how things had progressed between them and the ease of being in his company. He had introduced her to pretty much everyone at the White Rose by now, always with a huge smile. He raved about how wonderful she was and how lucky he was to have her as his girlfriend. Hope sighed contentedly. Everything was perfect right now.

Well, not *quite* perfect. A certain other someone

still refused to be firmly pushed out of the picture. Even though nearly three months had passed since that night with Ben, Hope still couldn't get him out of her head, and it had begun to trouble her. She would just have to accept that she would need a little longer to get over him. She had to leave that incredible night in the past, stop wondering about what might have been, and focus solely on Adam going forwards. She couldn't risk losing Ben's friendship by telling him how she truly felt about him, but she also didn't want to jeopardise what she had built with Adam by holding onto her feelings for Ben. She simply had to forget about Ben romantically. Surely, she could do that.

Although her relationship with Adam was still in its early days, they'd spent so much time together during the last seven weeks that they felt as though they'd been dating longer. She could tell that he was already emotionally attached, not that he'd told her in so many words. Yet clearly her feelings for Ben also troubled him. He made light of things, but every now and then he passed a comment such as 'Well, you've got six boys' or 'that's if you don't run off with your other men', revealing his insecurity with the situation.

Hope stepped into the bath, and it dawned on her how hard it must be for Adam. She'd wanted to be truthful with him from the start. She'd wanted to be honest about her feelings for Ben and hold Adam at a distance whilst she either got Ben out of her head or made him fall for her. Yet maybe she'd been too honest and failed to appreciate how hard Adam now found it. Maybe she had also built Ben up to such an extent that Adam felt he could never compete. If only there were a way to allay his fears. Not that they were necessarily unfounded.

Hope sank back in the bubbles. The situation was becoming rather arduous. In all honesty, there really wasn't anything for Adam to worry about. Ben would never get to learn how she felt and therefore wasn't really a threat to Adam. But could Adam ever see it like that? Their relationship was futile if he couldn't deal with her feelings for Ben, even if she found a way to hide them away forever.

Jess clattered through the front door and into the kitchen, shouting, 'Hello?'

Hope bellowed back, 'Hold on, hun, I'll be down in a sec. Are you putting the kettle on?'

'I'm already on it,' Jess answered at the top of her voice.

By the time Hope came downstairs, Jess had made them both a cuppa. The girls both felt weary, even though neither of them had work the next day. As they sat nursing their coffees, Hope decided she wouldn't go to the pub. Adam would be staying over in Birmingham the following week to attend a training course, and he'd invited her to spend the nights in his hotel with him. So, this evening, she fancied some time with Jess and hoped he would understand. Sometimes he was a little territorial and made her feel guilty if her plans didn't revolve around him.

'Tell you what we need to wake ourselves up,' Hope said, getting out of her chair and heading for the fridge. 'We need vino.' Jess got up, too, and fetched glasses from the cupboard. She placed them on the kitchen table as Hope poured the wine. 'Let's have a girls' night in and then go shopping tomorrow. I'll call Adam to tell him I can't make it tonight. What do you reckon?'

'Great idea,' Jess agreed, chinking her glass against Hope's.

Not until they finished that bottle of wine and moved on to a second one did Hope suddenly realise she hadn't rung Adam yet. She picked up her mobile and called him at the pub. He immediately knew she had been drinking—something she flatly denied, although her giggles and angelic attitude gave her away.

'I don't drink, Adam. I'm a total teabag. I mean teatoppler. I mean teetotaller.' She burst into raucous laughter with Jess, throwing her head back and thwacking it on the wall behind her. 'Ow, why did you do that?' she grumbled into the phone.

'What are you doing, Blossom? Why did I do what?'

'I banged my head from laughing too much. Ouch.'

'I wish I wasn't working tonight. You two sound like you're having fun. Are you coming over in a bit?'

'Do you mind if I don't tonight, honey? It's just that Jess and I haven't seen each other for ages. We're having a girlie night, and you . . . you are a man!'

Jess chuckled at her friend's amazing perception, which started Hope off again. But Adam wasn't laughing.

'Okay. Be good. Got to go,' he said, hanging up.

Was Hope imagining it, or was there an edge to his voice? 'I am good, I'm lovely,' she babbled into the phone to no one before taking another sip of wine. Then she looked searchingly at her mobile, but it was left to Jess to reassure her that she was indeed lovely.

With the phone call over, the girls wondered what to do with their night. They felt like having fun but were both so tired. Jess put on some music, and then Hope's phone whistled and sang. It was Ben, and Hope realised that Jess would finally get a chance to speak to him.

'Hi, Ben, it's Hope,' she screamed into the phone, motioning for Jess to turn the radio down.

'I know, I called you, you moron. Have you been drinking?'

'Jess is here. Say hello to Jess.'

'Okay, put her on then,' Ben requested.

Jess took the phone from her friend and chatted to Ben for a few minutes whilst Hope stood up and moved across the kitchen. Realising she'd barely had anything to eat all day, she lifted a loaf of bread up in the air and motioned that she was going to make toast. She raised her eyebrows to see if Jess wanted any. Her friend's thumbs-up gave her the go-ahead to make enough for two, and she busied herself toasting the bread and buttering it before applying a generous layer of Marmite. Toast ready, she placed the plates on the kitchen table and gestured for Jess to put the call on speakerphone. The girls polished off the food and chatted away to Ben for another hour or more before he had to shoot off.

'I still think I love Ben a little bit,' Hope admitted, feeling lightheaded because the toast hadn't quite soaked up the wine yet.

'No, you don't,' Jess scolded, 'you're just unwilling to let him go. Adam is lovely, and with him you could have a real future. Isn't that what you want, marriage, babies, and all that happily ever after? You know Ben isn't ready for that; he might never be. You and Adam are great together. Please don't let Ben mess that up.'

'How are you not a little bit drunk?' Hope sat up

straight in her chair, eyes wide in astonishment that her friend had coherently strung so many words together.

'Because you drank like a fish whilst I was chatting to Ben.'

'Oh! But don't you think he sounds lovely?' Hope looked all dreamy-eyed.

'Yes, but I also thought the same about naan bread recently. And look where that got me.' She showed Hope where the button had popped off her trousers.

A few hours later, Hope stirred and sat up in bed, trying to focus on the clock in the dark. She'd been having a nightmare, but it wasn't all that uncommon. Ever since her mum, Lisa, had died suddenly from a brain haemorrhage, Hope had often woken in the early hours, forced to relive the anguish of the night it happened.

In the recurring dream, she always saw her dad carrying her mum's limp body in from the car and onto the sofa after they'd been out together for the evening. This had actually happened in real life more than a decade ago. Hope had been left to sit alongside the lifeless body for an eternity whilst her dad waited in the road to flag down the ambulance. The experience had haunted her in the early months after her mum's death. Fortunately, the nightmare happened less often these days, but it still always woke her with a fright.

Hope sniffed away a solitary tear. Over the years, she had come to terms with her mum's death, but sometimes Hope wished she could still call on her for advice, a listening ear, or even just a cuddle. Settling back into bed now, she shut her eyes and ordered the mechanical parts of her brain to switch to power-saving mode. Time for sleep.

Disappointed that Hope had chosen Jess over him for the night when he'd anticipated seeing her, Adam felt out of sorts. After a seemingly eternal fifteen-hour shift, he'd got rid of the staff, locked up the pub, and now sat in his flat, feeling hungry, lonely, and disgruntled. He would be away from Cheltenham for four nights the following week, and his mind turned to what he would miss whilst away. He was pleased that Hope would be staying with him in Birmingham, but she couldn't satisfy *these* cravings. Picking up his phone, he made a quick call.

***

Angelisa ventured out into the cold, guided only by the light of the Blue Moon. It seemed that Adam was still struggling to come to terms with Hope being unable to let go of her obsession with Ben. Yet he was clearly falling for Hope. Feelings were certainly progressing quickly between the pair of them, but did that mean she would have to step aside soon? Was she no longer going to be called for?

18

First thing Monday morning, Hope and Adam once again found themselves standing on platform two, waiting to catch the seven twelve to Birmingham. This time around, Hope had packed a little suitcase, planning to spend the next four nights in Adam's hotel room. Although she had work that day, she'd been able to re-jig the staff rota to give her an earlier finish than usual, in order to see Adam shortly after his training ended at four.

In a stuffy training room the next morning, Adam was busy thinking about Hope, rather than concentrating on the instructor's lesson. Hope was so thoughtful, constantly doing cute little things to show him how much she cared. Like when she'd made him a framed picture for his flat with a message spelled entirely out of Love Heart sweets. Or when she'd taken on the mammoth task of ironing all of his clothes, after he'd admitted that he didn't have any in his wardrobe and simply ironed whatever he needed from the washing basket each morning.

Whilst Adam learned about risk assessments and environmental health officer visits, Hope spent her day off trawling the high street, hunting down little gifts for him which had sentimental value, souvenirs to commemorate the time they'd spent together since first meeting. When Adam met up with her later, she presented him with a beautifully gift-wrapped box full of weird and wonderful things, each with a special hidden meaning.

Hope had admittedly been a little embarrassed to explain the reason behind each gift in front of Adam's work colleagues, who had tagged along for the early part of the evening. She cringed now as she remembered pretending the medal was for putting up with her PMT. She'd had to think on the spot, rather than say it had actually been for tolerating her inability to quash her feelings for Ben. She hadn't wanted to embarrass Adam by revealing the truth in front of his workmates. *Adam still doesn't realise just how much I admire and appreciate him for handling the Ben Situation so well. I'll have to tell him how much it means to me later.*

Adam and Hope were now alone again, after breaking off from the group to share a romantic meal and drinks back at the hotel. They discussed the pub trade and how much he enjoyed his job, as well as their respective short- and long-term future plans.

'That's why I want to buy my own pub, somewhere rural, within the next year or two, ideally,' Adam said, looking at Hope. 'The venue will need to be in a perfect location to become the heart and soul of the community. But it should also allow easy access via main roads, with its reputation for outstanding food enticing people to travel from far and wide. I can really see myself running the business whilst being a hands-on parent one day. Living above my own pub would mean I could easily work shifts around the needs of a family.'

Hope enjoyed hearing about his aspirations and that he saw children in his future.

Not wanting the night to end too soon, they decided to go for a walk and ended up in a tacky nightclub. Hope kept trying to drag Adam onto the dance floor, under his protests, but in the end he gave in and actually seemed to enjoy himself. He twirled her around as she danced away, barefoot. They would have stayed all night had someone's stiletto heel not pierced Hope's left foot mid dance move. She had to hobble back to the hotel room in agony, aided by Adam.

Hope's second day off that week followed straight after her first. So, whilst Adam completed another day of training, she popped back home for fresh clothes and a change of scenery. She knew Jess was off, too, and had arranged to meet her for a workout before they spent the afternoon together in town. Hope's sore foot meant that her time at the gym wasn't as productive as usual. The pair later treated themselves to indulgent hot chocolates and Danish pastries before doing some serious Christmas shopping. All too soon, it was time for Hope to return to Birmingham.

She arrived back at Adam's hotel a little after eight and opened her newly packed suitcase to reveal two bottles of chilled white wine (stored in the freezer earlier); a huge bag of Maltesers; a hamper of crackers and cheese; and a Roku stick, complete with a remote and the necessary cables to connect it to the room's television. They settled in for the night with a soppy film, tucking into all of the goodies after polishing off the pizza that Hope had arranged to be delivered at nine.

'How did you know takeaway pizza is one of my weaknesses?' Adam asked.

'I didn't,' she replied, passing him the last slice, 'but who can resist pizza?'

All too soon, it was their final night in Birmingham. Adam would return straight home once his training ended on Friday. As she finished up at work, Hope thought about their last few days together with a contented smile. She realised that Ben had been fading from her mind as the week progressed, and it pleased her more than she'd expected.

Hope got back to the hotel room a little after six and gave Adam a kiss before getting changed. They hadn't booked anywhere to eat because they wanted to feel free whilst enjoying their last hours in these new surroundings. Hope suggested they meander into the heart of the city to see what food options took their fancy.

They walked past a few eateries near the centre, rejecting a pub or two because Adam always ate from the White Rose's menu unless he was cooking for Hope. They narrowed their choice down to a stunning Thai restaurant or an American steakhouse, yet neither could make a final decision. A coin toss determined their fate; they would eat Thai cuisine tonight.

A bouquet of fragrant spices welcomed them into the restaurant, and they were shown to a table.

Unsurprisingly, the food was incredible, and they felt happy to end up there on their final night. For starters, they opted for a platter of assorted canapes, comprising chicken satay, spring rolls, spare ribs, gung hom pah, and tung tong. They dove in the moment the huge dish was placed in front of them, then licked their fingers as they devoured every last morsel and washed it down with wine. For the main course, they shared green chicken curry, sweet and sour chicken, and stir-fried pork with ginger, all accompanied by generous portions of steaming Thai jasmine rice.

After eating, they sat back in their chairs and chatted about their plans for the next few weeks. Hope excused herself and went upstairs to the toilets. The upper dining area, not currently in use, was decorated with lotus flowers, orchids, jasmine, and hibiscus, all possibly artificial but looking so stunning under mood lighting that it was impossible to tell and really didn't matter. She felt as if she'd entered an Asian floating garden. The only other person in the room was an elderly Thai lady, seated at a table and making gung hom pah from scratch. She had hundreds of them sitting at attention on a tray in front of her. Fascinated, Hope felt as though the staircase had whisked her away to Thailand, but it wasn't the alcohol taking her there, only the ambience.

She returned to the table where Adam sat, perplexed by the goofy facial expressions he kept making. Then she spotted a little boy outside the window, pulling faces through the glass. Adam was mustering the craziest expressions he could, and the child's laughter was infectious. Hope got a glimpse of how Adam would be as a father, and she wondered whether a family was in *their* future together. *I so desperately want to be a mum one day. I have ever since the day that—*

'Ah, Hope, I'm just entertaining our little friend here.' He indicated the boy, who was dancing around outside the window whilst his parents enquired whether a table was free. Adam poked his tongue out, then put his hand over his mouth and acted bashful as though he knew he'd been naughty. His new buddy doubled over in stitches.

Looking around, Hope saw that all of the tables seemed full. It wasn't surprising, given the sensational food served here.

'Let's make a move,' she suggested, 'so that family can have our table.'

Adam nodded in agreement. He paid the bill, and they vacated their seats to move outside.

Wandering out into the dark, Hope reflected on how wonderful the last few days had been. They were both silent for a few moments, a little down now that their last night in Birmingham was drawing to a close. They'd been on a fabulous mini-break, and now they would soon head home again to their mundane daily lives. They walked for a while, letting the delectable Thai food settle in their tummies as Adam expanded on future plans for his own pub. He hinted that maybe it was something the two of them could do together one day, and she realised she wasn't averse to the idea at all.

As they walked back to his hotel, he pulled her close for a kiss. Hope realised how at home she felt with this man.

'Thank you for another lovely evening, Blossom.'

Adam smiled down at her.

'It's so nice to be away from the rest of the world for a change, isn't it? None of your staff or customers around . . .' *No mention of Ben getting in the way of things any more*, she added silently.

'It is. Now let's settle in for the night so I can have you all to myself.' He smacked her on the bottom, moving her forwards, and she giggled. They still hadn't taken things any further than kissing, although Hope had begun to feel that things might soon change.

But oh, how quickly a glorious week could go sour in an instant. With the worst possible timing, just as they were about to climb into bed for their last night in Birmingham, just as Adam thought about telling her he loved her, and just as Hope had begun to feel that tonight might be the time to turn on the green light in the bedroom . . . Ben's name lit up her phone as it trilled and begged her to answer.

She knew what she should do. She should ignore her phone and hope that Adam hadn't seen who was calling on the display. But one look at his face told her that he had already noticed.

'Take it,' he said dejectedly, not realising what had been on her mind seconds earlier.

Hope knew that whether or not she answered the phone, the evening was now ruined. Ben had gate-crashed their refuge just as she was hoping she'd shut him out and bolted the door. She reluctantly answered the call.

In an attempt to minimise Adam's anguish, she wandered through to the bathroom, phone to her ear, little knowing that he thought she was doing it only to keep secret whatever she said. *I can't help but admit that it does feel good to hear Ben's voice. I can't even remember the last time he found time to chat on the phone, but of all the nights.* It was around midnight, as was often the case when Ben did manage to call, so he'd probably just finished working for the day. Hope slid down the cool, tiled wall and sat on the floor. She pulled her knees up to her chest in an attempt to keep warm, as she was dressed for bed and felt a little chilly.

After speaking for twenty minutes or so, Ben reminded her that she and Jess had promised to visit soon. It suddenly registered that she'd actually spoken to him a few nights earlier, when he'd phoned her on their girls' night, and Jess had pretty much commandeered the conversation. Hope couldn't remember mentioning any visit. *Was that something Jess discussed with him whilst I was doing something else?* Her memory was still very patchy. *Wasn't I making toast or something?*

Hanging up the phone, she returned to the bedroom, feeling guilty. She needed to tell Adam she would be seeing Ben again at some point, but she didn't think he would be happy about that. It really put a damper on the amazing few days they'd just shared.

She climbed into bed and leaned over to talk to him, but he'd fallen asleep. She looked at her phone. The display read 2:27 a.m. She'd been on the phone with Ben for hours. Now she felt doubly guilty. She'd gone and ruined their last night away together. Adam had a right to be mad at her when he woke up, and she was sure he would be. She planted a kiss on his forehead and whispered, 'Sorry', into the silence.

19

Adam acted distant from Hope at breakfast.

It's totally understandable, she thought. They'd both got up late, and she had to rush off to work straight after they ate, leaving Adam to check out and go to the training centre alone. She prayed that he'd call her when they were both back home that evening, but she had a nagging feeling he wouldn't.

Her gut instinct turned out to be right. Although Hope reached out to Adam through numerous text messages and voicemails that night, they ended up barely speaking again for a couple of days. When she went to the pub quiz with Jess, Adam claimed that he'd been busy at work in the run-up to Christmas, but Hope knew he was simply using that as an excuse.

Attempting to repair the damage she'd caused, Hope spent her lunch hour the next day planning a romantic night for them. She knew Adam had the evening off and sent him a message, inviting him around to her house for a meal. She suggested that she'd love him to stay the night, too, if he could. He didn't reply, and by the time she'd finished work for the day, she still hadn't heard from him.

Hope arrived home around half past six, having stopped off for groceries on the way back from the station. Then she got busy with cooking anyway.

'Hi,' she called out as Jess came through the front door. 'Thank you for agreeing to make yourself scarce tonight. I really appreciate it. What are you going to do with yourself, and do you want me to plate you up some tagliatelle for later?'

'I've arranged to meet Tomasz at the cinema,' Jess shouted, walking towards Hope's voice. 'We plan to watch that action film he's been going on about lately, but I'll probably use the time to catch up on sleep whilst he's glued to the screen.' She laughed before adding, 'Then I'll go back to his for a bit and come home late if you like. Yes, please, to the pasta. How long do you want me to stay out? I'm a little worried that Tom will get his guitar out and start singing if he has me as a captive audience. Have you heard him?'

Hope smiled. 'No. Luckily for me, by the sound of it. Don't stay out later than you want to. If you'd rather come back straight after the film, that's fine. I can't have you enduring torture on my behalf. I think Adam and I need to have a proper chat, though. He seems to be getting more and more distant since Birmingham,' Hope replied forlornly, looking at her phone for messages. But there were none.

Jess went upstairs to get ready. Hope tried to call Adam again whilst keeping an eye on the pasta sauce bubbling away gently. She wondered at what stage of the cooking it would be safest to have a quick shower without ruining the food. There was no need to wash her hair tonight, but she'd cleanse her face and reapply her makeup after showering.

An hour or so later, Jess was out, and Hope was ready, as was the food. But Adam was MIA. Hope had sent him four messages since returning home and felt like she'd phoned him a hundred times. Her calls and messages had all gone unanswered, though. She turned off the hob and moved the pans off the heat before opening the bottle of Adam's favourite wine. She hoped he was okay. She was a little worried about him now. She rang the pub to see if someone could go up to his flat and check on him. Dillan happily obliged, but Adam was nowhere to be found.

When Jess returned home a little after ten, she crept into the house, not wanting to disturb whatever might be going on between the troubled couple. She was surprised to see Hope sitting alone, nibbling at plain pasta straight out of the saucepan.

'I guess I've been stood up,' Hope said, unable to hide her sadness.

Jess tossed the pasta through the pan of sauce that was still on the hob, heaped two plates with generous portions, and popped first one and then the other into the microwave. After filling the empty glass on the table with some wine for herself and topping up the other glass, she placed the food down and sat opposite her friend. Hope said very little.

The moment the girls began to tuck into the pasta, a message arrived from Adam.

> So busy. Been taking my focus off work too much lately, and business is struggling. Can't make it tonight. Sorry. Adam X

Hope put down her fork, immediately losing her

appetite. She handed Jess the phone to read the text herself. 'It's all going wrong, Jess. I wish I'd never told Adam about my feelings for Ben in the first place. We had such a wonderful time in Birmingham that Ben was losing his grip on my heart. We still message all the time, but it's only whenever he phones that I'm left wondering a little.'

'Wondering what, honey?'

'Whether I'm truly over him. I'm really falling for Adam. I can't deny it. I haven't told him yet, but I know I am.'

'That's great, Hope, isn't it? Why haven't you told him?'

'I'm not really sure. I thought if I took things slowly with Adam, then at some point I would be one hundred percent clear about my feelings for each of them. It just worries me that whenever Ben rings, I still get a few doubts. That's probably why I haven't told Adam how I feel yet. I know I've always unintentionally compared them both, but what I have with Adam is real and pretty amazing. Perhaps I'm unwilling to let go of Ben simply to protect myself from falling too deeply for Adam now.'

'That makes sense. Maybe you *are* over Ben then, and you're simply scared to admit how much you like Adam.'

'Maybe.'

'You know what you need to do?' Jess looked at her friend earnestly.

'Give up on men altogether?'

'No. We need to get our backsides to Portsmouth, pronto, so you can figure out once and for all if you're definitely over Ben. Have you sent him the dates we're both free yet?'

'Yes, but it might be months before he gets a weekend off. You know how long I had to wait to meet him the first time around.'

'Well, it might not be. At least, if you see Ben again in person, then you can work out exactly how you feel about him and where that leaves you and Adam. Then you'll just have to take it from there.'

'You know what?' Hope looked at her friend wistfully.

'What, sweetie?'

'If I had to choose between them right now, then, of course, it would be Adam. He's the only sensible option.'

But love was a very strange thing. It seemed to be the most nonsensical emotion of them all. People couldn't choose who they fell in love with, and that was the annoyance of it all.

'In the meantime,' said Jess, 'for a start, maybe don't answer the phone to Ben when you and Adam are together.'

'Good point,' Hope replied, looking shamefaced.

It was one in the morning by the time they finalised the younger girl's next steps. They agreed that the only way for Hope to walk a less complicated path was to visit Ben again, in pursuit of closure. Fingers crossed, it wouldn't be too long before the opportunity arose.

The following day, Hope tried to reach Adam again on her lunch hour. Her calls went straight to voicemail, so she sent him a couple more texts but still heard nothing in return. She tried again to get hold of him on the train home. By the time she got back to the house, she decided there was no point continuing to message and call if he was going to ignore her. So, she and Jess eventually went over to the White Rose to see if they could track him down. Adam wasn't working, though, and no one there seemed to have any idea where he was. Returning home after an hour or so and feeling utterly dejected, Hope tried calling him once more. This time, the call didn't go straight to voicemail, but it still wasn't answered. A few short minutes later, all she received in return was one lousy text message.

Sorry. I think I need a week on my own to miss you. Adam

There isn't even a kiss at the end, Hope noticed as she looked down at her phone screen.

Adam knew he wasn't being fair to Hope, but he was hurting. He'd never been in love with anyone before, despite being in his mid-thirties now, and he couldn't cope with all the emotions. Even though Hope repeatedly tried to reassure him that she had begun to get over Ben, he was always on Adam's mind.

He picked his phone up off the kitchen worktop, knowing he should call Hope to apologise. Unfortunately, though, he hadn't ever been good at admitting when he was wrong. So, instead, he made another call.

***

Angelisa was having a moral dilemma. She'd spent so long on the side-lines, forced to merely sit back and watch as the person she wholeheartedly loved continued to, somewhat unsuccessfully, seek love elsewhere. She couldn't just walk away, though. It was no secret that Adam and Hope were struggling. She was well aware of the recent ups and downs in their relationship. Her instinct told her that Adam would leave Hope soon, but could she rely on a hunch?

20

Luckily for Hope, it didn't take Adam a whole week to miss her. One evening, a few days later, he popped around to apologise in person. He told her that he was really struggling with the Ben Situation, but he did want to be with her. Hope knew she expected a lot from Adam. It had to be extremely hard for him every time she heard from Ben. *Maybe I still haven't appreciated quite how difficult he finds it.* She wasn't one to hold a grudge, so she accepted his apology without hesitation, wrapping him in a hug and telling him not to feel bad. He felt awful, though, given recent events.

Adam could only stay for five minutes because it was now less than a month before Christmas—a very busy time of year for the pub trade with all the office parties booked right up until the big day. 'Please come up to the White Rose when you get back from work tonight and tomorrow and the next day,' he begged as he left. He looked sheepish.

'Of course, I will,' she replied, smiling fondly at him.

Hope kept her promise and saw Adam every evening for the next few days, which were busy but uneventful in comparison to the recent ups and downs their relationship had suffered.

When she went to the pub the following Monday, shortly after getting home from the store, she expected him to be working again. But he'd managed to get some cover for his shift in order to surprise her.

'Keep your coat on, Blossom,' he ordered, 'we're going out.' He kissed her on the cheek and ushered her back out through the wooden doors.

'Where are we going?'

'Well, I think it's about time I treated you to something a little bit Christmassy,' was all he would give away. They climbed into his car and sped off.

Fifteen minutes later, Adam parked up at Gloucester Quays, and they continued for a short distance on foot. He had such a spring in his step that she had to half-run to keep up the pace. As they neared their destination, Hope could hear carol singers, their beautiful harmonies filling the air with the melodious notes of 'Silent Night'. Turning the corner and stepping up to the harbour, she noticed it brimming with a multitude of stalls, all resembling tiny little log cabins, with traders busily promoting their wares.

'A Christmas market. Oh, it's so beautiful,' she murmured, feeling as if she'd been delivered to Santa's village.

'And that's not all.' Adam grinned and pointed to the far right. 'There's also an ice rink,' he revealed, his eyes glinting, 'and I've booked us in for nine o'clock.'

'Seriously?' She hugged him tightly, almost at a loss

for words.

The pair sauntered from one stall to the next, sampling the craft gins and vodkas, marvelling at the Christmas ornaments, tasting a huge variety of cheeses and chutneys, and purchasing one or two gifts for friends and family along the way. At one booth, Hope couldn't believe her eyes. She tugged at Adam's sleeve to get his attention.

'Look,' she cried out, pointing to the Christmas tree toppers adorning the busy stall. 'That angel is exactly like the one Mum used to have. It was given to her by my great grandma, and we had it on the top of our tree every year when I was little. We couldn't ever find it in the attic after Mum died, though. It must have got thrown away by mistake. That one honestly looks identical.'

'How much is the angel, please?' Adam asked the stallholder.

'No, not that one, the one to the left. No, my left. Yes, that's the one,' Hope said, nodding.

'It's a collector's item, that one. From Selfridge's the year they opened in 1909. They don't make them like that anymore. Let's see. I've got it priced up at two fifty.'

'Thank you,' Adam replied before turning to Hope.

'That's one expensive angel, Blossom,' he whispered.

'Never mind,' she murmured, knowing that two hundred and fifty pounds was far more than she was willing to pay, in spite of its sentimental value. 'It's beautiful, though, isn't it?'

'Not as beautiful as you,' Adam replied, dragging her away. He kissed her before putting his arm around her shoulder as they moved on.

Just before nine, they walked over to the ice rink and booted up in readiness for their time slot on the ice. It had been ages since either of them had last skated, but it didn't take them long to remember the ropes. Soon, they were gliding around together, trying to avoid bumping into other skaters and wincing as people around them thudded down onto the cold, hard surface.

'It's so magical. Thank you so much for planning this,' Hope enthused as they took a breather at the side of the rink.

'Anything for you, Blossom,' he replied. He dragged her back onto the ice for a few more laps before their time was up.

When Hope queued to hand in her skates and change into her shoes, she realised she'd lost sight of Adam in the crowd. She wandered around aimlessly for a few minutes, trying to locate him, and then phoned him. Little did she know that he'd disappeared intentionally and was now racing back to his car to deposit a gift for her safely in the boot.

'I'm getting us some hot chocolate,' he lied, hot-footing it back to a stand where he was then able to do just that. 'Have another look around the market, and I'll meet you at the tree in fifteen minutes.'

As they drove back to her house later, Hope was in her element. Christmas was all around them, and she couldn't have been happier. Adam wouldn't have a whole day off now until after Boxing Day and would be run off his feet for the next few weeks before closing the pub in the late afternoon on Christmas Day. But none of that mattered as long as they could squeeze in a few more dates like tonight before then. They already had tickets for the pantomime at the local theatre the following week and had pencilled in an afternoon with Jess for putting up Hope's tree the week afterwards.

With the big day now fast approaching, Hope ran through a mental checklist, figuring out the presents she needed to buy and when to do the Christmas food shopping. Adam dropped her off and kissed her goodnight.

'See you tomorrow?' he asked as she got out of the car. Nodding, Hope reminded him that he still hadn't confirmed whether his friend would join them for Christmas dinner. Then she reluctantly bade him farewell.

The days continued at such a pace that Hope began to wonder whether she'd get everything done in time. She spent the entire morning wrapping the last of her gifts, taking those with miles to travel to the post office and stashing the others away in hiding. Jess had wrangled an early finish today so would be home by four. In the meantime, Hope and Adam would get everything laid out in the lounge, in readiness for the big task ahead.

The tree they would decorate was artificial but so lifelike that it was hard to tell. Hope had purchased it a few years earlier, and it currently sat in its box in the attic, alongside all of her decorations. It was now midday, and she had only half an hour left before Adam would arrive, so she sent Ben a quick message.

> Putting up the tree with Adam and Jess this afternoon! Yippee! Have you got yours up yet? Are you going to be able to slow down a little for Christmas? Mwah Xxx

His reply was almost immediate.

Have fun decorating the tree and make sure you send me a pic. I think I should be able to get Christmas Day off this year, but I'm not going to count my chickens. Or should that be turkeys? No tree here yet. Mwah backatcha X

Adam arrived a little late, laden with the groceries he'd purchased especially for the occasion, on Hope's instructions. They carried all of the boxes down from the loft and heated up the oven to prepare the finger food for later. They'd enjoy the spread once they'd worked their magic on the tree, just as Hope had always done with her family when she was young.

There were frozen mini sausage rolls to cook, mince pies to warm, vol-au-vents to bake and fill with cream cheese, prawns to defrost and douse with Marie-Rose sauce, crusty breads to pull apart and butter, and a whole host of cheeses to unwrap. Hope salivated as she put the Bailey's in the freezer to chill, the only item that hadn't been on the menu during her childhood tree-decorating celebrations.

'Honey, I'm home,' Jess cried out a while later. She pulled the front door shut to keep in the heat. 'You haven't started without me, have you?'

'Only on the food. Preparing it, not eating it, that is.' Hope banged some ice-cubes out of the tray and poured a generous serving of Bailey's over the top before handing Jess the glass and pouring two more.

'Hi, Adam.' Jess hugged him. 'Thanks, Hope,' she added before taking a sip of her drink. 'Yum. Right, let's get this show on the road.'

And with that said, they sorted the tree sections into numerical order and unfurled their wired, snow-topped branches, bringing the magnificent specimen back to life once more.

A little after eight, Hope stood back and admired their handiwork. The tree looked stunning adorned with silver, red, and gold baubles, interspersed with bows and the array of intricate ornaments she'd collected over the years. She couldn't wait to see them all illuminated by the strands of simple, warm-white lights once they were turned on. The only thing left to do was place the star on top and commence the countdown before flicking the switch.

She wandered into the kitchen and grabbed the footstool so she could reach the uppermost branch. Back in the lounge, she picked up the star, but Adam immediately took it away.

'One minute,' he said. 'I have a present for you to open first.'

'But we're so close to seeing it all lit up,' Hope retorted.

'Trust me, I think you'll want to open this first,' he insisted, winking at Jess, who seemed to be in on whatever was happening.

Realising any further protests would only fall on deaf ears, Hope slid the ribbon off the parcel and carefully unwrapped the paper. She took the lid off the box and gasped. It was an angel. No. It was *the* angel. The one she'd spotted at the Christmas market a fortnight ago.

'Oh, Adam . . .' she stammered, 'it's too much!'

'It's just enough!' Adam retaliated, helping her remove it gently from the box. He held the step-stool so she could place the angel on top of the tree.

'Three,' began Hope, stepping off the stool.

'Two,' the others joined in, and Adam moved across to the socket in readiness.

'One,' they chorused, as the tree was illuminated in all its glory.

'Thank you, Adam. Thank you so, so much,' Hope whispered, turning to him. 'You can't begin to know how much that means to me.'

'Almost as much as you mean to me, I'm sure.' He beamed, delighted to have been the reason Hope's face was now lit up even more brightly than the Douglas fir they stood in front of.

21

The next ten days went by at a hundred miles an hour, with Jess and Hope delighted to finally finish up at their respective stores on Christmas Eve. After getting changed and having a bite to eat at home, they spent a few leisurely hours catching up with all the regulars at the White Rose. Then they sat down with Adam and the staff once the pub finally closed for the night.

As the last member of staff left the building half an hour later, Jess and Hope made a move to follow. Adam took Hope's hand and pulled her back towards him for another kiss.

'What are you hoping Father Christmas will bring you tomorrow?' he asked.

'An uncomplicated forever with you,' she confessed.

'Then I hope you're not on his naughty list this year,' he teased, kissing her one last time before seeing the girls to the door. 'Merry Christmas, Hope! Merry Christmas, Jess! See you tomorrow night.'

'Merry Christmas, I hope it all goes well tomorrow,' Hope called out as he shut the door behind them.

The next morning, Hope jumped out of bed and ran to the window, just as she had done every Christmas since childhood. Someone had transformed the scene outside her window into a snow globe during the night and then shaken it vigorously. She shrieked with joy.

She raced into Jess's room and yanked the duvet off her friend. Then she grabbed Jess's arm and dragged her to look outside. Hope drew the curtains back with such ferocity that she broke four or five hooks, leaving the fabric hanging off the rail.

'Jess, look,' Hope half-whispered. She feared that if she spoke too loudly, the beautiful blanket of soft snow transforming everything into a magical winter wonderland would disappear.

'Merry Christmas, hun,' her housemate answered, rubbing her bleary eyes. She grinned and threw her arms around Hope. 'Let's go have breakfast and see if Father Christmas has filled our stockings.'

Of course, he had, or at least the girls had each filled a stocking for the other. They spent breakfast opening up their multitude of gifts whilst munching thick slices of ham on multigrain toast, topped off with mustard. They wouldn't eat again until early evening, once Adam had finished serving 182 Christmas dinners and locked up for the day, so they didn't intend to scrimp on breakfast.

Hope had agreed that she wouldn't contact Adam during the day, as he'd be ridiculously busy working through two seatings at full capacity. So instead, whilst Jess was in the shower, she called her dad and then her brothers to wish them merry Christmas. Next, she jumped in the shower, singing Christmas carols at the top of her voice.

Once both girls were dressed, coiffed, and ready for the day, they went to the tree to rummage through the presents underneath. Some gifts had arrived in the post from family members; others were presents they'd wrapped for each other; Adam had dropped off a few during the last week; and there were presents for Kev and Adam from the girls. As always, they discovered an odd few whose labels had fallen off and could have been for anyone. They'd match those parcels with their tags later by analysing the wrapping paper imprints left on the sticky tape, *if* they managed to locate the labels.

Jess turned on the Christmas radio station before helping Hope lug the turkey into the oven. Singing along merrily to the festive songs, they opened up a few more presents. Hope wanted to save the ones from Adam until he arrived, so he could see her open them, but they made short work of many other gifts. They spent the next few hours preparing the rest of the meal which they'd cook later on. Then they set and decorated the dining table, nibbling on nuts and Turkish delight.

Not long after five, Adam and Kev arrived. Hope raced along the hallway to let them in. Adam looked shattered, and Hope hugged him tightly. *Oh well, he can finally relax now. I'll look after him tonight.* She fetched him a beer whilst Jess poured Kev a lemonade, as he was the designated driver. Hope had asked Adam to stay the night, but she wasn't sure if he would. He'd never slept at hers yet, in spite of her having spent many a night at his. She might suggest it again later and then give him an extra special Christmas present.

An hour later, they all sat down for dinner. Hope had erred on the side of caution by planning it late, in case Adam got held up at the White Rose. Jess did the honours and popped the cork on the champagne Hope had saved for today. She had received it from her area manager following a record month of sales in November. As they all tucked into their avocado and prawns with gusto, the girls talked excitedly about the presents they'd already opened and how they'd spent the day.

'I can't believe I forgot to ask how everything went at the pub!' Hope squealed, turning to Adam. She whispered an apology.

'Well, I certainly feel a lot more relaxed now than I did a few hours ago,' he admitted, patting Kev on the back and thanking him for mucking in when they'd been rushed off their feet. 'But all the customers seemed more than satisfied with both the food and the service. I don't think we had a single complaint.' He kissed Hope on the cheek as she congratulated him with a cuddle.

Once they'd finished the starters, Hope and Adam cleared the crockery and the cutlery into the kitchen. There, he plated the turkey and sharpened the carving knife whilst she dished vegetables into large heated serving dishes. Hope wanted everyone to help themselves to the portions they wanted. *I know I'll be going back for seconds and possibly thirds, even if that doesn't leave me any room for Christmas pudding later.* Christmas dinner was one of her favourite meals, and she was starving tonight. She opened up a bottle of prosecco, as the champagne had vanished very quickly, and then sat back at the table. Adam entered, carrying the mighty bird.

Two and a half hours after sitting down to eat, the foursome finally left the dining table and staggered into the lounge. The meal had been a huge success, but they'd all eaten far more than they should have. Hope couldn't help but admire the Christmas tree again. It looked so beautiful in the semi-darkness, with the room lights dimmed and strands of tiny white tree lights flickering and dancing like fairies. She looked up at the precious angel on top and smiled.

'Merry Christmas, Mum,' she whispered, raising her glass to the heavens. *I wish you could let me know whether to forget about Ben and trust in what I have with Adam,* she added silently.

Once they had given their stomachs plenty of time to settle, they opened up the remaining presents. Adam was so taken with the photo album Hope had put together for him that he spent ages poring over it whilst the others chatted. It was packed full of pictures from their dates and had witty anecdotes and inscriptions on every page. After he finally put it down, he scooped Hope up in a hug and carried her off into the kitchen for some alone time.

When they eventually returned to the lounge, red faced and heady, it was time for games. Of course, Monopoly was one, along with charades, and, with the prosecco still flowing, they were in high spirits. Around ten, they felt peckish enough for the final course. The girls had put together a huge selection of crackers and cheeses, but somehow they polished off the lot.

Hope's phone rang as they were about to play Trivial Pursuit, and she looked around for it. Adam saw it on the sofa cushion and passed it to her. She realised from his disdain that it must be Ben calling. Gingerly placing the phone on the mantelpiece, she let it go to voicemail, planning to listen to any messages when Adam wasn't around. A few seconds later, a notification beeped, but she ignored it and sat on the sofa.

Just before midnight, they packed up the last of the games. Whilst the others went into the kitchen to top up their drinks, Hope had a quick look at her phone. Ben hadn't left a voicemail but had sent her something on WhatsApp.

Merry Christmas, Monkey. Try calling you again in a bit. I'm sure you're still up. Mwah X

Hope put her phone on silent mode and joined the others in the kitchen. 'What shall we do now?' she asked, hugging Adam.

'I'll have to make a move shortly,' Kev confessed. 'Otherwise, I'll fall asleep on your sofa.'

'You're welcome to stay over,' Hope suggested. 'It's actually a sofa bed in the lounge, and'—she looked at Adam beseechingly—'you can sleep in my room.'

But Adam shook his head. He was shattered, and when he was tired, he wanted to sleep in his own bed. Hope said she understood, but she felt disappointed. They hadn't started the day together, so she really wanted them to end it together. It was Christmas, after all.

'Okay, another half hour, then? I was about to make some turkey doorstops,' Jess joked, knowing Hope didn't want Adam to leave yet. Their stomachs groaned in protest, but they agreed to stay. So, whilst Kev and Jess wandered back into the lounge, exchanging phone numbers, Adam and Hope stayed in the kitchen on the pretence of clearing up. They really just wanted more privacy.

Hope's phone immediately interrupted their kisses, jumping about on the worktop and vibrating erratically. They both looked over at the screen. It was Ben again. Guilt ate away at Hope when she saw anguish on Adam's face. *Wasn't silent mode supposed to stop your phone from vibrating, too?*

She moved to divert the call to voicemail, but Adam, thinking that she was going to answer it, stormed off into the lounge. Instructing Kev to get his things, he bade Jess goodnight and marched down the hall to the front door, with Kev in hot pursuit.

'Way to ruin Christmas, Hope,' he shot at her when passing the kitchen.

By the time Hope realised Adam was leaving, she was too late. The front door had slammed, and a car engine was already running as she hot-footed it after the men. If racing across a gravel drive with bare feet was nigh on impossible at the best of times, adding a thin layer of snow didn't improve the situation. Instead, it impeded her progress and turned her feet into icicles. Luckily, the elderly next-door neighbour had placed her wheelie bin in the perfect position to make manoeuvring out of the driveway a little tricky for Kev. That gave Hope just enough time to catch up to the car before it drove off.

Reaching the vehicle, she banged on the window, and Adam wound it down slightly.

'Adam . . .' She couldn't find any more words.

'I can't keep doing this.'

'I'm sorry, Adam—'

'The more I fall in love with you, the more it messes me up every time Ben rings you!' he interrupted, winding the window up tightly.

'In love with me?' she asked the empty space around her. The car and its occupants had gone.

Arriving back at the pub, Adam was broken. He couldn't keep torturing himself by loving Hope if she would never get over Ben. It was getting harder and harder to deal with the whole situation. His finger hovered over his phone button. *Should I call her?*

***

Angelisa floated out of Adam's flat a few hours later and slipped off into the darkness unseen. Things were obviously still not good between Hope and Adam at the moment. She was becoming ever surer that their relationship was not destined to last, in spite of the fact that Adam clearly loved Hope. Maybe it was time for her to take things into her own hands and do a little meddling. There must be something she could do to bring a swift end to Adam and Hope's relationship once and for all—and an end to everyone's heartache.

22

Hope lay awake in bed, staring at the ceiling. She had tried to call Adam over and over, but he hadn't picked up. *Why do things keep going wrong between us? That's a stupid question, as the answer is obvious. If Ben were out of the picture totally, then I feel sure that Adam and I would have a long and happy future together, so is it selfish of me not to want Ben out of the equation entirely until after I visit him once more? Will things keep going wrong between me and Adam unless I cut all contact with Ben for good? And is that even something I can do?*

She managed little sleep and padded downstairs shortly after five to sit at the kitchen table alone. *Adam is in love with me. He told me so. Okay, so it wasn't the most romantic declaration of love, having been spat out rather than whispered lovingly, but the sentiment is surely still the same. I know that I love Adam, too, something I've been reluctant to admit over the last few weeks. But where does that leave Ben? Am I totally over him yet?*

She'd written and deleted countless messages to Adam before finally falling asleep. She simply couldn't find the words to tell him how she felt and concluded that a text message wasn't the way to convey such strong feelings. She wished he'd answered the phone so she could have told him she was in love with him, too. He wasn't the only one who wished Ben didn't keep unwittingly interfering in their relationship.

Jess joined her at the kitchen table a little after six. They talked briefly about the previous night until it was time to get ready for work and set off. The girls' stores had been closed on Christmas Day, but, like Adam, they both had shifts on Boxing Day.

It's going to be a very long day at the store, Hope thought. All she wanted to do was rush around to Adam's and declare her love for him. *I never wanted to cause him such pain. How can I find a way to make everything better again? I know we both need Ben gone, once and for all, but there's only one way to make that happen.* She shuddered as an icy chill passed through her body. Ben had been such a big part of her life during the last two years, long before Adam had come on the scene. He was one of her closest friends, and the thought of a future without him was too much to bear.

Adam was torn. Yes, he was hurting. More than he ever had before if he was honest. But he also knew that he loved Hope desperately and that he'd never had anywhere near such strong feelings for a woman in the past. He had to harness his emotions and find a way to cope until this Ben guy was left out in the cold. If only he could make Ben vanish—out of sight or, at least, out of mind—with a quick click of his fingers. Or more realistically, get Hope to see through the vision she had created, because Adam doubted

Ben was as incredible as she made him out to be.

Maybe he would have to step aside and let Hope pursue Ben fully, with faith that things between them wouldn't last. Then Adam would race in to rescue her when it all went wrong. But he realised he couldn't run the risk of losing her to Ben whilst waiting in the wings, praying she'd come back to him. Hope had told him that her romantic thoughts of Ben had all but disappeared now. Yet that wasn't the impression Adam got from the way her eyes lit up every time Ben got in touch. No, Adam needed him gone, for good, and wished Hope would cut all contact with Ben once and for all.

Adam poured himself a coffee and looked down at his phone. There were numerous missed calls from Hope, spanning all the early hours of the morning, and also a message that came through a short while ago. He opened it to reveal a YouTube link to 'I Don't Know Much' by Aaron Neville and Linda Ronstadt. He clicked on the link, and a familiar song filled the room. Adam listened to every word, realising how much it meant to hear that Hope loved him, too. He felt guilty about how he'd behaved the previous night, but he didn't want to think about that. He would speak to Hope, and they'd put everything behind them. *No looking back and no regrets.* He'd wait for her to contact him, though, rather than reaching out himself.

Adam didn't have to wait long. He was taking a quick break before opening up the pub when his phone flashed that Hope was calling. He'd forgotten that he'd put it on silent mode in the early morning hours when she'd phoned incessantly. After waiting a few more seconds, he picked up the call. A breathless

Hope thanked him for answering and told him she loved him. She was crying. He could tell. She was trying to hide her sobs, but it was clear how upset she was.

'It's okay, Blossom. It's okay. We can fix this. I love you, too,' he reassured her, hoping they would be able to come back from this. If they were to have a future together with no more hiccups, then there could be no more outsiders threatening to ruin their relationship.

The week leading up to New Year's Eve was notoriously quiet in the pub trade, as most people had overdone it on the alcohol on Christmas Day. Adam was off the next day, and if Hope managed to get time off, too, they could go to the seaside to clear their heads and start afresh. Hope loved his idea and said she'd try to get her assistant manager to switch shifts. She ended the call by promising to head to the pub at around seven that evening with an overnight bag.

The weather the next morning was bitter, but it didn't deter them from making the trip. They set off bright and early, singing along to the radio and chatting, with the car heater on full blast. Hope's grandparents used to live not far from Exmouth, so she knew her way around the seaside town well, having visited often over the years. She hadn't been there since the new harbour-side development had been built, though.

When she and Adam entered the car park and saw the colourful wood-clad buildings, a striking mismatch of pastels that all went well together, they couldn't help but marvel. The water was soothing, the boats were enchanting and, although the sea was choppy today, it reminded them of how up and down their relationship became every time Ben showed up on the scene.

Having neglected to eat breakfast before leaving Adam's flat, they were ravenous by noon. As they moved away from the harbour and strolled along the promenade, they fancied only one thing for lunch. It had to be fish and chips. Hope had been brought up to believe it was bad manners to travel to the coast without ordering the iconic dish, and Adam was inclined to agree.

After a quick recce of the fish and chip shops in close proximity, they found one they could dine in, right on the seafront. It was ideal, with a huge glass front that allowed diners to sit and watch the sea. They chose a table as close to the water as possible, watching the tide crash against the harbour wall. Their meals were brought to them before they'd even started on their drinks, and the aroma wafting up from the plates made their mouths water.

'I really do love you,' Adam told her, taking her hands in his.

'I really love you, too,' she replied. 'I'm just so sorry that—' But he stood up and leaned across to kiss her, interrupting her. Then he sat back down so they could tuck in whilst the food was piping hot.

After wandering along the beach and watching the tide turn as they talked about the future, they returned to the car park. Daylight had begun to fade. Adam couldn't resist buying a bag of mussels from a fishermen who'd just come into dock. He planned to cook *moules marinières* when they returned to his flat. They would stop off on the way home to buy the ingredients they'd need, along with some crusty white bread to dip in the delectable sauce and a bottle of wine to complement the dish.

Their talk was interrupted on the journey when Adam received a phone call from the pub. He chatted away on his hands-free kit for fifteen minutes or so, but Hope paid little attention to either side of the conversation. She'd finally decided what to do about the Ben Situation, given that they still hadn't booked a date for a return to Portsmouth.

'Damn,' Adam exclaimed, ending the call. 'Debbie's been signed off for two weeks, so I'll have to work the weekend straight after your birthday. Sorry, Blossom.'

'Don't worry,' Hope replied, 'I'm pretty sure Jess is also off that weekend, so I can do something with her instead. I've neglected her since you and I got together, so I should spend some quality time with her.'

'Okay. Then how about I throw you a big birthday bash at the pub, on the day itself?'

'Oooh, I'd love that.'

'Excellent.' He set out his ideas for the party and asked her about gifts she'd like, failing to notice that she was distracted.

The mussels were sensational but Adam didn't eat many. Hope had just mopped up the last of the sauce with huge hunks of bread whilst half-watching the film her boyfriend was engrossed in. It was still early, but she was itching to get home and put her plan into action. Adam didn't object when she made a move to leave around half nine. She had expected him to ask her to stay the night again, but he now seemed a little distracted himself.

'Are you expecting someone?' She was only joking, of course.

'I'm just tired,' he lied, yawning. 'That sea air has taken it all out of me.'

She knew what he meant. Something about the sea breeze seemed to sap all her energy, in spite of how it invigorated her whilst she was breathing it into her lungs.

Shortly after Hope left his flat, Adam picked up his phone to make a call. He had been pleased when she'd decided to leave early, but now he felt guilty about how he planned to end the evening in her absence. He opened the contact list in his phone and dialled the top entry, unable or unwilling to resist temptation.

***

Angelisa busied herself with supervising the Christmas tree being packed away for another year, whilst trying desperately to stay grounded. As soon as the tree-topper had been removed from the uppermost branch, she dusted off her wings and went upstairs for some thinking time.

Adam and Hope's relationship had been on her mind ever since she'd returned home, and her forehead was now furrowed in worry. The wrinkle lines were only temporary; she hadn't aged at all in the last ten years, but her concerns were fast becoming more permanent. She couldn't ignore a sombre sense of foreboding.

23

Having spent the rest of the evening finalising her plan, Hope now sat at the kitchen table in the early hours, tapping away on her phone. Adam had competed with Ben for too long, and it wasn't fair to him. He needed Ben off the radar, and she believed she had found a way to achieve that. As far as what she herself needed, well, that wasn't her priority. She'd worry about that later. She took a deep breath and hit the send button.

Ben,

Don't panic, but there's something important I need to tell you that I've been too chicken to admit before. Please don't let this ruin our friendship!

Hang on. How do I say this? Um, let's see. During the weekend I spent at yours in August, I really fell for you. I never said anything because you must have told me at least five times that weekend that you run scared whenever anyone falls for you. I didn't want to risk you running away from me and out of my life forever, as you've always been such an amazing friend, so I kept my feelings to myself. At the time, I thought that if I gave you space, you might end up falling for me, too. Silly as that sounds. But things have changed.

You know lots about Adam, but one thing you don't know is that I told him all about my feelings for you from the moment we started dating. I didn't want to lead him on and hoped that the more I got to know him, the more I'd stop holding onto a dream that you and I might end up together.

I'm so lucky to have two amazing men in my life. You are both incredibly special to me. But two men is one too many, and having feelings for two men at the same time was just greedy.

I've fallen in love with Adam. But the trouble is that he's still worried I have feelings for you, or that you might feel that way about me. Please respond, as I think Adam and I have a chance for a long and wonderful future together, but only if I can convince him that you and I will only ever be friends.

Hope
Xxx

Minutes later, her phone pinged, and she had the response that she needed. Well, the response Adam needed, at least.

> Hope, I had no idea. Sorry. You're lovely, but you know me. I'm just not cut out for relationships, so Adam has nothing to worry about. I doubt I'll ever settle down with anyone after what happened with Laura. Of course, this won't affect our friendship! I have to dash off for a meeting in a minute. Sorry, roller-coaster life of mine. Good luck with Adam, I hope everything works out for you both. Big Mwah X

Hope heard Jess stirring in her room above the kitchen and knew she would have some explaining to do. Yet she didn't want to face that now. Instead, she popped the iPhone into her pocket, pressed the switch on the kettle, grabbed her coat and keys, and was half-way down the hall when Jess appeared at the top of the stairs, bleary eyed.

'You seen my phone, Hope?' she asked, raising her hand to muffle a yawn.

'Kitchen table. Kettle's boiling. I've got to run.' And with that, Hope was out of the front door in a flash.

24

Work dragged by at a snail's pace that day. When Hope eventually made it back to the station, she drove straight around to see Adam and asked if he could take a five-minute break. She had something important to show him on her phone. He read the messages slowly, looking up at her only when he'd digested both of them. His eyes searched hers.

'Happy?' she asked him, eagerly.

'No more Ben Situation?'

'No more Ben Situation!'

'But how do you feel? Are you okay? I know it must be hard for you.'

'I'm okay. But how about you?'

'I'm pleased, of course . . . well, no, not pleased . . . well, pleased for us. Are you sure you're okay, Blossom? Honestly?'

'Yes. Now we can finally move forwards. Just the two of us.'

'You're right, Blossom, we can.' Adam pulled her towards him, and she buried her face in his chest.

After checking that enough staff were working to finish up for the night, Adam ordered some food from the bar to be sent up to his flat.

Hope was quiet all evening. They discussed plans for New Year's Eve and the impending New Year, which would be a whole new start.

Hope drove home a little after ten, tears of anguish falling from her eyes. She tried to blink them away and focus on the short drive, but she felt wretched. She recalled how Adam had very sweetly tried to disguise his joy, in an attempt to protect her from the hurt and humiliation he'd anticipated her feeling. But all she felt was guilt.

'The thing is, Jess,' Hope confided, 'I didn't send that message to Ben or receive any reply from him. It's Tomasz's fault. No, I can't really blame him, as it's not *exactly* his fault, but . . . well . . . something he said the other day gave me the idea.'

'Slow down, you've lost me,' Jess pleaded, 'and get to the point!'

'I pinched your mobile yesterday morning to set up a fake WhatsApp account for Ben, uploading a photo of him to make it look realistic. Then I messaged that profile from my phone and replied to myself from yours, pretending to be Ben. I feel awful. I shouldn't have done it, and I'm sorry I used your phone without asking. It's just that you were asleep when I decided to go ahead with the plan, and . . .'

Whilst her friend paused, Jess tried to catch up.

'I could tell Adam was over the moon when he read the messages, even though he tried to hide it for my sake. But the guilt is tearing me apart,' Hope croaked, 'and I still haven't solved the problem because Adam may be happy now, but . . .'

'But what, honey?' Jess probed.

'I feel so bad for lying to him, and Ben does still pop into my mind every now and then. Which doesn't help.'

'So, why did you do it? I'm baffled by what you intended to achieve.'

'I needed to help Adam because he's not coping with the Ben Situation too well. I stupidly thought that if I could show him that Ben would only ever see me as a friend, then things would be fine between us again. I didn't want Adam to have to wait until you and I visit Ben together for closure. I still don't know when that will be, or if you'll even come with me now.' Hope sighed and dropped her head, shaking it sadly. Then she looked earnestly at Jess, hoping she could figure a way out of this fix.

'Okay, so Adam thinks that Ben now knows you have feelings for him but that he's not interested in anything other than friendship?' Jess asked.

Hope nodded.

'None of which is true,' Jess scolded.

Hope was silent. What was there to say?

'But you said Adam seemed really happy when he read Ben's supposed reply. So your plan worked. I guess that's a start,' Jess stated in a pragmatic tone. 'What's the problem now, the guilt or the fact that you might not be over Ben?'

'The guilt, I think. Adam was so lovely. He ordered us food and, oh, the White Rose's new menu has just launched, and it's got so many wonderful dishes on there. I tried the hunter's chicken tonight, and it's absolutely to die for. You have to try it next time we go to the pub. But don't have the curly fries that it comes with. Switch them out for cheesy chips instead. The curly fries aren't—'

'Hey, the food can wait!' Jess interrupted and then smiled at her troubled friend. 'Obviously, your guilt hasn't affected your appetite tonight—or maybe you've simply been drowning your sorrows in barbecue sauce.'

Hope had to laugh. 'Well, Adam was thrilled, no question about it, but sweet enough to console me, knowing it would have . . . *should* have been hard for me to hear. We ate our meals and chatted for a while. But then, rather than stay over, I made excuses and left because I felt so terrible for deceiving him.'

'I know how strongly you feel about lies and deceit.'

'I've been fooling myself with thoughts of fairy-tales and divine intervention ever since Ben came into my life, and that's brought nothing but heartache. Ben was never a sensible option, and you know that "logic" is my middle name.'

Jess laughed and said, 'Your list of middle names is now longer than the Great Wall of China. So, is Ben still unaware that he's causing all this trouble?'

'Totally unaware,' Hope confirmed. 'He's known about Adam ever since we've been dating and is aware we've had ups and downs recently, but he doesn't know it's all because of him. I've always been transparent with Ben about Adam, as well as being transparent with Adam about Ben.' She looked Jess in the eye before correcting herself. 'Well, semi-transparent because Ben doesn't know I've harboured feelings for *him* all this time, of course, and Adam doesn't know the WhatsApp messages aren't genuine. Oh, what a total, utter mess!' Hope shook her head from side to side, groaning.

'It's all rather complicated,' Jess admitted. 'Couldn't you just send your WhatsApp message to Ben now, so that everything's out in the open?'

'I don't think so.' Hope blushed. 'I fear it would ruin our friendship if he knew how I really felt about him. Otherwise, I'd have done that in the first place.'

The girls deliberated long into the night. Hope heard from Adam via a text message at one point, checking in to ensure that she was okay, but she kept her reply short and sweet. She worried that if she didn't, she would end up blurting everything out. Should she admit the truth? Tell him what she had done and why? Confess that she had thought it was the only way to save what they had? Hadn't Adam taken too much punishment already?

25

Adam's euphoria, now that he believed Ben was no longer a threat, had put him in the best of moods, and it was infectious. He treated Hope so delicately during the next few days that she began to relax again, pushing away her guilt and falling for him more deeply. The fact that her plan had eradicated Ben from Adam's thoughts pleased Hope, but she would never be able to own up to her deception now.

That meant there was only one thing to do: follow through with Jess's plan to visit Ben one more time and pull the plug on romanticising him. Hopefully, Ben would have some time off that coincided with the days she and Jess were free, but it might be many weeks or months away.

On the morning of New Year's Eve, Adam was racing around, trying to get everything ready for the huge ticket-only party he would host at the White Rose. Hope and Jess were obviously at the top of the guest list. He had promised them free tickets in return for spending the previous few nights helping him prepare the decorations. Now he would take these down to the pub while it was closed for a few hours. All the staff had to do, at this point, was fill the balloons with helium, decorate the tables, and check whether any barrels or optics needed changing.

At five o'clock, Adam pulled open the heavy front doors, and a few regulars strolled in. He greeted them and insisted they try some of the buffet food laid out near the entrance. More customers followed, and by eight the pub was already packed, with thirty or forty more guests still to arrive, according to the bouncer's ticket count. They didn't expect any trouble tonight. As an out-of-town pub, the White Rose rarely had any disturbances, but the hired doorman would ensure that only people who'd paid the hefty admission fee could enter.

The evening was a roaring success. They didn't serve any cooked dishes from the menu that night, but plenty of finger food was on offer. It was included in the admission cost, along with the entertainment Adam had organised: a magician, a comedian, and a live band. The drink sales indicated that they'd make a fortune tonight. Alcoholic beverages sold at such a speed, one would think it was the end of the world, rather than the end of the year. All through the night, Adam kept topping up the buffet from reserves in the walk-in fridges, chatting away to the locals, and providing table service for anyone who ordered more drinks.

Hope didn't see much of her boyfriend during the evening, apart from fleeting glances whenever he raced around to check that customers were happy. She and Jess sipped on mulled wine and chatted to other partygoers, looking forward to seeing in the

New Year. Hope, especially, wanted this to signify her and Adam's fresh start now that Ben had been eliminated from Adam's thoughts.

At a few minutes to midnight, the landlord took the microphone and beckoned Hope over to the temporary stage erected for the night's proceedings. He rallied the customers for the striking of the last hour of this year and the first hour of the next. Checking that they'd all picked up their party poppers and streamers and were ready to join him in the countdown. Hope smiled at Adam, happy that they were in a great place again.

The entire pub erupted in cheers and salutations as the band launched into 'Auld Lang Syne,' with everyone joining in. Hope looked up at the handsome man standing in front of her as he bent down and kissed her. He wished her a happy New Year and hugged her tightly. As she kissed him back, she felt her phone vibrating in her pocket. The sound was obscured by the merriment around them, but she cringed because it was probably a message from Ben. Making excuses a few minutes later, she went to the Ladies and read the content when no one was close by.

> Happy New Year, my favourite girl. I hope you've had a great day. I have a birthday present for you here that I've been meaning to post, but I've just had a business trip cancelled next weekend. I know you and Jess are both free then, so come and visit me, then I can give it to you in person. I'll have to pop into the office on Saturday morning, but we could meet up after lunch. I know it's quite late notice, but

what do you think? Let me know. Big Mwaaaaaahhhh X

Hope had decided, quite a while ago, not to tell Adam about going back to Ben's until the opportunity presented itself. Especially as she'd thought it could take months to finalise a plan. She hadn't imagined that an opportune weekend would come around this quickly. If she would be visiting Ben in a matter of days, then she had to bite the bullet and check that Adam would be happy for her to go. She wasn't looking forward to the conversation at all if she was honest. She knew, without a doubt, that she had a chance of a long and happy future with Adam, and it wasn't worth throwing it all away on a whim for something that would probably never happen with Ben. But she also needed to visit Ben once more to eradicate him from her heart. So she told Jess about the invite but asked her to keep it quiet for a few days, until she'd plucked up the courage to tell Adam.

Being in love with two men had taken its toll on Hope. It had torn her apart and had hurt Adam for far too long. She'd been able to help Adam by faking those WhatsApp messages, but it wouldn't help him at all in the long run if her feelings for Ben still existed. Not that she thought they did. She'd managed to move Ben into the platonic friends section of her brain. She hoped he'd stay there when she saw him next. *Lucky old Ben doesn't have a clue about all the trouble he's caused ever since Adam and I have got together. But then, he couldn't be blamed for unknowingly capturing my heart that fateful weekend and tying it in knots ever since.*

As the last few customers left the pub in the early

hours of New Year's Day, Adam locked the front door and sat down with Hope, Jess, and the staff. 'Hey, grand job, guys! That couldn't have gone better. Let me get you all a drink. Dillan, can you do the honours? Run it through on my tab, and I'll settle up later when I cash up.'

His number-one barman took everyone's orders and headed back to the bar. He brought the drinks over, one by one, before finally sitting down with a pint himself.

'Happy New Year, Blossom,' Adam whispered in Hope's ear before kissing her cheek. 'I have a feeling this year will be special.'

'Happy New Year.' She smiled back, caught up in her own thoughts.

26

The New Year brought a much slower pace at work for Adam, whereas the opposite was the case for Hope. During the last few days, she'd been incredibly busy with a half-price sale that attracted a vast number of additional shoppers to the store. She still hadn't got around to telling Adam about her imminent trip to Portsmouth.

On the morning of Hope's special day, she was greeted with a chorus of 'Happy Birthday'. One of the two visitors to her room belted it out and was now sitting on her bed. She hugged Jess and stroked Gizmo, who purred along to her owner's singing. Jess had strewn assorted gifts and cards all around.

'Happy birthday, honey.' Jess looked at her with anticipation.

Hope ripped open the wrapping of the first parcel to find a cashmere jumper inside. 'Jess, it's beautiful, thank you. I must go and try it on before I open anything else.'

Hope went to the bathroom, and Jess took the rest

of the presents and cards down to the kitchen. There, she made them coffee and toast. The birthday girl reappeared, wearing her new jumper and looking picture perfect, having brushed her hair and applied a little makeup. They ate and drank as Hope opened the rest of the gifts. Then they stood all of the cards up around the kitchen.

'I'll have to head to Adam's before the pub opens,' Hope said a short while later. 'He might not want to go ahead with my party once he knows about our trip to Ben's. Do you mind?'

'Course not, silly. Hurry back, though, because if I have to share you with everyone at the pub this evening and then with Ben all weekend, I should at least get a few hours with you this morning. And we should spend them shopping.'

'Great idea,' Hope replied, jumping up from her chair and blowing a kiss. 'I'll be back before you know it. Love you, honey, and thanks for all my presents.'

'You're welcome. Fingers crossed that Adam's okay about us going.'

As Hope walked down the hall to the front door, Adam appeared on the other side, his hand hovering over the doorbell. She sighed deeply, preparing for the inevitable. 'Hi, Adam.'

'Happy birthday, Blossom.' He wrapped her in a big hug and almost dropped the little gift box in his hand.

'Thank you,' she replied.

'I can't stay. I need to get straight back to the pub. I just wanted to give you this, in case you want to wear it tonight'—he handed over the wrapped box—'oh, and this,' he added before kissing her.

'Thank you. I'll see you tonight. Love you.' Hope shut the door behind him, pleased that he'd given her no chance to mention her weekend plans.

She opened the little box to reveal a charming silver bangle. Turning it over to admire it from every angle, she noticed it was engraved.

Hope, you're the reason my heart continues to beat, love, Adam X

She was taken aback. She'd never received a gift anywhere near as special as this, and she realised how invested Adam was in their relationship. *How can I tell him now?*

After a few productive hours in town, Jess and Hope went home to get glammed up for the party. Adam had really gone to town with balloons and banners adorning the walls of her favourite section of the pub. He'd prepared a magnificent finger buffet himself; displayed a plethora of beautifully wrapped presents alongside the food; and sat bottles of prosecco, chilling in ice buckets, on every other table.

Hope gave him a kiss and thanked him for all the trouble he'd gone to. Then she tucked into the food, devouring quiches and crustless sandwiches like there was no tomorrow. Trying on clothes all afternoon in town had given her a huge appetite.

The hours passed too quickly, with bar staff and regulars seeking Hope out to wish her a happy birthday. Some gave her cards whilst others handed over gifts. Adam doted on her all night, and everyone was full of the party spirit. As last orders were called, Adam played 'Happy Birthday to You' through the pub's sound system, and almost everyone joined in the singing. He pulled Hope into an embrace as the music ended and kissed her passionately.

'Happy birthday, Blossom. I hope you enjoyed your party.'

'It was wonderful, thank you so much,' Hope replied, knowing that soon they'd be alone and talk of her trip to Ben's would spoil everything.

After closing, Jess and Hope helped the staff clean down the tables, restock the bar fridges for the next day, and mop the floor. Adam turned the music up a notch, and the party carried on. The night ended abruptly for Jess after she jumped up on a table to dance, gesturing for others to join her. She lost her balance and fell in a heap to the floor. She needed help getting up and was then sent home in a taxi, under protest.

'I'll join you shortly, honey,' Hope said. 'Adam is going to walk me home in half an hour or so.'

Hope had intended to stay the night in Adam's flat, but when Jess had got injured, she'd told Adam she would have to go home to check that her friend was okay. She was only using Jess's injury as an excuse for a hasty exit, though. Adam had nodded agreement.

As Hope and Adam walked back to her house in the early hours, her heart was heavy. She summoned up her courage and started with, 'Thank you so much for tonight. The party was incredible, and I love all my gifts, especially the bracelet.' She twirled it around on her wrist, willing herself to continue as he took hold of the conversation.

'You're welcome, Blossom, I'm so pleased you had a good night. I hope Jess is—'

'Speaking of Jess,' Hope interjected, 'there's

something I've been meaning to tell you, and I'm so sorry I didn't say anything sooner. It's just that . . .' She took a deep breath. 'Jess and I are going away for the weekend.' She gritted her teeth. 'To Ben's.'

She struggled through another few sentences, trying to make Adam see how it was the last part of the puzzle she needed to complete. Adam remained quiet but seemed to understand, given that Ben would always be important as a friend. That being said, tension lay in the air as they arrived in her cul-de-sac and said goodbye.

Giving her a half-hearted kiss, Adam immediately turned to wander off. Hope thought about inviting him in or even offering to cancel her trip. Instead, she thanked him once more for the amazing party. *Fingers crossed that once I return from Portsmouth on Sunday, there will be no further ups and downs for us ever again. I'll give him some space now, and hopefully nothing will stop us from finally exploring the physical side of our relationship once I return.*

Before settling in for the night, Hope sent Adam a text.

> Adam, would you rather I don't go to Ben's tomorrow? I don't want to ruin things between us. I love you so much. Hope Xxx

But Adam didn't reply. He sank down into his sofa above the pub and yawned. He was tired out, frustrated, and irritated that they weren't even a week into the new year, yet Ben was already giving him cause for concern. Of course, he didn't want Hope to see Ben. It was unsettling. But he wouldn't beg her not to visit. Hearing that Jess would accompany Hope was some solace, but he still felt uncomfortable. He trusted Hope—but he didn't trust Ben not to try it on with his sexy girl, in spite of what he'd said in the WhatsApp message about seeing them only as friends. Adam knew he was punishing Hope by not responding to her message, and he'd apologise later. Still, he'd leave her to stew a little longer and pray that she'd decide not to go. Distractedly, he picked up his phone and made a call.

***

Angelisa had finally located what she'd been looking for, hidden away in the cloud. Adam and Hope's relationship was doomed, without a doubt. She now had the proof she needed. Admittedly, she shouldn't have had access to the file. But as her heart was in the right place, she felt vindicated. If Adam really and truly loved Hope, then the best thing for him to do would be to let her go. Otherwise, Hope would only end up heartbroken further down the line. Angelisa had just tried to get through to Adam, but he'd chosen to ignore her. Did that give her the right to put Hope in the picture herself? She knew it would destroy Hope if she did. Was she really willing to break the young girl's heart, even if it turned out best for her in the long run?

27

The next morning, Hope woke up bright and early, despite having a restless night. The sun ventured out to accompany her on this venture, but she had a feeling it might be her only companion. If Jess's back hadn't improved this morning, after her erratic table-dancing the previous night, then Hope would have to go to Portsmouth without her. She desperately wanted her best friend to meet Ben. It was so important that Jess be behind Hope's decision to forget about a future with him.

Jess stooped into the kitchen and tried to sit at the table. 'Morning,' she groaned.

'How's your back feeling?'

'So sore. I don't think I can even sit.'

'Here, take some painkillers.' Hope popped a couple of ibuprofen out of a pouch and handed them over with a glass of water. 'You won't be able to make it, will you, sweetie?'

'I'm sorry, honey, maybe you're meant to go there on your own. That way, you can figure everything out for yourself without me getting in the way.'

'You wouldn't have got in the way,' Hope reassured her, taking two mugs out of the cupboard and manoeuvring back around her friend, who had still not settled into her seat.

'Can you move to your left a smidge so I can get to the kettle?' Hope winced as Jess cried out in pain. 'Sorry!' *Okay, maybe Jess would have got in the way a little bit*, she thought, hiding a grin. 'Do you want me to stay home? I don't want to leave you here alone if you're in agony.'

'No way, silly . . . owwww . . . I'll be fine.' Jess gave up trying to sit down and hovered by the worktop instead. 'Don't you *dare* take a photo of me while I look like this.' Hope put her phone down, thwarted. 'I'll head back to bed for the day and hope it does my back some good. But you go, you must.'

Hope felt sad that she wouldn't be driving to Portsmouth with Jess, but she still looked forward to going. She wasn't due to leave until about ten, but she was already getting physically and mentally prepared for what lay ahead. A tiny part of her did wonder whether everything would change when she saw Ben. Whether her plans of achieving closure would be abandoned the instant she saw him, to be replaced by a desire for him to whisk her off into the sunset. But her heart was set on this being an end to any illusions she had about him. She knew that if anything were to happen between them, then it would be over for her and Adam when she got back.

She loved Adam, she knew that, and she didn't want to jeopardise their relationship a moment longer. She was one hundred percent sure of that now. Well, ninety-nine percent, at least. If only she'd met Adam first, life would have been so much simpler. Hope deliberately shaved her legs and armpits, knowing that when you don't, you always end up in an unexpected liaison with a member of the opposite sex. So, this was merely her attempt at ensuring nothing inappropriate would happen with Ben this time around. *Who am I kidding? Am I just covering all the bases?*

She'd chosen to wear a pair of jeans and her new cashmere jumper, which set off her year-round tan and clung in all of the right places to accentuate her tiny waist. Her makeup was minimal, and she wore her hair down, curling gently around her shoulders. At nine o'clock she was ready, prepared to face whatever this weekend would bring. Now she just had an hour to kill before leaving, so she went up to Jess's room.

Stretching out next to her on the bed, Hope chatted away like an excited child on Christmas Eve.

'You take care whilst I'm away. Ring me if you need me, and I'll come straight home.' Hope looked at Jess earnestly.

'I'll be fine, sweetie. Now go and figure things out.'

'I hope I can.'

'Me, too,' Jess replied wholeheartedly.

Hope carried her little suitcase across the gravel and threw it into the boot of the car. She should arrive in Portsmouth just after one, if she didn't take an unexpected detour again. There were two spare charging cables in the car, too, so no excuse for any Google Maps issues to arise. She would park in front of Ben's apartment before taking herself off to a pub and then suggest he join her there after his meeting. That way, she could check her appearance in the toilet mirror and have a sip or two of alcohol to steady her nerves before seeing him. Why hadn't she planned it this way the last time?

After a quick stop at the petrol station, to fill up and check the oil and tyres, she set off. The bright, crisp weather of early morning had changed drastically in the last few hours, and rain now beat down, making driving conditions difficult and extending the journey time. Just before she'd left the house, Ben had typed a few lines on WhatsApp, saying he was worried about her driving on her own, due to the severe weather. There were floods in Portsmouth, and he suggested she leave it till another time. She realised there was indeed clout behind his warning, but she could not put this off any longer. She needed her sanity back, she needed closure, and she wasn't going to leave Portsmouth without either.

Hope couldn't believe it when she pulled into the apartment's car park having not got lost once on the way. Even the rain had finally stopped, and the sun tried to peep out from behind the clouds. *The change in the weather surely signifies a fresh start for my relationship with Adam*, she thought. She sent Ben a quick text to let him know she'd arrived and then set off for the local shops and bars to freshen up. Ben replied that he would be out of his meeting in about half an hour and suggested she find somewhere to sit with a drink. Little did he know she had already executed that part of the plan and was currently inside the pub they'd sat outside on her last visit. She made herself comfortable on a sofa, sipping her glass of prosecco and nipping to the loo every now and then to check her appearance.

Now that she was here, the past seemed to whisk

her back to the last time she'd visited and threatened to take her sensibility away with it. Every time the pub door opened, her heart jumped into her mouth, and every time she had to calm herself down because it wasn't him. She wondered how she would feel the second she saw him again. Would it be like before, when the moment her eyes met his, she felt faint, her heart melted, and she felt like they were destined to be together? Would she still feel the same draw towards him that she'd felt the first time? Or would she be disappointed and finally know for sure that Adam was the only one she wanted? She imprinted an image of Adam's face at the very front of her thoughts. *Don't throw everything away, Hope*, she warned herself sternly.

Finally, Ben walked into sight, and she tried to analyse her emotions. He couldn't see her yet. She was tucked away in a secluded corner, indulging in her last few seconds of alone time. She lifted her mobile to her ear, planning to call him, and he walked around the corner to where she sat, his phone also to his ear as it connected to hers. They smiled at each other.

'Hello, honey.' She grinned broadly, getting up to give him a hug.

'Hello, Monkey.'

His voice still had an effect on her, of that she had no doubt.

He wrapped her in an enormous embrace and then sat opposite her, rather than beside her on the sofa. She felt awkward and half-wished that she was sitting here with Adam now because she was so comfortable in his presence. But she was here on a mission. In an hour or so, her nerves would go, and then she would no doubt see through the cracks of her illusions.

The two of them launched into conversation but were interrupted constantly, as Ben's phone rang every few minutes. He was clearly busy all the time with friends and work colleagues, leaving him little time for himself. Suddenly, Ben jumped out of his seat and ran to the window. He peered out excitedly like a small boy and ogled a ship approaching the harbour.

'Wow. Look at that one, Hope. It's German. Isn't it fantastic?'

To her, it looked like any other boat, but she didn't want to spoil his fun, so she tried to seem as excited as he was. Ships were his passion, his raison d'être, and this German spectacle was clearly the highlight of his day. As their conversation resumed, and he sat back down, she became aware of his intense love of all things nautical. Every few minutes, his eyes glazed over as he looked seaward. Hope wondered whether she could ever be as enthusiastic about the one thing which clearly meant so much to Ben. For the first time, she saw a tiny crack in her vision of the fantasy life she had once longed to share with him.

The rain had returned shortly after Hope had entered the pub and now incessantly lashed against the floor-to-ceiling windows. No doubt, the flooding Ben had mentioned earlier would get worse around the area. Hope realised that as much as she didn't mind the prospect of being stuck here with Ben, if the weather made it unfit to return home, she didn't like being stranded away from Adam for too long. She missed him already.

Ben asked her what she wanted to do for food, and she considered his question. What she really needed was time alone with him, far from the madding crowd, where she could shut out the world and work on her plan for total closure.

'How about we get some ingredients and I cook in your amazing kitchen?' she suggested. It was ironic that last time around, she had wanted him all to herself to give them privacy for something romantic to happen, but now she had a different agenda. Her time here was precious and she had more chance of removing Ben from her heart if she didn't share him with anyone else this evening.

They drove to the local supermarket and spent a hilarious twenty minutes whizzing around the aisles, with Ben on the back-bar of the trolley, whilst they pondered whether to choose garlic bread or ciabatta, white wine or prosecco, salsa dip or sour cream and chives. By the time they finished making their selections, they had enough ingredients to conjure up a feast fit for a king. Ben insisted on paying, despite Hope's protests, and they went back to the car as his phone rang again.

'Hi, Niki, we're getting something to eat. Where are you?' Ben chatted away and, to Hope's disappointment, promised they would try to meet up with Niki later. Yet Hope couldn't help but admit that she actually looked forward to seeing her again.

As they drove back to Ben's, Hope unwittingly compared him to Adam. Although being away from Cheltenham had given her time to realise how much she loved Adam, she still wasn't one hundred percent convinced that Fate didn't intend her to end up with Ben.

Back in his apartment, Ben looked over at Hope whilst unpacking the shopping. 'How are things going with Adam now?' he asked.

'Good,' she replied noncommittally. 'He threw me such an amazing birthday party at the pub last night, and'—she stretched out her wrist—'got me this gorgeous bracelet. It's inscribed, too.'

'Oh, that reminds me.' Ben rushed to his hall cupboard and returned with her black boots and a beautifully wrapped gift. 'The bracelet's lovely,' he said, placing the boots beside her suitcase. 'I'm glad things are good between you both again.'

She nodded. 'Ah, my boots, ooh, and a present'—she took it from him—'thank you. Wow, your wrapping skills are amazing.'

'Ha, I can't take credit for that, I'm afraid, that's the work of my wonderful PA. The present was all me, though. I'm not one of those awful execs who get their secretaries to buy all their personal gifts. Took me ages to work out what to get you and then find what I was looking for. I wanted to get you something special, as you're very special to me and always will be.' He handed her the parcel before adding, 'I really hope you like them.'

Hope unwrapped the gift and delighted in the stunning pair of tan leather, knee-length boots inside. They must have cost him an arm and a leg. She knew that once she put them on, she would never want to take them off, and they would also go with almost every outfit she owned. She sat on the sofa to try them on.

'Wow, they're stunning, thank you, I absolutely love them!' She stood up to give him a hug. 'They're so comfy, too,' she added, strutting up and down the lounge.

'Good,' Ben replied, smiling broadly.

Hope insisted that he relax whilst she prepared

their meal, so he sat down to read the newspaper. They would start with the ciabatta and dips, so she prepared them first before putting the pasta on to boil. She placed the hot bread in front of him when it was ready. They ate in silence. Ben was still busy scanning the print for stories that might have some impact on his business, and Hope was once again caught up in her thoughts.

She studied Ben's face, looking intently at his features: his quirky smile, his bright shining eyes, and his chiselled jaw. She wasn't quite sure what she expected to feel, but she somehow felt like a fish out of water. The last time she had seen him, the world had seemed to stop spinning, but now it seemed to be rotating at speed, making her feel dizzy. Had she merely used Ben to protect her from falling too deeply for Adam so she wouldn't get hurt? He was and always would be extremely important to her, but was it just an affinity with someone she'd craved for so long, rather than Ben himself?

She took another small sip of her wine and emptied the remainder of the bottle into Ben's glass.

Then she woke up from her reverie to the sound of water boiling over and a horrible burning smell. Before she could get to the hob to investigate, Ben was there. He pushed her out of the way, frantic at the mess from the pasta water. She had never seen this side of him before. It was as if, suddenly and for the first time, the spell was broken. He was, after all, merely human. Like everyone else. He was undoubtedly still a great catch, but he, too, had his faults, one being that he was far too pernickety about his kitchen equipment.

Hope tried to help clear up the mess, but Ben

flailed around, ushering her into a corner and tackling the not-so-huge problem himself. At one point, he seemed to sense that she felt bad and pulled her to him for a brief hug, saying everything would be okay. Yet he didn't look like it would be. Hope felt mortified. Admittedly, he seemed to go a little over the top. But she still felt bad. He gently stroked the hob with a soft cloth, bending down until eye level with it. Staring at it from different angles to see if there was any permanent damage. After two more attempts to remedy the situation, Hope gave up and left him to his precious never-to-be-used kitchenware. She wondered if she'd be invited to the memorial service if the hob didn't pull through. Standing out on the balcony, as far away as possible from the seemingly major catastrophe she had caused, she took a deep breath as a realisation hit her: Ben was no longer immortal in her eyes.

She messaged Jess.

Having a nightmare. Was cooking for Ben, but I've killed his hob. What should I do? Xxx

Jess's reply beeped straight back onto her screen.

I knew you should have stuck with MasterChef (Adam), instead of channel hopping over to Can't Cook, Won't Cook (Ben). Greedy! X

When he'd finally done as much as he could for the poor appliance, they dished up the now ruined food and ate in silence again. Ben seemed to notice how sheepish Hope looked and appeared to feel guilty. He apologised profusely and tried to explain how easily the hob scratched and how he never really cooked anything on it himself for fear of ruining it. Hope found it all a little bizarre and longed to be in Adam's flat where the kitchen was clean but always in disarray and most certainly never out of bounds.

With her spirits dampened and most of the meal left on their plates, the pair decided to brave the rain and meet Niki and her friends. It was good to have some other people to carry the conversation for a while, leaving Hope to sit back and listen to the others chat. She had words with herself for not taking proper care of the cooking. When Niki heard the story, though, she told Ben off for being petty. Hope clearly saw that they had a very strong bond, for *she* would never have been able to tell Ben to stop being a control freak. He went quiet and looked guilty for making such a fuss.

'It's just my way,' he protested, 'and I'm worn out with work.'

Hope realised there was an awful lot she still didn't know about him.

As the evening continued, a twinge of loneliness hit Hope. The only place she wanted to be right now was in Adam's arms. Yet if she hadn't made this trip, she wouldn't have witnessed Ben fall off the pedestal she'd put him on. She also knew that it was unfair to compare Adam to Ben. *It's like trying to choose between your favourite comfy jeans and a pair of rare, never-been-worn vintage ones, having only tried them on once for size*, she reasoned. *It's never been a fair contest.*

Excusing herself on the pretence of needing the toilet, Hope moved out of sight and took her phone from her pocket. She desperately needed to speak to Adam and tried calling him, twice. But there was no answer either time. She typed a heartfelt message and sent it on its way, eager to hear from him before too much time passed. Why hadn't she realised how much she loved him? Why did she put up barriers by always bringing Ben into the equation, instead of being brave enough to know that Adam was the only one for her? And why did he not reply to her message?

Returning to the group, Hope saw that the others were getting ready to leave. A taxi had been ordered, as it was still pouring with rain outside. The few staff members clearing up obviously wanted to get rid of them and go home. So, they all walked to the front of the pub and waited for their lift to arrive. The girls were dropped off first, leaving Hope and Ben to continue on alone, back to his apartment. They slipped quietly in through the doors and wearily sat on the sofa.

Ben clicked a remote to put some music on in the background whilst Hope put the kettle on. Things between them now seemed back to normal after the Hob Incident. They'd named it once Ben had finally seen the funny side, and Hope was glad. Ben had no idea that he'd kept inadvertently throwing a spanner in the works right from the start of her relationship with Adam—making things anything but plain sailing lately. Hope smiled inwardly at her apt idiom, given Ben's nautical passion, and wonder whether she and Adam were at long last headed for calmer waters. It was getting late, and she still hadn't heard back from him.

Seeing Hope yawn, Ben suggested they hit they hay. Now she felt a little awkward. Where should she sleep?

Saving her from asking the question, Ben said

he'd made up the spare room for her. 'I wasn't sure whether to bother when Jess couldn't make it. I'd have been happy letting you bunk in with me for the night, but I didn't want either of us getting in trouble with Adam,' Ben half-joked.

Ben respects that I have a boyfriend. Of course, he does. I'd expect nothing less from him. He was intent on doing the right thing by Adam, but have I done the opposite by coming here alone? She hadn't even told Adam that Jess hadn't been able to accompany her. He wouldn't be happy about her being one-on-one with Ben.

After a quick visit to the bathroom to change into pyjamas and clean her teeth, Hope padded into the guest room.

'Knock, knock,' Ben called out, wandering in through the open door, 'I just wanted to check you had everything you needed.'

She reassured him that she did and hugged him goodnight, thanking him for the meal earlier and apologising once more about the hob. As Ben turned and walked away, Hope stood and watched him for a split second. Then she slowly closed the door on him and, more importantly, on her delusions of the fairy-tale life she'd foolishly believed they could have together. She climbed under the covers thinking only of Adam, safe in the knowledge that she could finally give him all of her heart.

The snoring from the room next door, minutes later, made her chuckle and served as further proof that the bubble had finally burst. Not that she needed any convincing. *Nice touch, Ben*, she thought, realising he was totally oblivious to the painstaking journey she'd taken to get here. *Ben clearly has no problem sleeping tonight, but then again why would he? He isn't the one with a thousand thoughts going through his head. He isn't worrying that he might have jeopardised something precious to chase a dream. He isn't the one tossing and turning, wondering why on earth Adam still hasn't been in touch.* No, she was.

Unbeknownst to Hope, Adam was well aware that she was at Ben's alone, and he was not impressed. Not one little bit. He'd popped around to her house with the birthday presents that had been left at the pub after her party, intending to leave them on the front porch. But when Jess had opened the door, the cat was out of the bag. *How could Hope stay overnight at Ben's on her own without even telling me?* When her text came through that night, Adam barely read it and immediately deleted it. *Jess must have been in touch with her to admit she'd spilt the beans*, he thought, *and now Hope is trying to do damage control.* Without hesitation, he accessed the number at the top of his contact list and pressed the call button.

***

Angelisa had just caught up with recent events and was now in a much better place. She couldn't deny that she was incredibly pleased that things were going wrong for Hope and Adam once again, though it made her feel a little callous. Maybe the fact that Hope had gone to Ben's alone this weekend would be enough for Adam to break up with her, once and for all. If that were to happen, then Angelisa would, of course, make sure she was close at hand to step in and mop up after the fallout, in any way she could.

She was convinced that it would be best for everyone if the pair called it a day sooner rather than later. Yet it would be far better if that happened without her interfering. She'd have to be patient and see what happened next, which was hard when her heart was so invested. Also, patience was a virtue she'd never possessed.

28

When Hope woke up the next morning, she immediately looked at her phone. She slowly reread the text she had sent Adam the previous night.

> Adam, I was so stupid. I know now that I fell in love with the fantasy of Ben, not the reality of him, and I'm so desperately sorry for putting you through so much heartache over the last few months. I feel so far away from you tonight and just want to be there with you now. You are everything to me, Adam, and you are REAL!! I love you so much. I want to spend my whole life with you. I miss you like crazy, and I wish I hadn't come here today. I'll see you tomorrow. Please reply! Love, Hope Xxx

She had sent it shortly after ten, and it was now almost eight the following morning. Yet still no reply from Adam. She placed the phone to her ear and called him, but after a few short rings the call was intercepted by the answerphone. This unsettled her. He must have read her message by now. Was he blanking her? Was he hurt that she had gone to Ben's, despite not asking her to cancel the trip? Was he worried that she may have been unfaithful? Or had he simply had enough? She tried calling again, still no answer. The sooner she got back to Cheltenham, the better. She needed to see him to know that everything would be okay. Her heart beat fast with worry. Surely, she hadn't wrecked everything in the short space of twenty-four hours or so, had she?

Hope left Ben's at the first opportunity that morning. She wished she hadn't had a drink the previous night. If she'd stuck to soft drinks, she would have driven home when they'd returned to his flat after seeing Niki—provided it didn't appear rude. Ben hadn't sensed her urgency at wanting to go, and she couldn't explain it to him. He'd had to pop back into the office for an hour or two first thing and suggested she have a nice lie before meeting him later for lunch. Told her not to worry if the cleaners turned up. But Hope had said that she'd leave the apartment at the same time as him and look around the shops for a while. Little did he know that rather than shopping, she'd got straight into her car and started driving as soon as they'd parted ways.

Hope now turned her full attention to the journey ahead. The road which all too slowly was taking her back to the man she truly loved, the man she now knew she wanted to spend her whole life with and never again wonder whether she'd turned her back on something incredible with Ben. Why hadn't she been able to figure that out sooner?

She was driving far too fast this morning, but she

felt everything slipping away from her. She had to get back home to sort it out before she lost Adam for good. Putting her foot down and battling against the wet roads, she remembered the last time she had done this journey. Last time she had been in just as much of a rush but hadn't wanted to leave Portsmouth, feeling that everything she wanted was there. This time, though, she knew that everything she really wanted was back in Cheltenham. This time there was no train to catch, no work to get back in time for, just a sorry mess to fix, if it wasn't too late.

At eleven fifteen, she finally managed to get hold of Adam by calling the pub. 'You didn't reply to my text. Is everything okay?' She wasn't sure, but he didn't seem all that thrilled to speak to her.

'I didn't get it until I woke up this morning, sorry,' he lied.

'Adam, I was so worried when you didn't reply. I know I must have hurt you so much.' The conversation continued for a few more minutes, but it didn't give Hope the reassurance she needed. He was distant, cold, and still so many miles away. Hope choked back tears and tried to concentrate on the road. The rain was pelting down now, slowing her up and frustrating her even more.

An hour later, when she was only a few miles from Cheltenham, her phone rang. It was Ben, saying he wouldn't be able to meet her for lunch after all because his meeting was running late. She told him she'd just left Portsmouth anyway because she had things to do back at home, and she thanked him again for the boots. He would always be a good friend, and she loved him dearly, but it would be a long time before he was ready for a relationship. *And I'm already in one*. She hoped that was still the case.

As she was about to pull into her cul-de-sac, Hope saw Adam's car driving on the main road in the opposite direction. She flashed him down and stopped her car at the side of the road, then ran up and motioned for him to wind down his window. He was on the way to the post office to bank the takings and seemed in a rush to get away, so they arranged to meet at the pub that evening. She could sense a real sadness to him, and she knew she'd caused it.

Adam hadn't been able to get away from Hope fast enough. He'd spent all weekend consumed by imagining what might have gone on, once he'd learned that Hope had gone to see Ben alone. He had missed her, but he wasn't going to stand around with his arms wide open and let her run straight back into them again. She needed to know that she'd hurt him, and he needed to fit in a shower before he started his shift.

When Hope made her way to the pub that evening, Adam was nowhere to be seen. They'd arranged to meet at seven, and it was now quarter past. She tried calling him, but he didn't answer. A few minutes passed, and then a text message appeared on her screen.

Change of plan. Out with the lads. Sorry. X

Had her trip to Ben's just lost her Adam?

Adam had been struggling. He knew how much he loved Hope and had been tormented by demons when she was gone. He also knew he was the one who had acted badly and that he ought to try and fix things. Hope was relieved that when she next called him the following evening after work, he answered the phone. They arranged to meet up in an hour at her house.

Or should I be worried? Hope wondered. *Is he planning to break up with me for good? Is that why he's coming to my house, instead of suggesting I go to the pub?*

Adam arrived at eight, looking sheepish and uncomfortable.

'Is everything okay?' she asked gingerly, waiting for him to throw the grenade.

'I want it to be,' he mumbled, 'if you do, too, but only if there's definitely nothing between you and Ben.'

'I promise there's nothing between me and Ben. I love you so much. I'm sorry I went to see him. But it really helped. It's you I want, though, and only you.'

Adam held her and kissed her, mumbling, 'I'm sorry I was distant.'

It hadn't taken him long to feel guilty. He knew he'd behaved like a jerk. He hadn't even gone out with the lads at all the previous night, had just hidden away in his flat for the evening. Jess had gone around to the White Rose to see him a few hours earlier, having had the day off. She had told him that he had nothing to worry about because the weekend had helped Hope realise her visions of Ben had never been real. Adam knew Jess wouldn't have said that if anything *had* gone on between Hope and Ben. He felt really guilty and was glad Hope didn't seek further explanation for his behaviour. Perhaps they could now leave the past in the past.

Hope didn't expect everything to be perfect with Adam straight after she'd spent a weekend at Ben's alone. Yet she hoped they could start rebuilding the foundations again and work from there.

29

After that minor wobble, Hope and Adam found the following days a real breath of fresh air, with things finally back on track. Realising, with hindsight, that her return trip to Portsmouth was the only way she could shut down the Ben Situation, Adam was no longer annoyed.

During the next month, he and Hope became inseparable, sharing lazy days off, seeking out treasures in local charity shops, spending a day at the zoo, and trying on the most outrageous outfits they could find for each other in town. Any evening when Adam wasn't working, they dined out or he cooked for her in his flat, and they often played word games until late into the night. Every moment they spent together was filled with laughter and joy. Adam couldn't envisage his life without Hope in it, and, thankfully, she was finally of like mind.

As Hope made the familiar drive from the station to the White Rose, she realised she wanted to talk to Adam about something tonight. She'd been staying over at his flat more often than she'd slept at home recently, but they still hadn't taken things any further in the bedroom. Both were keen to ensure the dust had fully settled after her trip to Ben's. Neither of them had broached the subject since her return a month earlier, but Hope now felt more than ready to take that next step in their relationship.

Adam greeted her with a kiss and made them both coffee. Then he took the lid off the Scrabble box and began setting up a game.

'You beat me again last night, but I have a feeling your winning streak is about to end,' he teased.

'Ooh, I almost forgot.' Hope got up from the sofa and went to her handbag, then she presented him with a heavy but delicately wrapped gift. 'You know how we said we needed a dictionary to act as our Scrabble bible, instead of always using the Internet to check whether words are allowed and getting different results from every website. Well . . . open it,' she urged.

Inside was a bulky hard-back dictionary whose original wraparound cover had been replaced by one Hope had created on her computer and printer. It depicted a Scrabble grid filled with words that had special meanings to them. She'd added *Adam & Hope's Scrabble Bible* as a title at the top.

'I've inscribed it, too.' Hope gestured inside the front cover.

selfish
sel-fish
adjective
concentrating on one's own needs, without considering those of others

> Adam, I've been so selfish ever since we first met. I'm so sorry.
> Love, Hope Xxx

'I love it, thank you.' Adam swooped her up into his arms and kissed her. 'So, no more cheating from you tonight?'

'From *you*, you mean!' Adam's cheeks flushed red, but Hope didn't seem to notice. 'Hang on, look in the back, too,' she added. Inside the back cover, she'd used photo corners to create a purpose-built holder containing personalised score cards. 'Now we don't need to use scraps of paper anymore.'

'When did you find time to do all this?' Adam asked, noting how professional the cover looked and overwhelmed by the effort she'd put into such a meaningful gift.

'Oh, I've been working on it for a while,' she replied nonchalantly. She sat back down and readied herself to place the first word on the Scrabble board.

'You weren't selfish, though, you know,' Adam piped up moments later, adding a word to the board. He waited for Hope to finish topping up her tiles so that he could do the same. 'You were in a tricky situation when we met. And I really didn't handle things as well as I should have.'

'Well, that's all in the past,' Hope replied, placing an S and an X down on the board and putting *sex* on the table. 'And now that you have me all to yourself, when are you going to make a dishonest woman of me?' She looked over at him, a naughty smile tugging at the sides of her mouth.

He kissed her hungrily and felt tempted to take her

off to the bedroom right there and then, but he hesitated. He had planned to do something before he and Hope slept together, but he couldn't do anything about that tonight. Buying himself some time, he came up with a cunning suggestion. 'Well, given how close it is to Valentine's Day, only the most romantic day of the year, why don't we wait until then? We've both got the fourteenth and fifteenth off, so let me arrange something special.'

'Ooh, yes, that's a fantastic idea!' Hope kissed him again.

Hope was up before the sun on Valentine's Day. She knew that Adam had plans for them and eagerly anticipated something romantic, already aware of how the night would end.

Unbeknownst to her, Adam had booked a hotel in the heart of London and had a few surprises up his sleeve to make the occasion memorable. He'd also ordered red rose petals and balloons for the hotel staff to decorate their suite and arranged for a hamper of chocolates, champagne, crackers, and cheese to be sent up to the room in the evening.

Hope showered, dressed, and finished packing, then sent Jess a quick message before setting off for the pub. Adam had instructed her to pack an overnight bag and to include something glamourous for the evening. She hoped that the new dress she'd splashed out on would not only be suitable but would also blow him away. She'd treated herself to matching lingerie, too. It had cost her a pretty penny but was technically a gift for Adam.

Arriving at the White Rose, Hope saw Adam standing beside his car with the boot open, ready to drop her suitcase in and head straight off.

'Happy Valentine's Day, gorgeous girl,' he greeted her, wrapping her in a warm embrace. 'I love you so much.'

'Happy Valentine's Day. I love you, too,' Hope managed to reply once he let her up for air. Then she handed him a card and his gift.

They set off on the road. Hope had no clue where they were going, but she soon guessed they were on their way to the big city. At that point Adam, couldn't resist telling her a little of what he'd planned. 'We're staying in Westminster, right near the London Eye, and I have tickets for a show this afternoon and a table booked for a meal tonight. We can spend a few hours exploring when we get there and then freshen up in the room before we head out to eat later. Does that sound okay?'

'It sounds wonderful.' Hope smiled at him. 'What show are we seeing?'

'It's a secret.' Adam smiled back and zipped his lips with forefinger and thumb.

They pulled into the hotel car park just before midday, and Adam hopped out to pay the parking fee. It was too early to check in, so he raced around to Hope's side of the car to let her out, nearly colliding with her as he did. She giggled.

'We have a few hours to kill before your first surprise, so is there anywhere you fancy exploring?' he asked.

She pondered for a while and then had an idea. 'I'd love to go to the Serpentine, to see if they still have the pedalos there. We went once as kids with Mum and Dad, but I've never been back since.'

'Right, let's get you to the Serpentine then,

Blossom, and really get this day started.'

She pulled him towards her for a kiss. Knowing how this day would end was all she could think about. This wonderful man, who had stuck by her and had now planned a special trip away, was *finally* going to take her to bed this evening, with an X-rated agenda. Her cheeks flushed as crimson as the lacy underwear in her suitcase.

'I love you,' she spluttered.

'Serpentine,' he ordered, 'but now I wish I'd paid extra for an early check-in.'

Arriving at the lake, they were disappointed to discover that it was out of season, so no boats were available for hire. 'Another time,' Adam promised her as they walked around, admiring the beautiful scenery.

'Whenever we went on pedalos when we were younger, my dad always cracked the same old joke. There used to be some in Exmouth when I was little. They've gone now, but we always used to go on them whenever we visited Gran and Grandad.'

'What was the joke?' Adam asked, curious.

'Come in, number six, your time is up. Oh, no, number nine, are you in trouble?' Hope shook her head, cringing at the memory, and then looked directly at him. 'You don't ever talk about your parents. Is there a reason for that?'

'It's a little awkward between us,' he admitted. 'They've never been behind me moving into pub management. We've not spoken much in the last few years, apart from at Christmas or on birthdays. I should probably try to fix things with them, but I keep putting it off.'

'You must talk to them,' Hope urged, knowing all too well how easily a parent could be snatched away when a person least expected it.

'I will,' Adam promised.

'Do they even know about me?' Hope asked.

'No. Sorry,' he replied, shamefaced.

They walked for a while longer, immersed in their thoughts whilst the afternoon sun sparkled in the water.

Adam broke the silence, taking her hand. 'Hey, let's get a Subway.'

'What are you, American?' Hope stared at him, her head tilted to one side.

'No, not the underground. I really fancy a footlong Italian.'

'A what?' *What on earth is he talking about? Have I misheard him?*

'A Subway. Surely, you've had a Subway before. It's a sandwich chain. You create whatever sub . . . submarine sandwich you fancy, choosing the main ingredients and then adding all the salad items you'd like on top. They're delicious.'

Trusting him implicitly without knowing what she was getting into, Hope let him pull her along.

Forty-five minutes later, they sat on a bench in Little Venice, and Hope was making all the right noises. 'I can't believe I've never been to a Subway before,' she said, finishing her food. 'How did I not know this place even exists? Is there one in Cheltenham?'

'Sadly not.' Adam looked over to gauge her reaction.

'Oh, no, really?'

He laughed. 'We've got two in Cheltenham, I think. I'm glad you enjoyed it.' He gave her a kiss before continuing to eat his sub. At one point, when she eagerly eyed it, he let her have a bite. He'd chosen one twice the size of Hope's, but she'd stacked hers up with so much salad that she'd barely managed to get her mouth around it.

'Time for us to make a move,' Adam said a few moments later.

'Where are we going?' Hope asked, but he wouldn't say.

He'd arranged for them to see a matinée performance of *Les Miserables*, knowing it would bring back more fond memories of Hope's childhood. Yet he hadn't expected how glassy-eyed she'd look when they left the theatre afterwards.

'Did you love it?' Hope asked as he stopped to buy a programme at the exit.

'Yes, Blossom, I loved it. Not quite as much as you, though, by the look of it.'

'It's just how I remember from when Henry and I watched it with Mum and Dad. My older brothers must have been old enough to do their own thing that day, so it was just the four of us in London. Dad bought some last-minute tickets off a tout near the entrance. I think it was this very same theatre. Last time around, I couldn't see most of the performance, though, because Dad had paid over the odds for two pairs of really cheap tickets. He and Henry were stuck right at the very back, and Mum and I sat directly behind a pillar.'

They both laughed.

'I bought the soundtrack a few days later and played it over and over to learn all the words. It drove my brothers bonkers!'

'I know, Blossom, you told me.' Adam hugged her, still laughing. 'Enjoying Valentine's Day so far?'

'So much!' Hope reassured him, throwing her arms around his neck and kissing him.

'Well, there's still more to come,' Adam teased.

They wandered back to Little Venice, but this time for coffee. Finding themselves back on the same bench they'd sat on earlier, they watched barges making their leisurely way down the canal as if time were irrelevant. The peace was short-lived because a little girl raced up to them, excitedly searching for pennies dropped by passers-by. But the interruption was not unwelcome. They looked on fondly at the girl's joy whenever she found a coin.

Hope felt a familiar yearning for a child of her own and wondered whether Adam could read her mind. *Would that scare him off?* She didn't think so.

When the young girl was looking in the opposite direction, Adam fished into his jeans pocket to gather loose change and threw the bounty over his shoulder onto the grass. As the child continued to search a little way off, he called out to her, 'I think I can see one over there.' He pointed, and it didn't take long before she'd found one and then another.

'Coin! More coins! Look, a penny, ooh . . .' she squealed, 'and another one. Ooh . . . look at this really shiny 2p, Mummy.'

Her Mum absentmindedly congratulated her and then got back to whatever kept her busy on the phone.

'And a silver one. *Lots* of silver ones. I've found a whole treasure bank of coins here, Mummy. What's this pointy silver one called again? Mummy . . . Mummy?'

Adam looked over at Hope. They tried to hide their smiles for fear of being rumbled. As he pulled her up off the bench and put his arm around her shoulder, they heard the little girl ask, 'Have we got enough to go to Hamley's yet, Mummy?'

'That's a great idea,' Adam said, steering Hope towards the nearest tube station. 'Let's go and have some fun in Hamley's.'

An hour passed by in a flash in the giant toy store. Adam left one stand wearing glitter tattoos all the way up both arms, and Hope had bumblebees and ladybirds painted on her fingernails at another. They took dozens of selfies by the giant Lego figures and raced remote control cars around a track. Then they watched magic tricks being performed before nearly knocking someone out with a giant Frisbee.

'Next floor?' Adam asked, when they found themselves at the bottom of another escalator.

'Definitely,' squealed Hope, her eyes sparkling.

Entering the floor for newborns and toddlers, Adam picked up two baby sleepsuits. 'Which shall we have first, Blossom?' He held the blue one out in front of him. 'A boy'— he switched the pink one to the front—'or a girl?'

'A boy first and then a girl,' Hope replied. 'That way our daughter will have a big brother to always look out for her.'

'Then we'd better get practising.' Adam winked at her.

'Ready when you are.' Hope smiled, her cheeks reddening.

'What about names?' Adam spluttered, running his finger around the inside of his collar.

'I've always loved the idea of Faith for a girl and Harry for a boy. What about you?'

'Faith's a lovely name. But it would have to be

Charlie for a boy, I think, after my favourite book when I was young.'

'*Charlie and the Chocolate Factory*?' Hope guessed correctly, with Adam nodding.

'Charlie has a nice ring to it,' Hope said firmly. 'So, Charlie and Faith?'

'Agreed! Just *one* of each flavour then?'

'I don't think you get to choose what flavour you get.' She grinned. 'But one of each would be perfect.'

He put down the Babygros and kissed Hope.

'I lost a baby once.' Hope spoke so quietly that Adam barely heard her.

He put his arm around her shoulder and pulled her closer, whispering in her ear, 'I'm so sorry, Blossom.'

'I was seeing a Dutch guy, Pietje. It's actually spelt p-i-e-t-j-e, but you pronounce it pit-juh. You have to kind of say the word "picture" fast but ignore the "c" in the middle. Pit-juh. Like that.'

She had the knack for drifting right off topic whenever she had something difficult to say, but Adam didn't rush her.

'We started dating before Mum died. He wasn't right for me at all, but I ended up staying with him for months afterwards, as I was so desperate to be loved.' Hope trailed off a little before continuing the story. 'I fell pregnant unexpectedly, when we'd been together for nearly a year. But as soon as I told him, he hot-footed it back to Holland, never to be heard from again. I lost the baby at eleven weeks. It was for the best in the end, though. I was only eighteen and far too young to have a baby. But at the time, I'd planned to go ahead with the pregnancy, thinking that a baby might replace the emptiness I felt from losing Mum. I still desperately want to be a mum one day.'

'You'll be an *amazing* mum,' Adam whispered in her ear. 'I have no doubt about that.' He pulled her close and wrapped his arms around her.

'Anyway,' she continued, attempting to lighten the mood, 'could be worse. I could have ended up marrying him and becoming Mrs Van den Wijngaard. Can you imagine that? What a mouthful!' She extracted herself from his embrace and smiled.

Adam looked at her fondly. 'Come here, Mrs Van den Wijngaard,' he beckoned, laughing. They went down the escalators and out of the store.

A little after six, they arrived back at the hotel and checked in. The staff had done a fantastic job of decorating their suite. It was the epitome of romance and the perfect setting for this monumental evening. Hope admired the view of the London Eye from their window, illuminated in transitional colours as it tirelessly revolved.

They planned to get changed and head out for a few drinks before their meal. But the moment Adam saw Hope reappear from the bathroom in her floor-length black dress, he was unable to resist her. They fell onto the bed, kissing, both knowing that this time there would be no holding back.

'I'm glad our table isn't booked until nine,' Adam whispered.

'We're supposed to be getting ready to go out, though,' Hope reprimanded playfully.

'Then you shouldn't have worn such a sexy dress,' Adam responded, trying to remove it.

'If you like the dress, then wait until you see what I'm wearing underneath,' Hope teased.

It had certainly been worth the wait. Their abstinence during the last five months had fuelled such a build-up of desire that their passion was almost insatiable. As Hope lay in Adam's arms a while later, her mind was on one man only, the one currently by her side.

'I'm sure the restaurant will keep our table if we're a little late,' Adam said, pulling her towards him again. This time around, Hope didn't protest as she surrendered to his touch.

They finally tore themselves away from the room at around half eight and took the tube to Covent Garden. Adam had known that Hope had never tried sushi but wanted to, so he'd booked a table at a beautiful Japanese restaurant. They sampled all sorts of different dishes, accompanied by glasses of prosecco, and discussed their future.

'You know how we've toyed with the idea of running a pub together one day?' Adam said whilst Hope tucked into the food. 'I was talking to Jane and Edward last week, and it got me thinking.'

Hope remembered the kind couple she'd met in Birmingham on the night she and Adam had first travelled there together. 'Thinking what?' she asked in between mouthfuls.

'Well, they've finished their training and been offered a pub to manage in Birmingham. Maybe you could apply for the management training scheme. After ten weeks, you'd be given your first pub to run, somewhere on the area, and then we could make plans to run our own pub together one day.'

'Leave retail?' Hope sat back and dipped her dragon roll into the pot of soy sauce, contemplating Adam's proposal.

'I know it would be a big move, but the industry has many similarities,' he ventured.

'Do you really think they'd accept me on the course?' Hope asked, still trying to wrap her head around the idea but liking how danced around in her brain.

'I can have a word with my area manager, suggest you for it and see what he says,' Adam said.

'Okay.' Hope was too busy thinking—and eating—to say much more. Could she really leave her career in retail to go into pub management with Adam? She knew she loved him deeply and could see him in her future, but did that involve a change of career, too? *Perhaps it does*, she realised, with little hesitation.

Adam had pulled a small box out of his jacket pocket and was presenting it to her. As she reached for it, holding her breath in anticipation, he twiddled the bracelet on her wrist that he'd given her for her birthday. 'You already know that you're the reason my heart keeps beating. Now I'm giving it to you for safe keeping. Open it,' he requested.

She removed the lid of the box to reveal a stunningly simple heart pendant, inscribed with his name, on a delicate silver necklace. 'It's beautiful, thank you.' Hope kissed him, and he jumped up to fasten it around her neck.

'Promise to look after it. It's still fragile after all you put me through,' he joked, finally able to make light of the Ben Situation.

'I promise. Thank you, I love it.'

'Back to the room?' Adam asked.

'Just one more piece of sushi first,' Hope pleaded, in spite of being full. The day had been filled with so many wonderful firsts, and she wanted second helpings of everything.

As they went up to their room in the lift, they were barely able to keep their hands off each other. The hamper Adam had organised was now on the bed, and he moved it to the desk, taking out the bottle of champagne and uncorking it.

'To us,' he toasted, raising his glass to Hope's. 'Happy Valentine's Day, Blossom.'

'Happy Valentine's Day. It's the best one I've ever had.'

'Then here's to many more in the future.' Adam finished his glass and set it down. He tackled Hope and threw her onto the bed, spilling her drink all over them in the process.

Sometime later, Adam rolled over and looked at Hope lying beside him. Fast asleep, she looked so serene. The peaceful look on her face made him wonder whether the intense passion he remembered from moments ago had all been in his mind. Her cheeks were flushed red, though, and her lips wore a contented smile whilst she softly breathed in and out, oblivious to his gaze. The curtains flapped in the breeze from the open window. Adam checked the wall clock; it was just before three. He finally felt that the woman he'd wanted from the moment he'd first set eyes on her, his beautiful Blossom, was truly his and only his, heart, body, and soul.

Hours later, Hope yawned and stretched, then bent over to kiss Adam on the cheek. She sat up and reached for the *Les Miserables* programme on the bedside table. As she flicked through the pages, reliving the magic of the show, he stirred.

'Morning, honey,' she greeted him. 'How did you

sleep?'

'Like a baby,' he replied. 'And speaking of babies, I haven't finished with you yet.' He sat up and leaned towards her.

'Let's try out the hot tub first,' Hope replied in a high-pitched squeal as he tickled her. 'It would be a shame to go home without making use of it, and I still have glitter absolutely everywhere from your Hamley's tattoos. I'll fill it up.'

She wandered into the bathroom and then returned.

'I'm sure it will take a while to fill.' He raised his eyebrows. 'Plenty of time—' He was silenced with a kiss as Hope climbed back under the covers.

Swathed in their bathrobes, after a luxuriously steamy soak in the hot tub, they now sat on the bed, tucking into their breakfast, which had just been delivered.

'This suite is so beautiful, Adam, thank you,' Hope said as she finished eating. 'I'll be rather sad to leave. It's so . . . so sumptuous.'

'I know. It's rather special here, isn't it? I thought you'd like it.' He kissed her and rose from the bed. 'And that brings me nicely onto what I have planned for today.'

'Oooh, what are we doing?'

'Well, you've spent so much time at mine lately, so I thought we'd go home via Ikea and buy some things to make my flat more welcoming. You can put your feminine touch on the place. Make it cosier for when you're there. You choose whatever you want, my treat.' He hadn't failed to notice that she'd begun to leave more and more of her things at his flat, but it still looked like a bachelor pad.

'I love that idea!'

'Right, let's get moving.' He began to get dressed whilst Hope went into the bathroom to do the same.

'We can't fit much in the Porsche, though,' she called out through the open door.

'That's okay. We can order anything you like and have it delivered.'

'Great. But do you know what you can't ever leave Ikea without?'

'No.'

'Either a hot dog, an ice cream, or a milkshake.' Hope wandered back out of the bathroom and perched on the bed to pull on her boots. 'They have a hot dog stand at the end after the checkouts, with machines where you put in a token to pull your very own ice cream or pour your own milkshake. It's so much fun!'

'Then we'd better get all three.' Adam grinned, kissing her. 'You're very easily pleased.'

30

Hope's and Adam's staff rotas for the rest of February and the beginning of March had robbed the loved-up pair of any further opportunities for quality time off together. They had to make do with Hope spending her evenings at the White Rose whilst Adam worked, as well as joining him there for his lunch breaks whenever she wasn't working at the store.

Thankfully, though, her days off this week perfectly aligned with Adam's plans. He had an area meeting in Bristol to attend today, followed by an evening meal and drinks, all paid for by one of the breweries. Hope had been invited along as Adam's partner. Accommodation had been laid on, too. When his car pulled up in Hope's driveway, she opened the front door, and he gave her an enormous hug and a kiss.

As they neared the brewery, Adam phoned his area manager to get directions. They found the little pub and checked in. It was quaint but homely, and the bedrooms were basic but clean. Whilst Adam had his brewery tour, all Hope needed was somewhere to lay her head for a few hours and then wash and get ready for their night out. So, the room was more than adequate. Adam kissed her cheek, then kissed her hard on the lips, before leaving to walk down the road and meet the other managers.

Hope was absolutely shattered. She'd had ten long work days in a row because of staff shortages, due to a bug going around. Now exhausted, she finally had two days off. She left the room to buy a bar of chocolate and some magazines and then returned a few minutes later, planning to read and watch television in bed. But the second her head hit the pillow, she was fast asleep.

It wasn't until Adam returned, at half past five, that she finally awoke. Now she had only an hour to get ready before they would meet the others downstairs in the bar. Hope felt a little touchy after waking up and was still tired from her work schedule, so she was not pleased that time was against her.

Adam looked over at her racing around, cursing under her breath because she didn't have long enough to dry her hair and apply her makeup and could never be ready in time. *She looks so funny. Even cross, she still looks beautiful, and even if she goes down to the bar in her dressing gown with wet hair, as she is right now, she will still be the most stunning woman there. She just doesn't see it somehow. It's a shame she can't see herself through my eyes. Maybe then she would realise how special she is to me and how gorgeous she always looks.*

When they eventually made it downstairs, fifteen minutes later than scheduled, only two of the group were there already. Hope needn't have rushed after all. Yet in the end, she relaxed. She'd wanted to look her best, she didn't look too bad, and she would soon have a drink inside her and the courage to meet all these new people. It was strange how she was extremely confident professionally, yet socially she was always a little shy and nervous at first. She felt so desperate to be accepted by people and didn't realise she had nothing to worry about.

The evening began properly once the area manager, David—only an hour and ten minutes late—finally made his appearance. Adam introduced Hope, and it was clear that he had told David about her previously because David's first words were, 'Well, you told me she was pretty fantastic, and you weren't lying.'

Hope blushed.

The three of them chatted about what Adam did for a living, and she was fascinated to learn more about the industry. David said she was just what the business needed and asked whether she had ever considered the pub trade. Upon hearing that she and Adam had discussed running a pub together in the future, David joked that maybe he should kick Adam out of the White Rose and get her to run it instead. Hope knew he was only kidding, but if he meant what he said about her potential, she would have to pursue that in another conversation with him.

After stopping off in a couple of pubs for drinks, they reached their final destination, a beautiful tavern overlooking a river with a menu of mouth-watering home-cooked delicacies. Hope felt a sense of belonging as she listened to people chattering about their customers, their jobs, and their lives.

After dinner, Adam suggested that Hope use her party trick to play a joke on David. At university, she had learned to down a pint of beer in less than five seconds without losing a drop. She hesitated before agreeing, hoping she wouldn't regret it. When David took a visit to the toilet, Adam filled the others in on the plan, and everyone was happy to play along.

Ten minutes later, Adam stood up to make a speech. On behalf of the whole group, he thanked David for a fantastic evening and then challenged him to a pint-downing contest. If Adam won, then David would have to offer Hope an interview for the management training programme. If David won, then Adam would buy the next round of drinks. David accepted the challenge but threw in the joker they all hoped he would.

'The thing is, Adam, because Hope is the one to gain from me losing, I think she should compete. But you can still buy a round when I win.'

The challenge was set, and David and Hope rose to it, with Hope protesting loudly that she couldn't even drink a pint of beer, let alone down one. The countdown was on, and they raised the glasses to their lips.

Five seconds later, Hope looked over at Adam's area manager, her empty glass in hand, to see that he hadn't even taken a sip. *The swine, he must have known he was being conned*, she thought.

Everyone rolled around in laughter as David realised he'd been set up. He looked at Hope incredulously. 'I have never seen a woman do that quite so fast, I must admit. I almost missed it. I think you ought to do another one, and I'll join in this time.'

'One's more than enough for tonight, David,' she said. After drinking that pint so quickly, she would have soft drinks for the rest of the evening. Then she grinned before adding, 'I'll down another one after I've had an interview and you've accepted me for the management training programme.' It had been an unorthodox way to get an interview, but this was an unconventional industry.

'You're on,' he replied. He raised his glass and downed his own pint, to applause all around.

Hope felt full of the party spirit, or at least full of a glass of wine, two lime and sodas, and a pint of lager. But the evening now seemed to be drawing to a close, with a couple of the managers talking about heading back to the pub and to bed. Hope didn't want the merriment to end. She suggested that they go dancing and tried to persuade her newfound comrades to join her. Hope looked at Adam imploringly. It didn't take much for him to twist everyone's arm.

The club was playing seventies and eighties throwbacks but was nearly empty. Hope was the only one brave enough to dance at first, but she soon persuaded the others to join her. The hours passed all too quickly. Afterwards, they congregated outside the venue, and David searched for a number of a taxi firm. Then a double-decker bus pulled up, and they decided to take it back to the hotel instead.

The inebriated group hijacked the entire top deck, crammed towards the front and looking out of the window. It had been years since any of them had been on this mode of public transport, and they all bellowed out the tunes they had soaked up that evening. After a happy twenty minutes, they jumped off at their stop, walked quietly through the inn's front door, and said goodnight to the world.

Hope had really got a buzz out of talking to these people about their jobs. She thought about how exciting it would be to run a pub and wondered whether she *should* switch careers. Jumping onto the bed, she looked over at Adam. He seemed to be ready for sleep, so she kissed him, trying to get him to wake up because she felt anything but sleepy herself.

Under the covers, she pressed her body against his, kissing him more passionately now. She knew how she wanted to finish off this wonderful evening. Yet he didn't seem to be in the mood. As she moved closer to him, he pulled away, muttering that he was absolutely shattered. She felt uneasy. What was wrong? Didn't he want her?

Hope stopped kissing him, and Adam rolled over to face away from her.

She lay awake, staring at the ceiling. The alcohol fuelled her emotions, and tears welled up in her eyes. Had she done something wrong tonight or was Adam going off her? Why did he seem so distant?

'Adam, do you still love me?' she had to ask.

'I'm tired, Blossom, that's all. Of course, I do.' He reached over and grasped her arm, then pulled it over both of them before settling down for sleep. It wasn't enough reassurance for Hope, though. Adam seemed preoccupied. She felt as if something were wrong, but she doubted she would find out what it was until morning.

31

Hope felt subdued. She had an awful lot of thinking to do. Firstly, she still felt rejected after Adam pushed her away the previous night. She'd wanted to talk about it, but he seemed fine again this morning. He kissed her when they woke up and started the morning the way she'd hoped last night would end. They were so late for breakfast afterwards that they totally missed it.

After packing their bags to return home, Hope assumed the alcohol had made Adam too tired for anything but sleep last night. She decided that unless the same thing happened again, she would let it lie. She was probably being insecure and oversensitive.

She reassessed what she wanted to do with her life as far as career was concerned. She loved the idea of pub management, but was it only because she wanted to run a pub with Adam eventually and become his wife? Would the dream be complete only if he were a part of it? If she planned to apply for the management training course, she needed to be sure she was doing it for herself, in case she and Adam one day went their separate ways. Admittedly, that thought broke her heart, but she needed to consider it, just the same.

She kept worrying about Adam's behaviour the previous night. She looked over at him, and he returned her gaze, smiling and placing a hand on her knee. He squeezed it gently before returning his attention to the road.

'Are you okay, Blossom? You seem quiet this morning.'

'I'm fine, honey. I just got worried last night that you might be going off me.'

Adam turned to look at her with a genuinely shocked expression.

'Of course, I'm not going off you,' he said. 'If anything, I'm falling more deeply in love with you. My colleagues were drawn to your magnanimous personality, and I loved showing you off to my boss.'

If truth be told, he had been a little agitated that he himself had been pushed out of the limelight the night before, whilst Hope and David had spent most of the evening talking business together and seemingly getting on a little too well. Maybe there was a twinge of jealousy on his behalf, as David had seemed very keen on getting Hope to run one of his pubs. Fuelled, no doubt, by the Stella Artois he'd been drinking, Adam could remember having been a little disgruntled that he no longer seemed to be his boss's golden boy. But he hadn't deliberately tried to punish Hope by being distant in bed, had he? He certainly hadn't meant to cold-shoulder her.

He remembered having been tired when they'd

finally got into bed last night. Then he remembered what had been playing on his mind and distracting him. There was something he'd been meaning to do before they'd first slept together on Valentine's Day, but he'd still not got around to it. Now he knew that he couldn't put it off any longer. It was time to put all his eggs in one basket, without further delay.

His words had put Hope's mind at ease, and they chatted away for the rest of the drive. She was happy he'd confirmed that nothing had changed between them. Now she needed to think about her impending decision. *Yesterday was such an insight into the pub industry. Meeting all the other managers, hearing more stories, and speaking to David, who really did seem to think that I have what it takes to run a pub. But was it all said in jest in the heat of the moment, as the alcohol and party atmosphere took over? Would he consider me a suitable applicant if I sent him my CV?*

Near midday, they arrived back in Cheltenham, after stopping off for a bite to eat. Adam dropped Hope home and jumped out to fetch her bag from the boot. He gave her a huge cuddle and a heartfelt kiss, then sped off around the corner. Hope waved as he left and watched his car disappear into the distance, unaware that she stayed rooted to the spot for a couple of minutes. She walked up to the front door and let herself into the house, then sat in the kitchen whilst the kettle boiled.

She had another whole day off today and would do nothing but indulge in her thoughts. As the cuckoo clock next door faintly chimed one o'clock, she tore up the stairs and jumped into her tracksuit bottoms and white vest top. After racing back downstairs and out into her car, she set off. If she could guarantee one thing, a session at the gym would clear her head and let her look at things objectively before deciding whether to take a risk.

The gym worked its magic. An hour and a half of rigorous exercise enabled her to mull over everything. If she gave up her career, she would be starting out in a business that could take over her life. She loved retail management, but would she enjoy pub management the same way? What was there not to love? It would combine her managerial and customer service skills with her passion for fun. Instead of selling clothes, she would be selling an experience.

There would be financial benefits, too. She could let her house, which would more than cover the mortgage. And if she and Adam did end up together, it would be a bonus entering the industry now, before they bought a pub of their own. She could either stay in a job she enjoyed but that left her little extra money at the end of each month, due to the daily commute, or she could throw caution to the wind. She knew what she wanted to do. She had to get an interview for the management training programme. Anyway, hadn't David already promised her one after she'd downed that pint last night?

Hope charged through the front door and tore upstairs to run a bath. She laid some clothes out on the bed whilst the water filled the tub. After turning off the taps and leaving the bathroom, she booted up the computer downstairs and busied herself typing. The bath was cold by the time she had finished, but she was too rushed to soak for long anyway. She needed to get her hair washed and dried, apply a little makeup, and then drive to the White Rose to show

Adam what she'd written before sending it to David. She hoped Adam would be behind her decision now that she had made up her mind.

Adam read the printed document that Hope handed him in silence. It was a well-written formal request to be interviewed for the training programme, with a copy of her CV attached. He gave her the email address to send it to, along with a brown envelope, and she sped back to the house, where her computer awaited this vital piece of information.

She had to kill time whilst trying to be patient. Busying herself with the ironing, she played the waiting game. Was Adam pleased that she'd finally reached a decision? In all the haste, she hadn't paid much attention to his enthusiasm or lack of it. Of course, he would be supportive. She chastised herself for doubting him.

Shortly after Hope left the pub, Adam told Debbie he was popping out for a couple of hours and pulled on his jacket. Checking that he had his wallet and phone, he stepped out into the sunshine.

***

Angelisa had recently found out that Hope and Adam were getting ever closer again, with Hope possibly giving up her career to move into pub management. So, Angelisa sensed that Adam would soon feel compelled to give her a ring and dreaded what might lurk around the corner.

Of course, Angelisa knew something about Adam that Hope was still blissfully unaware of, but she couldn't exactly blurt it out. She and Hope had been extremely close in the past, but they hadn't spoken for many years. If she did try to get through to Hope now, it was unlikely that Hope would believe her, even if Angelisa somehow got Hope to listen.

32

Unaware that Adam was up to something he wouldn't want her to know about, Hope put the ironing board away. A brown envelope on the worktop caught her eye. Adam had given it to her earlier, along with David's email address. She'd found it odd at the time but forgot about it in her haste to email David her CV. She opened the sealed brown envelope to find a printed menu with various choices for a three-course meal that Adam planned to cook for her that evening.

Hope looked at her watch. When she'd left the pub, Adam had been busy working, but he would finish his shift in an hour. He had invited her to head back there as soon as he knocked off. After consulting the menu for a few more minutes and cursing herself for being too preoccupied to pay attention to it earlier, Hope called him with her choices. She had to leave a voicemail, though, because he must have been too busy to answer. She followed it up with a text message to be on the safe side.

Tonight's meal would be special. Adam had gone

to a lot of trouble with the menu, laying it out professionally and decorating it. With time ticking, she changed her clothes and checked her appearance in the mirror.

Returning to the White Rose, she felt disappointed that she hadn't heard from David yet. But as her dad always said, 'No news is good news.' This was indeed true. Maybe David hadn't even read her email yet. She would have to be patient, a trait that had never been in her genetic makeup.

She wandered through the pub entrance, and Adam pounced on her, then swept her up into a huge embrace in front of all the locals.

'There you are, Blossom!'

'Hi.' *What did he look so delighted about?*

'I've just had David on the phone. He wanted to talk to me about a manager's vacancy on the area that may suit Debbie, but he also mentioned interviewing you for the training programme. He loves the idea of you moving into the industry.'

'Wow!' *This could be the start of a whole new life for me*, thought Hope, *a life that would also fit so well with Adam's. How exciting and yet how utterly nerve-wracking.*

Adam called over to Debbie, letting her know that he'd be going off duty again, although he'd only got back from a recent jaunt shortly before Hope arrived. He ushered his girlfriend out of the bar and upstairs to his flat, instructing her to sit on the sofa, relax, and watch television. Hope couldn't bear to be in the next room when Adam was in the kitchen, though. She kept sneaking in to see him, wrapping her arms around him as he tried to cook. It made him smile but at the same time got in the way of his culinary creations, which were rather slowly coming together.

'Right, you, away with you until this is ready. You're distracting me with your sexiness, and I'll never get it done. Go downstairs and tell Dillan to take a quick break and keep you company.'

His severe tone was unmistakably bogus because his mischievous eyes revealed that he might abandon the cooking, right there and then, and instead carry her off into the bedroom. Obeying his orders, Hope went back down to the pub, where she and Dillan sat with a drink and talked about her impending interview.

Less than twenty minutes later, she was summoned upstairs like a naughty girl. She giggled when she realised she was allowed to return provided she promised to behave. She sat on the sofa and waited patiently. Her mouth watered as Adam appeared with their starters. A delicious baked camembert oozed onto her plate, accompanied by warm chunky bread, caramelised onion chutney, and a side salad. They chatted away as they worked through the first course, washing it down with white wine.

Hope still felt surprised that she had found a boyfriend who interested and fascinated her. In most of her relationships, she had been the entertainer, always wondering whether she and her date would have sat in silence all night long if she stopped talking. It was different with Adam. She continued to polish off her food whilst listening intently as he talked about new sales incentives at the pub, told her what to expect at her interview, and explained the company's history so that she could sound knowledgeable if asked about it.

He'd hardly touched his starter, even though they'd begun eating at the same time. That was the trouble with cooking a meal. Adam spent so long poring over the food and nibbling tit bits while preparing it that he rarely enjoyed the finished product as much as his guest did. They weren't in a rush to devour their next course, so they cuddled on the sofa and devoured each other instead, happy to have more time alone in their own little bubble.

A bit later, Adam got up to turn on some music and then popped into the kitchen to fetch their main courses. This dish was even more incredible than the first. King prawns in a mouth-watering sauce, with al dente pasta twirls and a gentle hint of garlic to tantalise the taste buds. They ate in silence, hungry after their passionate kisses, each racing through the course so they could continue where they had left off.

Placing her empty plate down on the table, Hope snuggled deep into the arms of her chef. 'Thank you. That was incredible. I think I need a rest before dessert, though.'

Adam pulled her closer and kissed her forehead as she closed her eyes.

As the night drew on, they wearily tore themselves off the sofa and made for the kitchen, carrying the remnants of the meal. Adam insisted on washing up, so Hope jumped up onto the worktop. She perched on the edge, asking him to tell her more about the pub trade.

'You'll have to do your food hygiene certificate, all about bacteria and cooking and storage temperatures,' he warned.

'Teach me stuff. I want to learn,' Hope begged.

Tired as they were, they chatted in the kitchen for another hour or so. After finishing the washing up, Adam also hopped up onto the worktop and sat opposite her. He reeled off things he had learned on his courses and then tested her to check her understanding. Hope was inspired. It was all so fascinating, so new and exciting.

'More. Tell me more.' And Adam could do nothing but oblige.

Finally, Hope admitted that tiredness had got the better of her. Adam jumped down and made his way over to where she sat. They shared a lingering kiss before dragging each other off to his bedroom. How unfair that they didn't both have a luxurious lie-in to look forward to tomorrow.

As they climbed under the covers, Hope suddenly realised they'd forgotten to eat the pudding. She couldn't even remember what she'd ordered from Adam's menu.

'What was for dessert, honey?' she whispered.

'Mmm. You are.' He pulled her closer and covered her lips with his. She hungrily kissed him back, her body arching towards him. She had begun to build her life around Adam, and there was no going back. Now that the Ben Situation had been put to bed, they could once again finish a perfect evening with a perfect night.

33

As had been her routine for a while, Hope drove back from the station after another day of work and made straight for the pub. By now, she had a few items of clothing tucked into Adam's new Ikea drawers and wardrobe and had duplicated her toiletries, hot brush, and makeup there. It was easier than going back home when she needed something. She'd certainly gone to town in Ikea. Now that all of the furniture and furnishings had been delivered, built, and positioned, Adam's bachelor pad had been transformed into a cosy abode. Hopefully, he didn't feel that things were moving too fast, or that she was trying to suggest moving in together.

As she entered the pub and wandered over to Adam standing behind the bar, she was greeted with a whoop, followed by, 'Blossom, what are you doing tomorrow?'

'Jess and I are going shopping, why?' Hope asked, intrigued.

'Change of plan. David's been on the phone, and

he can interview you down in Bristol if you can get there at two o'clock. What do you think?' Adam was beaming.

'I think I'm going to Bristol tomorrow,' she said. Then she rang David to confirm she would be able to attend. Hanging up the phone, she kissed Adam and ordered a soft drink. *Wow. I'm really doing this*, she realised. *I'm really about to change careers.* Remembering she still needed to get a job offer first, she sipped her drink and settled back on the sofa. Jess would join her there shortly, but now she wouldn't be letting her hair down tonight. She would need to be fresh as a daisy for her interview.

When Jess arrived, Hope filled her in about the last-minute change of plan. Jess fully supported Hope's eagerness to move into pub management and also her relationship with Adam.

Jess wasn't at all worried about where that would leave her. She knew Hope wouldn't kick her out of her house, and they'd already discussed possible arrangements. Hope had mentioned renting out the two other bedrooms, along with Jess continuing to rent hers. Hope would keep her own room empty so she'd always have a bolt-hole to return to. Jess knew she would eventually follow Hope to whatever town she ended up in anyway. She could easily transfer to another store. Vacancies were always cropping up, and her friendship with Hope was more important than staying in Cheltenham.

Hope's thoughts drifted to Adam as she admired him from their comfy seat, serving drinks to customers at the bar. He had definitely been acting strange again lately. She hoped he wasn't getting cold feet. Was she making a mistake by rearranging her whole life around him? If she got a job offer, she'd talk things through with him again to check that he was fully behind the idea, before she handed in her notice at work. He'd certainly seemed excited about it a few minutes ago. Maybe she was just imagining things. If she were to be offered the job, then she'd have a big decision to make.

The following day, after last-minute cramming the previous night, Hope woke up more than ready for the interview. She'd spent most of the morning doing extra preparation, and Jess had run her through some practice questions to settle her nerves. Now that she was mentally prepared, it was time to get dressed and made up.

With her shopping plans disrupted, Jess decided to spend the afternoon of Hope's interview at Adam's pub. She wandered in with a book, ready to while away the next few hours until Hope arrived, but first she would eat. After ordering a drink and a burger, she went to her usual sofa.

Around two thirty, she glanced up from her book to see Adam accompany a mystery woman down the stairs from his flat. As Jess watched the woman step up to the bar and Adam return upstairs, she noticed that he looked very shifty. *Surely, he isn't being unfaithful to Hope whilst she's attending her interview, about to change careers to have a future that revolves around him? Should I question him about it or mention it to Hope later? Oh, of all the days! What should I do?*

Hope's interview went brilliantly. In fact, within the first three minutes she felt that she'd got a place on the training programme, guaranteeing her a management role at the end. So, she wasn't surprised when David offered it to her after they'd sat down together for around an hour.

'Talk to Adam and have a think about it, but the position's yours if you want it. Just let me know by the end of the week,' he said, standing up to shake her hand.

'Thank you so much, David. I will. I'll let you know as soon as I've talked to Adam.'

Hope couldn't contain her excitement as she headed back to her parked car. Then she realised she was walking in the wrong direction and had to turn around, almost bumping into a passer-by. She fished her phone out of her handbag and dialled Adam's number.

'How did it go?' His voice was full of anticipation.

'I got the job!' Hope screamed into the phone.

'Hey, I had no doubt you would. Well done, you. Come back to the pub and we'll celebrate.'

'Okay, but can you promise not to tell anyone until I get there, please? I'd love to tell them myself,' Hope requested.

'I promise,' was his reply.

Hope wandered into the pub an hour later, excited to tell all the regulars her news. She hadn't expected to have a job offer on the day of the interview itself, so she felt as though she was in a whirlwind, given the events of the last twenty-four hours. She'd originally planned on spending the day shopping, after all. As she approached the bar, looking around for Adam, one of the barmen swooped up to her to offer congratulations, followed swiftly by another. Then all the regulars launched into a round of applause.

Adam had obviously not kept shtum. Hope was

greeted and congratulated by one person after another. She felt a little disappointed that he'd told everyone because she'd wanted to break the news herself, but at least they were all happy for her. Jess joined the throng, and Hope quietly confided that Adam wasn't supposed to tell anyone. Jess smiled wanly and gave Hope a huge hug and a kiss on the cheek.

Adam had been busy changing a barrel in the cellar when Hope arrived. After all the back-slapping and shrieking had subsided, he joined her, then pulled her close, kissed her, and whispered in her ear, 'You're amazing, Blossom. I knew you'd get the job!'

They spent the rest of the afternoon and evening with the regulars and some of the staff, talking about the future. Everyone envisioned how Hope and Adam would one day have babies crawling around their feet as they ran their own establishment together. Hope let her mind drift, seeing a long and happy future ahead.

Jess smiled at Hope but couldn't help feel troubled about the woman who'd been in Adam's flat earlier. He was behaving normally now, but he'd definitely looked like he was hiding something then. She would have to tell Hope at some point, but not tonight.

***

Angelisa had tried, yet again, to persuade Adam to end things with Hope, on her most recent trip to the White Rose that afternoon. However, he'd once again refused to hear a word she'd uttered. She didn't know what to do next, but she couldn't simply sit back and watch the turmoil that would soon unfold if she didn't intervene to prevent it. Perhaps it *was* now time to pay Hope a visit, in spite of knowing just how unproductive or disastrous that could be.

For weeks, she'd been preoccupied with the disturbing information she'd uncovered in Adam's cloud file. She'd been searching for proof that he and Hope should go their separate ways, but she certainly hadn't expected what she'd found. She finally accepted that she couldn't divulge her findings to Hope, who still desperately held onto the idea of a long and happy future with Adam. Yet Angelisa had to try something. She needed to act, and she needed to act fast. Time was of the essence.

34

Hope felt as if her life was playing in fast-forward ever since she'd been tasked with tying up the loose ends at work. She'd received her job offer from David only eight days ago and subsequently handed her notice to her regional manager. But with two weeks of un-used holiday allowance, she had only five more shifts at the store. Today was Easter Sunday, meaning the girls' shops were both closed. A restless Hope had silently crept around the house since dawn, not wanting to disturb Jess's long lie-in.

Shortly after eleven, Jess plodded downstairs, yawning. 'I'm so glad we're both off today,' she said, upon locating Hope in the kitchen. 'It's been ages since we spent the day together. I hardly see you anymore.'

'I'm sorry I've been at Adam's so much lately. There's a lot to talk through.' Hope took one last gulp of her drink. 'I can't believe my training starts next Monday.'

'Do you know where you might end up

afterwards?' Jess let out such a yawn that she risked breaking her jaw.

'No, not yet, but the area's not *too* huge, so with luck it will be close enough to Cheltenham for me to see you and Adam regularly.' Hope looked down into her mug as if attempting to read the tea leaves, even though she'd been drinking coffee. She still felt nervous about where she might end up but was excited to see what the future held.

'It won't be for too long, anyway, if you and Adam still plan on running your own pub together.' Jess acknowledged. 'Any idea where or when that will be?'

Hope told Jess a bit more about Adam's dream of purchasing a charming little village pub somewhere rural. 'He's got grand ideas about thatched roofs, stone walls, and a beautiful beer garden. Wants good schools nearby, too, as'—she acknowledged Jess miming rocking a baby in her arms—'we've spoken about babies. Yes.'

'Good.' Her friend yawned again.

'I'm not sure what time scale we're looking at, though. It will depend on how soon a suitable property comes up for sale. In the meantime, Adam's devising menu ideas and getting me to taste loads of new dishes. I think I'll have to up my gym sessions to work it all off,' she added, rubbing her stomach.

Jess laughed. 'I still can't believe you're going to be a landlady. I'm envious. Will you be sad to say goodbye to retail?'

'A little, but it would have been hard to stay in retail whilst having a family, whereas children will fit nicely around our future plans for the pub. What about you, still happy at Next?' Hope had noticed how Jess's eyes glazed over every time she passed a florist in town and wondered whether she missed her old job.

'Well, with you changing your life around so drastically, it did get me thinking. I do miss floristry and wonder whether one day . . . and I'm talking way off in the future . . . I might set up a little flower stall or shop of my own. Maybe right next door to your pub. What do you reckon?'

'Oh, I love that idea. You absolutely must!' Hope shrieked, picturing her friend creating floral masterpieces for the locals.

'Everything's perfect with Adam at the moment, then?' Jess asked.

'Well, I'm probably imagining it, as my brain is all over the place, but he has been acting strange recently,' Hope admitted, 'almost as though he's hiding something.' She stopped and thought for a few seconds. 'If he *is* being secretive, then maybe he's planning a surprise or something.'

Hope had seemed on top of the world lately, which is why Jess had decided not to mention the mystery woman in Adam's flat. But she now told Hope what she'd witnessed on the afternoon of her interview. 'I'm sorry I didn't say anything earlier,' Jess added, 'and I'm sure it's nothing to worry about, but maybe you should ask him to explain, especially since you're about to change your whole life around for him. I'm sure he's not being unfaithful. But if he were, you still have time to do a U-turn at work.'

Hope sat in stunned silence.

'I feel wretched. I should have told you before you handed in your notice,' Jess said. 'I'm a rubbish friend. Sorry, honey. Right, I need a long hot bath.' She got up from the table and fled down the hall to escape the awkwardness.

'Don't fret, I'm sure it's nothing to worry about,' she called out, already halfway up the stairs.

Hope leaned back in her chair, shocked. Adam had been acting weird during the last week or so, but she'd assumed he was adjusting to how quickly things were moving forwards with their life paths. She had never thought he might be seeing someone else behind her back. No, Jess must have got it totally wrong. Adam had invited both girls over to the pub later on, to treat them to Easter dinner, so she'd talk to him about it then. *There's nothing to worry about*, Hope decided. *There will be an innocent explanation.*

Before she could speculate any longer, her mobile sprang into life.

When Jess returned downstairs an hour later, she sat at the kitchen table, waiting for Hope to finish her phone call.

'That was Ben,' Hope said, hanging up. 'It's been ages since we last had a proper catch-up.'

'What does he think about your big career change?' Jess asked, tightening the belt on her dressing gown.

'He's really pleased for me,' Hope began, 'but a little concerned about the woman you saw at the pub. He told me to confront Adam as soon as I see him, to put my mind at rest, and wants me to call him later so he knows everything's okay. Cuppa?' She got up to flick the kettle back on.

Jess nodded. 'Is he still sworn off relationships?' She got up herself and put some bread into the toaster, hovering by the worktop to make the coffee.

'I think so. It's such a shame, as he'd love to have children one day and would make a great dad.' Hope sighed and told Jess how hard Ben found it having a niece and a nephew whom he couldn't be a proper uncle to because of his history with Laura.

'Yes, that must be really tricky,' Jess acknowledged. 'Is he still as busy as ever with work?

'He's actually about to fly to Barbados for a fortnight. For a holiday, would you believe? I think it's a great idea. He barely ever slows down and sounded absolutely shattered just then.'

Jess returned to the table with her breakfast and their coffee. 'Barbados, wow, has he got room for me in his suitcase? I can't remember when I last went abroad.'

Hope smiled. 'I'll ask when I speak to him later.'

'What about you and Adam, are you still planning to go abroad after your training?'

'Yes. He's booked two weeks' annual leave then. David says it shouldn't be a problem for me to have the time off, too, unless there's an urgent vacancy on the area they need me to fill immediately.' Hope took a bite of Jess's toast before continuing. 'So, we haven't booked anywhere yet, but I picked up some brochures yesterday. Hold on.' She got up and fetched them from the lounge.

'Ooh, let me see,' Jess cooed, flicking through the glossy pages. 'What about Ibiza?'

'Ibiza, are you kidding? I don't mind where we go, but not Ibiza, Jess. I'm not eighteen anymore,' she admonished. 'It will be a treat to have two whole weeks away somewhere warm, though. Maybe we'll splash out and go all-inclusive, too. It would be nice to get pampered.' Hope tried to steal another bite of toast but had her hand slapped away.

'Do you know if Adam's friend Kev is single?' Jess enquired, trying to feign disinterest.

'I knew it! Someone's finally ready to dip her toe in the water again!' Hope crowed.

'Maybe,' Jess retorted, shrugging noncommittally.

'I'll ask Adam later, oh'—she looked at her phone—'that's a text from him now. He says to delay getting to the pub until three, as our table won't be ready any earlier.'

'That's fine, gives me longer to get ready.' Jess's huge smile revealed toast crumbs stuck in her teeth. She went back upstairs to get dressed.

When the girls arrived at the White Rose, Adam stood outside the front door, waiting to greet them.

'I need to ask you a question,' Hope said urgently, stepping back from their hug and searching his face for traces of guilt. *He certainly looks cagey*, she thought, her pulse quickening. *Surely, there's no substance to Jess's concerns, is there?*

'Okay, Blossom, but first I need to ask you something,' he spluttered, leading her into the pub. He reached above her head to draw back the dividing curtain so the girls could walk through it.

Hope shuffled forwards and gasped. The small partitioned area of the pub was usually reserved for people who'd booked funeral wakes. But today's occasion would obviously be a lighter affair. The section was adorned with cream-and-gold helium balloons, beautiful flower arrangements, and confetti. Framed photos of a happy couple sat on some tables, while teddy bears sat on others. Looking closely, Hope realised the photos showed her and Adam. Then she saw the 'Will You Marry Me' sign, spelt out in gold letters on the far wall.

It dawned on Hope what was about to happen, and a huge smile lit up her face. But when she turned to see Adam down on one knee, her attention was drawn to a figure in the distance who didn't belong in the White Rose.

Returning her gaze to Adam, who now held out a tiny box containing an exquisite ring, she heard him say, 'Blossom, I don't ever want to be without you. Blakely Manor just had a cancellation for the second of July, and I know how much you love it there. I'll save the long speech for the wedding, but . . . will you marry me?'

Compelled to glance back towards the bar, Hope watched, transfixed, as the embodiment stared at her gravely before disappearing. She froze. Everyone around Adam waited with bated breath for her answer. He himself looked a little white around the gills and rather uncomfortable, having balanced precariously on one knee for far longer than he'd planned to. Jess gazed at her with an indecipherable expression.

But the silence continued. Gathering up the skirt of her dress so she wouldn't trip, Hope muttered a garbled apology and bolted out of the pub's front door.

35

Aware that someone was following her, Hope sped up. The strong wind acted like windscreen wipers on hyper speed, sweeping away her tears as they cascaded down her cheeks. She ran as fast as she could until she was far enough away to slow to a brisk pace. Then she turned to see who was following her, desperately wishing it to be Adam. She needed to properly apologise for her rejection, away from the prying eyes and ears at the White Rose. Yet it was far more likely to be Jess chasing her.

She quickened her pace again. Jess no doubt wanted answers and to check that she was okay, but Hope didn't have anything to say. She couldn't understand why she'd just turned Adam down. Her actions had taken her completely by surprise. Her only intent right now was to get as far away from the White Rose as possible, as fast as she could.

With every step, Hope felt guiltier. She could envision how much time and effort Adam had put into the proposal. He must have been eager to hear her say 'yes'. She would have to call him to explain. Fingers crossed, he would forgive her in time. But how could she make him comprehend why she'd spurned him, especially when she still struggled to make sense of it herself? *What on earth must he think right now? And how humiliated must he feel? I'd have caused him far less pain if I'd plunged a rusty dagger into his heart.*

Hope knew only one thing for certain: what she'd witnessed, prompting her to decline Adam's proposal, must have been a figment of her imagination. But the face she'd seen looking at her across the crowded bar had conveyed such overwhelming despondency and sorrow that she'd had to reconsider her decision. It was a face she knew so well, a face she trusted entirely, but a face that had no place in the White Rose. One that was more at home in her dreams. Yet even now, though she could make little sense of the whole confounding experience, Hope couldn't shake the notion that she'd somehow exercised good judgement, however preposterous that might sound to anyone else.

Turning to see that she had managed to lose Jess, Hope slowed her pace. She would have to confide in her friend at some point, but first she needed to reach Adam. Pulling out her phone, she took a deep breath and dialled his number. She had no idea what she would say if he did pick up. In spite of turning him down, she didn't want their relationship to end. On the contrary, she still loved him desperately and hoped they'd find a way through this. Sadly, her initial call went unanswered, and all subsequent attempts went straight through to his voicemail.

Having failed to catch up with Hope but assuming

she'd head home, Jess hastened there without delay. Racing in through the front door, she called out and then searched the entire house. Hope was nowhere to be found. She wondered whether Ben was part of the reason for today's outcome, but she also couldn't shake an uneasy suspicion that the mystery woman in Adam's flat might have played a role in Hope's decision. *Surely, Adam wouldn't have proposed if he was seeing someone else, though, would he? That must have been a misunderstanding.* How Jess wished she had questioned Adam herself, prior to today, instead of mentioning her concerns to Hope. Right now, all Jess could do was wait for Hope to return and then be there to listen when she was ready to talk.

When Hope finally slunk back into the house that evening, she felt physically and emotionally exhausted. She had tried to get in contact with Adam umpteen times since leaving the White Rose, but his phone had remained switched off. He was clearly blanking her, which was understandable. Yet he had to seek her out for an explanation at some point. She couldn't muster up enough courage to return to the pub any time soon, aware of the frosty reception she'd receive. She had no choice but to give him as long as he needed to come around. In the meantime, she had to work out how this affected her imminent change of career.

Five long days dragged by, with Adam ignoring Hope's calls and messages, in spite of having switched his phone back on.

As Hope finished off her last day at the store, she looked forward to returning home to Jess and wallowing in self-pity all weekend. Then she'd pull herself together to begin the management training programme on Monday. She'd decided to continue with her move into the pub industry, praying that Adam would take that as a sign that she still wanted a future with him. She hoped she wouldn't end up regretting that. As she said goodbye to the last of the staff members and handed over her keys, a text came through from Jess.

> Just been up to the White Rose to see if I could reach out to Adam on your behalf, but he's gone to Spain for a week with one of the chefs. Sorry, sweetie. Hope your last day went well. Hurry home, I'm cooking you something special and have a bottle of Baileys in the freezer! Jess X

This is no doubt Adam's attempt to hide from the embarrassment and lie low, Hope thought. She still hadn't said much to Jess about why she'd declined Adam's proposal. She'd simply muttered that she couldn't explain it but had felt it was the right thing to do.

For Adam, there was no coming back from this. He'd only ever planned on proposing once in his lifetime, and he'd expected his proposal to be swiftly followed by an acceptance, a wedding, a honeymoon, and then the pitter-patter of tiny feet. As he sat in the sun now, going over and over what had happened a week ago, he hid his misery from the holidaymakers around him.

He'd thought proposing was a great idea, given that Hope was changing her whole life around for him. He'd initially considered popping the question before he and Hope first slept together, but he hadn't found a suitable ring before Valentine's Day. After Hope had discussed the management training programme with David, Adam had been even more convinced it was the right thing to do. *Maybe I moved too fast, though. Will Hope even continue with her transition into pub management now?*

Adam wondered whether he'd been so busy planning everything that he'd missed the signs that Hope was getting cold feet about her career change. Perhaps his proposal was the final push to make her realise it was too much too soon. *No, she seemed sure of what she wanted to do with her life. We talked about whether she was doing it for herself or for our joint future together, and I'd have known if she was having second thoughts.*

His mind took him back to the day he'd nipped into town and impulsively purchased the engagement ring, the day Hope had sent off her CV. He'd felt so pleased with himself, having found the most perfect ring. The band had needed to be resized, and the jeweller in town, a regular at the pub, had very kindly offered to hand deliver it to Adam once it was ready. He didn't know that Jess had seen the jeweller leave his flat on the afternoon of Hope's interview and had then put two and two together to make five. He'd put so much effort into the proposal and keeping everything secret from Hope in order to surprise her. He'd kept it all quiet from the staff and the customers until the morning of the big day, too, fearing someone might give the game away.

The cancellation at Blakeley Manor had seemed like destiny because the timing coincided with the end of Hope's training. The pair of them had already arranged to spend those two weeks together, and it would have been ideal for a honeymoon abroad before Hope began her first managerial position. Adam had thought he'd left no stone unturned and, perhaps foolishly, hadn't even considered the possibility that she might say 'no'.

To be turned down . . . well, not only was that not part of the plan, but it was degrading. And it hurt like mad. She had injured his pride, bruised his ego, and belittled him in front of a whole damn pub full of people. Still, who was he kidding? He could pretend that he was protecting his ego, but he knew that most importantly of all, she had broken his heart.

Being with Hope in the early months, when she'd had Ben on her mind, had caused him so much anguish. He'd really thought that she had finally put her feelings for Ben away for good. But she clearly hadn't ever got over Ben. That was the only other logical reason Adam could think of for Hope turning him down. There was no coming back from this. He was done trying to compete with Ben. His heart couldn't take it anymore; it was already held together with sticky tape. He had no choice but to let Hope go.

His mind transported him back to the first moment he'd known he was falling for Hope. It was the evening of their train date . . . *shared commute*, he silently corrected himself, the first night he'd ever spent with her. A few days later, when he took her to the Italian restaurant and said he thought he could fall in love with her, he knew he already had. It took him less than a week. She was the only woman he'd ever loved, the only woman he'd ever truly connected with emotionally, and the only woman he'd ever been one hundred percent faithful to.

Adam recalled a young girl named Carrie whom he'd been seeing when he first met Hope. There had never been anything serious between him and Carrie, but they were involved in a physical relationship for a number of months before Hope came on the scene. Adam was so sure of his feelings for Hope that he immediately ended things with Carrie when Hope agreed to go on a proper date with him. That was the night she first told him about Ben. Admittedly, he broke up with Carrie in a cowardly text after fuelling himself with a mighty meatball pizza and two glasses of wine, but he at least did the right thing from the beginning. He'd never so much looked at another woman since Hope came into his life. He hadn't felt the need to.

When Hope continued to message and call him after fleeing the pub mid-proposal, his heart had been too shattered to let her try to explain.

The only way to protect himself now was to pretend she had never existed. He'd have to avoid her at any future area meetings if she did continue with the management training programme. He wasn't one to run away from problems, but he'd never given his heart to anyone before and never had to cope with how awful it felt to have it broken.

He hadn't taken advice from anyone since that day and had refused to listen to anybody except people offering their condolences. He knew there was no way back for either of them. He wondered whether Hope would understand and not hate him too much for making a clean break. Childish as it was, it was the only way he could function. He tore his thoughts away from Hope. It was simply too hard to think about her anymore.

'Damn,' he exclaimed aloud, stubbing his toe as he rose from the pool lounger. The sun had hidden behind the clouds and a thunderstorm had appeared out of nowhere. Tilting his head up to the sky, he let the rain cool down the heat thudding at his temples. When he returned to England, it would be time to move on.

***

Angelisa was on cloud nine. Hope had declined Adam's proposal, and, furthermore, the two of them seemed to have parted ways for good. Angelisa couldn't be sure whether she'd played any part in this outcome, but that was irrelevant. The important thing was that Hope had turned Adam down. Watching Adam and Hope dating had been one thing, but seeing them get married would have been too much for her to bear. She just prayed they wouldn't find a way back to each other after this.

Of course, she felt bad for Adam. She knew how much he loved Hope and that he must feel absolutely heartbroken. She also felt sure that one day, not long from now, he would realise it was all for the best. With regards to Hope, Angelisa was certain that in time, the young girl would meet someone else, someone she could spend her whole life with, without having any regrets about Adam.

No, Angelisa shouldn't feel bad for any part she may have played in this. After all, it would have been inhumane if she hadn't tried to get through to Hope, given what she knew about Adam.

36

Ten more drawn-out weeks passed. Adam refused to engage in any contact with Hope, hell-bent on erasing her from his memory. He was currently running around in a flap, getting very little done and making a meal of the task at hand. In a little more than twenty-four hours, he would move on to new pastures, and he felt pretty excited. He was supposed to be packing up the last of his possessions, but they still lay messily scattered throughout his flat. Only the bare essentials remained at the White Rose because he'd hired a van to take the bulk of his things over to his new pub.

Although he couldn't wait to start his new venture, he really would miss this pub. It had been his workplace and his lodgings for just shy of a year, and time had flown by until recently. Of all the venues he'd managed, this had been his favourite, so he felt nostalgic today. He would soon leave behind the staff, his regulars, and the little flat he'd come to call home. But he would at least take with him many fond memories. *As well as some unhappy ones*, he acknowledged.

Here, he had first met Hope. He sighed and tried to banish the thought because it did nothing but sadden him. It had been a little over two and a half months since she had declined his proposal. He'd gone out of his way to avoid her during that time, which included sending Debbie to the area meetings in his place. The White Rose had become such a success under Adam that David offered him all number of promotions and bonus packages, attempting to persuade him not to leave. Adam turned them all down. Along with terminating his contract with the company tomorrow, he would also leave employment and all memories of Hope behind him for good.

He stopped his useless attempt at gathering his belongings and decided to go for a drive. Walking through the pub on his way out, he noticed the posh ladies sitting at their favourite table, decorated with their usual gin and tonics. Heineken Man was in, too, with his pint and his newspaper, and Adam waved across the room to him. He realised he had never got to know the man's name, even though he came in every Wednesday, Friday, and Sunday. He was similar to Gammon Lady, whose real name was unknown to the entire staff—the only meal she ever ate became her identity when they referred to her amongst themselves. For instance, 'Gammon Lady is in again tonight' or 'These sauces need to be taken over to Gammon Lady, in area one'.

Adam wandered across the car park and climbed into a beaten-up Renault. He would miss his Porsche, but he'd made the sacrifice to help fund his new project. Starting the engine, he decided to venture up the motorway to Abberley, to take another look at his recent acquisition. He wouldn't be able to enter the premises before getting the keys from the planning consultant the next day, but it would be good to see the building again.

Half an hour later, he pulled into the deserted car park and stepped out. The metal sign hung on its pole, blowing in the wind. The World's End was a name that said very little about this magnificent venue. It was currently in a poor state of repair, with ivy growing up the sides of its run-down walls and its delicate thatched roof needing urgent attention. The cherry trees in the garden looked dazzling, though, with blossoming branches shimmering in the summer sunshine. The perfect name for this establishment suddenly came to him: *The Cherry Tree . . . no . . . Blossom Inn.* His thoughts were transported to Hope, but again he pushed them away. He chastised himself for thinking about her and wondered how many more rounds of this fight his brain would inflict on him.

The building would look fantastic inside and out in a few short months. This would be his most successful pub ever. He would make sure of that, come hell or high water. *Yes, onwards and upwards with no looking back*, he thought, ignoring a queasy feeling in his stomach as more unwelcome thoughts crept into his subconscious.

Peering in through the closest window, he saw the remains of a magnificent fireplace. He could easily envisage it restored to its former glory with a roaring fire in the winter months. He and the staff would congregate there on cold nights, sitting in comfy sofas and chairs, discussing the day.

He could visualise the newly refurbished interior,

from the colour of the walls and the furniture down to the floor's finish. He could even imagine the clientele: down-to-earth village types interspersed with passing commuters who would make a note to return with relatives and friends.

He moved around to the back of the property, where a larger window gave him a clear view of the vaulted ceilings. There was so much height to play with that he'd be able to display a magnificent Christmas tree every year. It would be a real tree, of course, with its fragrant needles adding a fourth dimension to the overall festive atmosphere. He could picture it decked out with baubles and lights, surrounded by a plethora of stunningly wrapped presents. Maybe they could do a gift drive through December and house all the donations under the tree before donating them to a local children's charity.

Once the refurbishment was complete, this venue would bring a real sense of community back to the village. Loved ones would meet up from near and far to celebrate special occasions, packing the pub and spreading joy all around. Generations would come together to celebrate Christmas Day in a place where people remembered the importance of family, camaraderie, and traditional values. He smiled until he was hit with the realisation that he couldn't quite imagine his own parents arriving here to spend the big day with him.

Adam poked his head through another window on a side wall of the building, where the glass had been smashed. This area would be ideal for functions. It was narrower than the main part of the interior, set back in a little dog leg with its own toilets, making it perfect for funeral wakes and christenings, engagement parties or proposals. His thoughts involuntarily went to Hope again.

After a final inspection of the interior, he went back to the car. The pub had so much potential. He was on the cusp of realising his ultimate dream, one he'd spent the last few years working towards. Yet without Hope as part of the vision, it now felt a little incomplete. He looked at the dashboard clock and realised time was pressing on. He had to get changed and ready for a party. After manoeuvring out of the empty car park, he drove home for one final night at the White Rose.

At noon the next day, Adam dragged himself out of bed. His staff had thrown him a wonderful leaving do, but he'd stayed there until the early hours after locking up. He'd poured himself one pint after another while sitting alone in the dark bar, reflecting. Finally, he had got what he wanted in his business life: a fantastic pub of his own. Yet the one thing he'd spent so long chasing didn't fulfil him as much as he had hoped. The previous day's queasy stomach returned as he once again grew preoccupied with thoughts of Hope. Pain thumped in his head, reminding him of how he'd drowned his sorrows at the end of his party. He moved gingerly into the bathroom to get some painkillers and wash the sleep out of his eyes.

The air today still threatened thunder, adding to the pressure inside Adam's head. A summer storm was no surprise, though, after the scorching weather they'd been blessed with lately. He plonked himself down on the sofa wearing nothing but his dressing gown and a scowl, then flicked through the channels, trying to find something quiet to watch that required no concentration. He lay along the length of the sofa, the Ikea cushions Hope had chosen positioned behind his throbbing head. He felt as if a tiny man were inside it now, singing away at the top of his voice and demanding his attention. Adam closed his eyes and willed himself to sleep, trying desperately to ignore the repetitive chorus. But there was no escape. *You were a moron protecting your pride, but now you are lonely and empty inside. Hope was the One and of that there's no doubt. Isn't it time that you tried to reach out?*

An hour later, Adam awoke with a start and realised he'd drifted off. He still felt groggy, but at least he could now move his head without shooting pains and flashes of light before his eyes. Unfortunately, the sing-song voice of his subconscious hadn't relented. If anything, it had increased in volume.

He turned the television off and walked along the landing to the bathroom, then found a fresh towel and dropped his dressing gown as he stepped into the shower. The water felt soothing as it cascaded over his aching body. He almost felt human again. He stayed under the warm torrent for ages, lathering every part of his body and massaging shampoo into his hair. There was something refreshing about getting himself scrubbed clean after a boozy evening and a long lie-in. It surely had similar medicinal properties to the post-heavy-night greasy fry-up. Perhaps everything would seem clearer to him now.

He picked last night's trousers off the floor and jumped into them, then tugged a clean white T-shirt over his head before running a hand through his damp hair. That was much better. Now he could think about what he had to do before leaving the keys in the door to the flat and slipping away quietly. He'd said all of his goodbyes at the party so would sneak off without a fuss once he'd loaded everything into his Renault.

As he gathered his belongings, he hummed along to the chorus in his brain. Had he really been trying to protect his pride by blanking Hope after she turned him down? He certainly was lonely without her. She'd tried to reach out to him over and over again from the moment she'd rejected his proposal, so why hadn't he given her a chance to explain? And why hadn't he reached out himself when she'd eventually stopped trying? He knew why, as did the voice in his head. Because he was a moron.

The pub was quiet when he crept out of the back door for the last time, said a silent goodbye to the White Rose, and set off towards the World's End. It was still early, and he had two hours before he would meet the planning consultant at his newly acquired premises. He decided to treat himself to one last takeaway pizza, for old time's sake.

He had phoned Angelo's Pizzeria for a late-night feast to be delivered to his flat at least once a fortnight since starting at the White Rose. It would be a change to go there in person today. He'd always indulged in this guilty pleasure alone because pizza somehow tasted better when he didn't have to share it. Yet he realised he'd give anything right now to halve a large stuffed-crust with Hope—however it may have compromised the taste. He couldn't keep pushing thoughts of her aside. He missed her terribly. He loved her desperately. Why on earth had he let her go?

Parking at the edge of town, Adam jumped out of the driver's seat and made to cross the busy road ahead. He'd been such a fool to blank Hope ever since that day. He had made the biggest mistake of his life by ignoring her. They would have been married and away on their honeymoon right now if Hope had accepted his proposal. He wondered whether to ring her and whether she'd even answer if he did. He desperately needed to tell her how stupid and thoughtless he'd been and how he wished he could rewind the clock. Maybe it was too late to put things right, but he could at least apologise for his immature behaviour and tell her he'd never stopped loving her. Perhaps it wouldn't be too late after all.

Adam fished his phone out of his pocket. Scrolling down past Angelo's Pizzeria, the very place he was heading to now and the only entry under *A* in his phone directory, he came upon the contact directly below, labelled *Blossom.* Taking one last deep breath, he prepared to dial.

***

Angelisa had her head in the clouds, still certain everything had turned out for the best—or at least as well as could be expected, given the circumstances. Hope had moved on and, from what she could gather, was clearly enjoying her new adventure with a bright future ahead of her.

Angelisa's thoughts now turned to Adam. She had checked in on him during recent months, and it pained her to know that she couldn't do anything to alter his fate. He still had no idea that time was fast running out.

As she set off, her superior called out in a tone of voice that made it unequivocally clear Angelisa was in big trouble. It must have finally become obvious that she'd accessed Adam's cloud file. Angelisa didn't know how she'd been found out, but she would have some serious explaining to do. *I'm done for*, she thought silently, preparing for the inevitable. She would face her punishment shortly. But right now, she needed to be by Adam's side.

37

Having completed her management training programme a few days earlier, Hope was now lapping up the sun with Jess in Tenerife. She would soon return to England to begin running her first pub.

It was Jess's idea for the girls to spend this week abroad, but she hadn't mentioned it was a singles holiday for the under thirties. Hope wasn't impressed, but she humoured her friend, even though her heart wasn't in it. She would go through the motions to prove she wasn't wallowing in her recent heartbreak. Yet after such a strong love with Adam, it would be a long time before she was ready to love again. All she needed now were the sun, some swimming, and a good rest.

After checking in at their hotel, the girls had gone straight to their room. They donned their bikinis, dumped their suitcases, and grabbed their beach towels, then headed straight to the hotel's impressive pool.

Lying back on her lounger a few hours later, Hope

remembered how overjoyed she'd been to gain her licence and be offered the manager's position at the Wishing Well, a quaint little pub on the Southampton coast. Having visited a few times to get a feel for the location, the pub itself, the staff, and the customer profile, she had gleefully accepted the offer. She would soon begin her first appointment as a full-fledged landlady.

This holiday with Jess would give her a new spurt of energy before she made the move to Southampton. There, she'd have to put in long hours to sort out the current issues at the Wishing Well. She'd accepted the post from another area manager, pleased to get far away from reminders of Adam. Now she was eager to get stuck in.

Hope didn't allow herself to think about Adam too often, knowing she had to move forwards rather than dwell on the past. Her mum's sudden death, more than a decade earlier, had taught her that all too well. She had a lot to look forward to, and the change of scenery would be an added bonus. She would always love Adam, but she had to lock away the hurt and move on.

If Adam had reached out in the weeks after she'd declined his proposal, they might have been able to make things work. Yet Hope couldn't help but feel that she'd had a lucky escape. He hadn't even given her a chance to explain. The fact that he'd made such a clean and permanent break had helped her move on with her life.

To this day, she still didn't understand why she'd turned him down, but she believed it had been the right thing to do. She often wondered where she would be right now if she had never met him. She knew she should thank him for her exciting new career path, so maybe that was the sole reason Fate had brought him into her life.

Focussing on the future and leaving Adam firmly in the past, Hope looked over at Jess and smiled. It thrilled her that Jess would soon move in above the Wishing Well, having snapped up a transfer at the local Next store. As an added bonus, Jess would always happily jump behind the bar and help out if ever Hope were understaffed. Plus, she would provide the emotional support that only a best friend could.

Living closer to Ben might also mean that Hope would get to see him more often. She'd really relied on his friendship since the fallout with Adam. They'd become closer than ever during the last couple of months. Yet she felt certain that all romantic thoughts of Ben were truly in the past now.

Hope turned to look at the magnificent infinity pool, stretching out to embrace the topaz blue sea. She felt a presence around her, even though the girls were alone. Picking up her cocktail from the table, she checked whether Jess had fallen asleep. Hope had never explained what had prompted her to decline Adam's proposal. Only now, while they basked in the sunshine two and a half months later, did she feel calm and at peace enough to open up about it. She knew Jess would laugh at her, but she didn't mind.

After a relaxing yet invigorating swim, the girls pulled kimonos over their bikinis and ordered drinks and pizzas at the poolside bar.

'Honestly, Jess,' Hope said, 'I know it sounds ridiculous, but that's what made me say "no" when Adam proposed.'

'An apparition made you turn him down, seriously?' Jess queried, laughing.

'I know it sounds insane. I can't explain it myself. But it was as if I were being sent a warning. Hey, stop giggling.' Then she gave up and joined Jess's laughter.

'I thought Ben might have played a part in your decision.'

'Ben? No, it had nothing to do with Ben.'

'And speaking of Ben? Are you *sure* you two will only ever be friends? He'll be only a short drive around the coast soon.'

'That ship has sailed,' Hope replied.

'Never say never, though, right?' Jess grinned.

'Isn't it magical here?' Hope replied, ignoring her friend's last comment.

After finishing their pizzas, taking their drinks back to the sun loungers, and enthusing about the massages they would book later, Hope felt as if she were in Heaven, here in Tenerife. She was, of course, totally unaware that Adam was currently headed there himself . . .

38

For a few seconds now, Adam had been lying eerily still at the edge of the pavement. Whilst he tried to make sense of what had happened, Angelisa appeared, kneeling at his side. Her face was contorted in pain and concern, yet she seemed unsurprised at his lifeless appearance. She spoke to him comfortingly, addressing him by his name, but he was sure he didn't know her. That being said, there was a familiarity about her presence he couldn't quite explain. Maybe his mind was playing tricks on him. He could certainly feel his brain struggling to function as the seconds ticked by. Was she just a figment of his imagination? His eyes, so tired and weary, slowly began to close.

Angelisa watched as passers-by raced to Adam's aid. Motorists stopped their cars in the middle of the road to get out and help, unaware that it was too late. Angelisa kissed him tenderly on the forehead and slowly drifted away from the scene, as though she'd never truly been there in the first place.

Adam could tell that he was dying. He wasn't sure whether he had been hit by a car or had been struck down by natural causes, but the overwhelming sense of peace he felt, combined with the brightest of lights in front of him, made him certain his time was up. Strangely, he had no cause for fear. As his whole life flashed before his eyes, he witnessed it like a cine-film playing in fast-forward on the inside of his eyelids. It raced through the years of his earliest memories right up to when he'd first met Hope, at which point the images slowed and brightened intensely.

Hope. He wasn't sure whether he'd managed to utter her name aloud, but his thoughts went to her now. Thank goodness, she hadn't witnessed whatever fate had befallen him. Thank goodness, she had moved on with her life without him. Thank goodness, she *had* turned down his proposal. Otherwise, she would soon be a widow.

***

Angelisa nervously hovered outside the monolithic door. Its sheer size alone was intimidating, and it also appeared to be suspended in thin air, with no visible hinges. She had just left Adam to his cruel destiny and was currently waiting to hear her own. Having been detained here for quite a while, she started to wonder how much longer she would have to wait before being called in. She still maintained that she had always acted entirely and unashamedly in Hope's best interests, but would that be good enough?

Upon discovering that Adam's days were numbered, she had felt she'd had no option but to step in. She couldn't have forgiven herself if she'd stood by and done nothing, to then witness Hope being widowed shortly after getting married, possibly with a honeymoon baby on the way who would never know its father. No. She'd seen first-hand how long it took for Hope to grieve the loss of a parent . . . and then an unborn baby. Letting Hope endure that gruelling process all over again, upon losing a husband, would have been beyond cruel.

If she could have saved Adam, then, of course, she would have, but she had no power over that. His date of death was clearly documented in his cloud file, impossible to ignore . . . or alter. She'd simply had no choice but to try and come between the pair. She had to have faith that she wasn't the only one who would see it that way. Yes, she was sad about being unable to save Adam from his fate, but she'd prevented Hope from experiencing further heartache.

And Hope's happiness would always be her number-one priority. After all, Guardian Angel or not . . . she would always be Hope's mum.

EPILOGUE

Angelisa had come down to Earth with such a bump that she felt hopelessly disoriented. Cloaked in anguish, she hung her head low in shame as she drifted around, not knowing which way to turn. She had just been advised that there were further entries in Adam's file. Further entries which she'd somehow failed to notice, further entries that changed *everything*.

She had been so sure that the best possible outcome for Hope would be moving on without Adam. Only now, with this new insight, did Angelisa realise what a monumental error in judgement she'd made. Furthermore, it had come to light that her presence at Adam's proposal was the sole reason Hope had turned him down. She'd thus been categorically forbidden from doing any further meddling. She supposed she ought to be grateful that she'd only had her wings clipped, as she'd anticipated a lot worse, but that didn't help allay her angst.

Mortification and desperation sank into her soul, pulling it apart with no reprieve and inflicting an unparalleled punishment.

Could she really step aside now and leave this whole sorry mess entirely in the hands of Fate? She wasn't sure that she could make any promises, especially since this tragic outcome was irrefutably her fault. Had she just put Hope's future happiness in dire jeopardy? Only time would tell . . .

Coming in 2023 . . .

Longing for Hope

by

Lainey Lawrence

The second book in

The Journey of Hope Series

Printed in Great Britain
by Amazon

14838638R00171